Tessa approached the darkly pensive man as Miles watched. The two briefly conversed, and Tessa's lithe body dropped down to the floor and scooted under the tablecloth. Miles witnessed her good work, seeing the expression on the young man's face. The man tried not to give himself away, but no one was watching except Miles. The man's last gasp of contentment was audible, though not so loud that anyone would notice. Seconds later, Tessa, with hardly a hair out of place, was strolling back to Miles, a pleased, amused, and sweetly triumphant look on her face.

"You didn't think I'd do it?" she asked Miles, while waving back to her appreciative lover.

"I assumed you would," Miles said, unimpressed by her willingness. "Let's go."

Outside, there was a chauffeur-driven car waiting for them. Miles was free to put all his attentions on Tessa.

Also by LIZBETH DUSSEAU:

Spanish Holiday
Caroline's Contract
Member of the Club
The Applicant

TRINKETS

LIZBETH DUSSEAU

MASQUERADE BOOKS, INC.
801 SECOND AVENUE
NEW YORK, N.Y. 10017

Trinkets

Second Masquerade Edition 1998

First Printing August 1998

ISBN 1-56333-668-5

Manufactured in the United States of America
Published by Masquerade Books, Inc.
801 Second Avenue
New York, N.Y. 10017

CHAPTER ONE

HE'D BEEN WATCHING her from an obscure corner of the cafe all night, obscure because that was the aura that Miles intended to convey when he was in a contemplative vein. Everything surrounding him took on a similar mysterious aspect. Looking at her dancing in the soft lights, smiling like sunshine, almost giddy with laughter produced by the wine flowing through her veins, he was deep in his thoughts of having her. And he would have her, there was no doubt of that.

Perhaps only he could see beneath the exuberant surface of her behavior to the darker woman residing there, the one that craved the control he could furnish. He was used to such women, but this one in particular was extraordinarily fascinating. He could devise a life for her that would be like no other. He could provide the wicked venue in which this Miss Tessa Cotille could safely play. There was no greater satisfaction for him than to possess such a creature.

He watched as she gyrated her hips, the soft swell of her belly undulating against the thighs of the man in front of her. Her bottom danced on the air, pert and fully round. It would take punishment well, he thought. She was naked underneath the short red dress with the cutouts at the sleeves. He knew that by the way her nipples pushed against the red fabric, the way one or two strands of pubic hair poked through the knit. Ah those nipples! Exquisite jewels! He imagined them lovingly adorned with gold ornaments pierced through the flesh.

It took only moments to know that she was the one, and just seconds to have his plan firmly laid.

Two weeks later she was in his house, his guest. The party was lush, and the guests were lewdly dressed. He was glad she'd chosen to wear leather. Her hips molded the soft cloth of the skirt, and her breasts, pushed together by the bustier, jiggled, threatening to spill out over the top.

He imagined her the centerpiece of a much different party—though it would take some time to nurture their relationship before he could have her that completely.

He'd begin this night.

"Miss Cotille, I'm glad you could join me," Miles Bryce said, as he strolled to her side. "You dance well."

"Thank you, Mr. Bryce," she said, her sultry eyes staring directly into his. "And I like your party."

"Why's that?" he inquired. He liked her fresh, innocent nature.

She danced around her words for a moment, her face flushed with expressive warmth. "Freedom, Mr. Bryce, freedom. I don't allow myself to be so brash many places. In your home it feels perfectly comfortable."

"I'm glad that pleases you, my dear, please call me Miles," he instructed her.

"Miles," she nodded. He was an older man, by at least ten years, though he didn't seem to care about the difference, so why should she? He was astonishingly direct in his manner, and she liked that. She liked men who took charge of things around them, who manipulated their environment in the ways that pleased them. So few were really adept at the art. In fact, only one man that she could remember had held her captive the way she liked. Unfortunately, he was not devoted to her. He was devoted only to his own sensual pleasure; the women he dominated were only a passing fancy in his heart. She soon passed from his fancy, discarded for another.

This man, this Miles Bryce, might be different, she thought.

She was eternally optimistic.

He was not obtrusive that night, at least not until the end. From 10 until 2 A.M., their paths crossed several times, though they didn't speak again. She found him staring at her while she danced; he discovered her searching for his staring eyes more than once.

By the end of such a night, so highly aroused, she was the kind of woman who could pick any partner to screw till morning. She'd land in most any man's bed, not discreetly choosing by any standard, but falling into the last arms that claimed her.

Miles knew this. She was easy to read, Tessa Cotille, a bawdy, wanton wench at heart. She would fall into the same pattern this night, except that Miles intended to rescue her for his own designs.

"Tessa," he said sharply, raising his voice. Her level of inebriation was so elevated, she needed his sharp tone to penetrate the woozy bliss she was feeling.

"Mr. Bryce!" she exclaimed, turning around. She was on the patio for a breath of fresh air.

"Miles...," he corrected her.

"Miles, you surprised me." She was beautifully disheveled, her golden locks, once piled high on her head, were now softly falling around her shoulders. A sweet tender smile drifted across her face, and her bright brilliant eyes still gleamed, though they'd softened in the hours that had passed. Her clothes were only slightly askew, but enough so that the aureole around her left nipple was beginning to show at the top of the leather bustier.

Miles stepped in front of her, his hands reaching around her bodice and twisting the garment so it was straight again. "You're feeling the effects of the evening I see," he said.

"Oh dear," she gasped, looking down as suddenly a nipple popped above the leather.

His fingers, on either side of the bud, tweaked it gently. "Watch yourself Tessa, too much wine and you might do something you regret."

"What could I possibly regret?" she said, deliberately pressing herself toward him.

"I would never take advantage of you this way," he said, tenderly pushing her away.

"No?" She looked disappointed.

"I'm not certain that you really want what I have to offer," he explained.

"And what would that be?" she asked curiously.

"We'll discuss that when you're completely sober," he suggested gently.

"Sober?"

"You're not now, you little wench," he murmured with a soothing voice. He would have liked to have taken her there, stripped her of her clothes and pushed her down between his legs, where she would have swallowed every last drop of his come. But that would have been too easy. This was a different kind of seduction he intended, one that would last far longer than just this night.

She looked at him as she was trying to sober herself. "No, I suppose I'm not thinking too clearly," she admitted. A pink blush rose on her cheek.

"You may have an upstairs room for the night if you like."

"Maybe for a few hours?" she suggested.

"As long as you like."

He led her away from the party and up his back staircase, where no one would see her. He was concerned that walking her back through the crowd might distract her. He'd rather have her sleep off the liquor, so they would talk about their sexual future together the next day—when she'd agree to be his submissive.

In the morning she came down the front stairs and found him in his breakfast room. Sunlight was streaming in through a bank of east-facing windows, making the light about them hazy with dust. He sat at a table by himself, a table for one. She had imagined them having breakfast together, but those hopes were quickly dashed.

"Come here," he commanded her. His words were given and received as an order. The agreement between them was tacit but clearly understood. He eyed her carefully as she approached him. She was wearing the leather skirt and bustier that she'd worn the night before, since she had nothing else to wear. He stared at her darkly, his playful eyes having changed to demanding cold ones, so cold she could not read his intentions. Then again, that was the way he wanted it.

Tessa liked the mystery, even though she trembled in its presence.

"You are as ravishing as you were last night," he remarked. Reaching for the bustier, his hand grazed its smooth surface where it covered her breasts. It buttoned top to bottom down the front. Carefully, he undid the top button, then made his way down until the garment opened. The flesh of her breasts shook slightly as they were freed into the warm air. The bustier had pressed them tightly to her; now released from their bondage they swelled in volume, two generous billowy mounds of milky white.

Tessa would have dropped between his legs and buried her face in his crotch right then, but something in his glance, the way he held her captive, prevented her from responding with anything more than just a sensuous gasp of breath from her parted lips.

"These will look exquisite when the gold studs

have pierced them," he said. He pinched them both hard, and she jerked with a pain that reached all the way down to her thighs. She remained silent.

"You're sober now?" he asked.

"Very," she answered.

A maid came and went with a steamy breakfast and coffee. She did so without as much as a raised eyebrow. Was this a common sight for her to see, a half-naked woman fondled as she served her employer his breakfast? Was it so common that she would hardly take notice of them?

"On your knees, Tessa," he ordered her.

She was prepared to serve him any way he chose, to caress and fondle his cock, to bring him to a vibrant orgasm. But Miles had something else in mind.

"Turn around," he ordered her, when she was on her hands and knees. She was puzzled, but complied, presenting her rear to him.

"You have a fine ass," he observed, his hand now caressing the leather of her skirt. In this position, it was beginning to ride up against her thighs, so that every aspect of her rear and cunt below was becoming visible for Mile's inspection. He raised the skirt further with his hand, exposing everything. He slapped her rear with a resounding smack. "This is the heart of a woman," he charged, as his hand made a thorough journey about her private parts. "Such plump labia," he observed. He pulled at the flesh of her cunt. "These too will be pierced."

She cried out as he slapped her rear again. She regrouped, and found herself taunting him, waving her rear at him, as if she were asking for more.

A finger pressed against her anus. She breathed

deeply and let him penetrate as far as he chose. Two fingers slipped into her pussy, and his whole hand began to pound its way deeper into her opening.

The night before had left her sexually charged with no satisfaction. In seconds she was at an edge, ready to explode.

Miles knew that, and withdrew his hand.

"You like this, don't you?" he teased. She groaned, waiting for him to fondle her more. But he wouldn't do that.

"Stand up," he ordered.

She hadn't had anything to eat or drink since she'd awakened, and she was suddenly feeling as inebriated as she had the night before. "You won't finish what you started?" she moaned, desperate to have him bring her to orgasm. "What can I do to please you?" Begging was a good sign, Miles thought to himself. "You can do many things to please me," he suggested, "but are you ready to do anything that I ask? Are you ready for pain and submission, and the reckless abandon that you really want? Or are you just toying with such radical notions?"

"I don't know what you mean."

"You appear docile, submissive, pliable. I could mold your sex life into something extraordinary. But I don't want a childish brat countering me at every turn. I want a serious decadent like myself, a woman who knows herself well enough to let me have her anyway I want, who will let me do with her anything I will, because it pleases me and arouses her."

Tessa didn't reply. Her clothes askew, her hair undone, her loins throbbing with need, she had no words to speak. Miles Bryce had stunned her loquacious nature into silence.

"I've overwhelmed you?" he suggested.

"Yes."

"Good. I intended to. Go home and come back when you want what I want of you."

She hesitated, still so bewildered, her limbs were frozen.

"Need I explain more?" Miles inquired calmly.

"No, not at all," she finally said. Then buttoning her bustier, she left the room and his house.

CHAPTER TWO

TESSA BURST INTO her apartment. She caught a whiff of some oddly familiar aroma, unexpected after a night away. Approaching the kitchen, she was aware that some fruity tea was brewing on the stove.

In the living room, she found her lover Martine, sitting on the sofa. The woman had her hands between her legs, playing with her pussy. It was juicy, and on another day, Tessa might have immediately succumbed to the surprise, immersing herself in that delightful cunt. Instead, Tessa plopped down on the other end of the sofa, ignoring the woman's masturbation.

"Where were you?" Martine asked.

"Miles Bryce," Tessa answered.

"The painter?"

"The dilettante."

"How impressive," Martine replied sarcastically.

"Did he fuck you?" She continued to finger herself. The robe she wore, Tessa's silk wrapper, was open down the front; not one important piece of her body was hidden from view.

"No, he didn't fuck me," Tessa answered.

Martine smiled, thinking she'd remained in control of Tessa's affections. "You're eyes are glassy," she observed, "he must have turned you on."

Tessa shrugged. She didn't want to talk about Miles with Martine.

"You're hot, aren't you?" Martine's voice deepened, its husky tones even more lecherous that usual. "Fuck me," she said, pulling Tessa toward her, so that she would drop between her legs, where her naked cunt was juicy and ready for lips and tongue.

Tessa fell against Martine's soft brown thighs and began to lap at her pussy instinctively, as she had a hundred times before. It was a habit, a pleasant one, though this time, her mind was not yet in the woman's sexual space.

"That's it, little bitch," Martine purred at her. Her long nails were clawing through her hair, her thighs beginning to flex and relax around Tessa's head.

As Tessa made the familiar journey into the folds and recesses of Martine's deep purple cunt, she began to wonder if this wasn't to her advantage. It was, after all, a place to put the raging sexual needs that had been left so unsatisfied at Miles Bryce's home.

Her mouth surrounded Martine's hard bud of a clit, as her brash friend demanded attention with the typical furor that Martine normally insisted on. Tessa sucked it until the bud was harder yet, and Martine was lying back screaming, "Arrruggh, ah yes, do that!"

Then, while Tessa's tongue flicked at the nasty throbbing head, two, then three, then four fingers prodded their way down her channel. Her cunt opened, so like Tessa's cunt had opened just an hour before. Tessa fucked her hard with her hand, as she watched the woman's sweating body claimed by one spasm after another.

"More, more, yes, yes," Martine screamed at her. "*Ah!* Ah yes..." She was a maniac in the middle of orgasm. Tessa clawed at her behind, scratching the skin with her nails. In her own way, Martine loved pain almost as much as Tessa did. But it wasn't something she submitted to, it was something that happened. When the last vigorous pulse died away, Tessa withdrew her hand. Martine collapsed back into the corner of the couch, and Tessa collapsed against her.

Martine stroked her hair. "You want your cunt eaten?" she asked.

"No, just stroke my hair," she replied.

The two remained in silent repose some minutes.

"How was the party?" Martine asked, finally sitting up. She took her long brown hair and pulled it into a ponytail, winding it on top of her head. Tessa's small dark-skinned roommate was the lover who sufficed in the lazy mornings and the lonely evenings, when neither were with men. They fucked when the mood was right.

It wasn't really right for Tessa, not this time; but she didn't have much will to resist something so simple. She was used to surrendering to Martine. But this time, despite the throbbing between her legs, it was thoughts of Miles that preoccupied her mind and kept her from letting Martine satisfy her.

"He wants me," she finally told the woman.

"Who?" Martine asked.

"Miles."

"Wants you how?" she queried.

"Sexually." Tessa answered. "He's a dom."

"And you're a passive little submissive, so what's the problem?"

Tessa didn't answer, except for the sly smirk appearing on her face, and Martine knew all she needed to know.

CHAPTER THREE

THEY MET AT the cafe again.

"You wanted to see me?" Tessa asked.

"Your message was on my machine," Miles said, as she sat down beside him. "I assumed you made your decision."

"I know I can't stay away from you," Tessa admitted.

He acknowledged her admission with a smile.

"Once you begin, it will be too late to reconsider," he warned.

"Why would I reconsider?" Tessa asked, her delicate eyes shining at him wickedly. Miles hadn't realized how easy it would be to have her, but then, too, she hadn't been tested yet.

"The man in the corner?" Miles said, nodding to a handsome young man, who was nursing a glass of Scotch.

"Yes?"

"You know him?"

"Only in passing," Tessa replied. She'd danced with him at the cafe a number of times. He'd remember her.

"I want you to go to him, tell him you'd like to suck him off."

"Now?" Tessa questioned.

"Now," Miles answered. "When he agrees, do it, under the table."

She was startled but didn't balk. "Do you know him?" she asked.

"Does it matter?" Miles asked. He wouldn't quit staring at her until she rose from her seat.

Tessa approached the darkly pensive man as Miles watched. The two briefly conversed, and Tessa's lithe body dropped down to the floor and scooted under the tablecloth. Miles witnessed her good work, seeing the expression on the young man's face. The man tried not to give himself away, but no one was watching except Miles. The man's last gasp of contentment was audible, though not so loud that anyone would notice. Seconds later, Tessa, with hardly a hair out of place, was strolling back to Miles, a pleased, amused, and sweetly triumphant look on her face.

"You didn't think I'd do it?" she asked Miles, while waving back to her appreciative lover.

"I assumed you would," Miles said, unimpressed by her willingness. "Let's go."

Outside, there was a chauffeur-driven car waiting for them. Miles was free to put all his attentions on Tessa.

As soon as the limousine was on its way, he had her kneel between his legs, while he pulled her dress up over her hips and then over her head. She was naked except for the black stockings and rose-colored garter belt. She wanted to please him, to see the approval written in his eyes, but he was far too cold and restrained to give himself away. He examined her carefully, then pulled at her nipples. She reacted without thinking, pulling herself away from the pain.

He slapped her face.

"Don't ever do that!" he ordered.

The slap stung, yet its sensations ran through her body, from breast to cunt. She would have taken more, but he wouldn't slap her again without provocation.

"Put your arms behind you and keep them there," he ordered.

She complied, grasping her hands together at the small of her back. Her breasts were thrust out in front of her, and he pulled her up, so he could fondle her more easily. One hand slipped down to grasp her cunt, while the other roved her flesh at will. He leaned in to kiss her face while he manipulated her sex.

"You're nervous," he said. He saw that she was trembling.

"I haven't had this happen before," she replied.

"It should please you," he said.

"It does," she said. Her body shuddered, even as his warm hands held her securely.

The limousine sped through traffic. Though the darkened windows wouldn't reveal their performance for an audience on the busy street, Tessa was aware of her nakedness, as if the world could see her.

"Look at me," Miles demanded. He wouldn't let her eyes waver from his. She was raw with desire, her responses becoming more fluid and less hesitant, as she lost herself in the rising sexual heat between them. He pulled her pubic hair, and she moaned. He slapped her rear, and she jerked against him. He grazed her lips with his teeth, and she bit him back. He drove her body with relentless zeal, his satisfaction drawn from the wanton slut now emerging.

The limousine jerked to a stop.

"Sir, we're here," the driver spoke through the intercom.

"We'll be here a while, be back in an hour," Miles instructed him.

Tessa reached for her dress.

"No." Miles stopped her with his hand.

His suit jacket, lying on the seat next to him, became her dress. The cool satin lining made her shiver as she put it on. As long as the dress she'd worn, it covered her, except that the deep neckline plunged low and wide, leaving half her breasts exposed. With any movement at all, the jacket swayed and her nipples peeked from inside.

"How novel!" was all she could think to say. She knew she was pleasing him and that was what mattered.

The walk from the limo across the street was exhilarating, even though most of the passersby didn't bother to notice her indecency, the blonde with the full lips and the half-naked breasts, walking in nothing but a man's suit jacket.

They stopped at the door of a small salon, tucked between a Chinese grocery and an upscale beauty parlor. The door rattled and the bell inside clanged, as they entered the curious little shop.

An exotic black woman sat behind a desk, looking as if she had been waiting for them. Her wares were ethnic artwork hanging on the walls, baskets along the floor, and gold jewelry in a display case. The air was filled with heat and the smell of exotic perfume, coming from the woman's body.

"I told you about Tessa," Miles said to the statuesque woman, indicating the smiling blonde in his suit jacket. "This is Maya," Miles told Tessa.

The proprietress was attired in a draping garment that clung to her body. It was vibrating with exotic colors, red, burgundy, and mauve, which blended with her dark chocolate skin. Gold dangled from her ears, bedecked each long slender finger, and pierced her nose with a tiny ring. Tessa could see the woman's smooth body through the fabric of her dress, especially as she walked toward them through the tiny sliver of sun that bolted through the window. She was nude underneath. She appeared to Tessa like a tribal flower, straight from foreign jungles, though her thick voice was clearly American.

"So white," Maya said, fondling Tessa's golden locks, which billowed about her shoulders. The woman stood before Tessa for some purpose that only she and Miles knew. Miles stood back and watched as the black woman inspected her, with careful attention to every aspect of Tessa's body. The woman parted the top of the suit jacket to view Tessa's chest: her full breasts, and her nipples that, caressed by the air, were tightening into hard knots.

"You want these pierced?" she asked Miles.

"Yes," he answered.

Maya pushed the jacket off Tessa's shoulders to better view the woman's body, her trim waist and the classic curve of her flat abdomen below. The jacket rested at Tessa's waist, covering her upper thighs and her pubic mound, but otherwise Tessa was quite naked in the small shop, being inspected like any other of Maya's trinkets.

"She's your submissive?" Maya prodded the naked breasts, pinched the nipples as Miles had done, and then took Tessa's face in her hand and inspected the line of her jaw, the startling dark eyes.

Miles nodded in reply to Maya's question.

"Then you'll want her pierced below too," she said, ready to remove the jacket completely to view the nether regions of Tessa's body.

"Not today," Miles answered without explanation.

"Too bad. She's like rich cream," the chocolate brown woman commented. She took Tessa by the hand and led her to a stool behind her desk.

"Sit," she ordered.

Tessa sat with Miles' jacket still draping her below the waist, her body vulnerable to any eye that passed by on the street and glanced in the window.

Tessa looked at Miles, while Maya turned to her work table, preparing the jewelry that would soon adorn her nipples. Tessa viewed him as her conqueror, so quickly had he climbed inside her elemental self and become the master of her body, and even of her thoughts. He caused her sex fires to roar by his cool detached claiming of her, his prize, his acquisition, his to do with as he chose. She'd dreamed of such subjection. Living it was something different. Something about it made her more silent and more sultry, as she waited for his command.

First, Maya applied a cold stinging disinfectant to Tessa's nipples. She pinched them harder than necessary with her cotton-covered fingers. When she let go of them, the air on them made them colder still, shriveling into ever tighter knots.

"They should bleed a day or two until they heal. Keep them cleansed." She showed her a bottle of clear liquid to apply to them.

The woman's hands moved so fast that Tessa could hardly see her work. She eyed the needle, thinking of the sharp pain to come. "I can't," she pleaded.

"Look at me," Miles commanded. His eyes were icy cold, his stare astounding for the effect it had on her. "You gave yourself to me, I should not have to remind of that."

Tessa bit her lip. She didn't want to disappoint him, or herself. She wanted to see the gold on her breasts, feel it hot and cold, feel the heaviness it brought, as a reminder of her station as his submissive love. Still, she was trembling too much. Her eyes watered with tears.

Maya turned away, and Tessa watched her pour a glass of amber liquid. "Drink this," she said turning back.

Tessa took the glass in hand and sipped the liquor.

"Gulp it, blonde one. C'mon hurry, I don't have all day." Maya sounded impatient, though she still moved in the same soft fluid manner, as if her body was floating.

Tessa gulped the liquor till the glass was empty, and she handed it back to the black woman.

"You should beat her ass for being so squeamish," Maya suggested to Miles.

"I'll consider it," he replied.

Tessa was left for several moments sitting on the stool, while Miles and Maya slipped into the back room, the two waiting for the liquor to quell Tessa's nervousness. It must have been some potent brew, for Tessa's head was soon swimming delightfully, her body seeming to drift into other worlds. When the two came back into the room, it was as if they'd awakened her from a sound sleep.

Maya was quick. The needle rapidly pricked Tessa's flesh, first one side, then the second. Tessa let out a quick gasp each time, though it was not as painful as she imagined it would be. Only after it was over did she realize that Miles was at her back, holding her arms firmly to her side, so she wouldn't jerk away. Tessa looked down to see the gold studs piercing her nipples. On either side of each tight bud, the studs were held fast by screw posts.

"She'll take well to chains and rings, once she's healed," Maya said, standing back and admiring her work. The gold sparkled as the sunlight brought out its brilliance. "Show her off Miles," Maya said. She pulled Tessa from the stool, placing the suit jacket back around her shoulders. "Don't let them get infected, and don't play with them till they're healed," the woman warned.

"You're telling *me* this?" Miles queried, feigning annoyance. Their sparring appeared a natural part of their relationship.

"I'm telling her," Maya bitched back, pointing to Tessa.

"She'll behave," he said, as he took Tessa by the arm. "This should suffice," he added, as he laid several green bills on her desk. Maya picked them up, counted them, and stuffed them down her dress.

Tessa was shivering, even though the shop was hot from the sun. She wanted to leave, sensing that if they stayed, they would all end up in the black woman's bed. Not that the prospect wasn't exciting, but Tessa was still too shaken by Miles' world, by the curious throbbing at her breasts, by the strange feeling of the gold studs pierced through her flesh. The liquor was making her too light-headed to feel coherent.

"I'll pierce her cunt next time," Maya insisted, walking Tessa and Miles to the door.

"When she deserves it," Miles said as they exited the shop. He raised his eyebrows playfully for the woman who was fast disappearing from their view.

When they reached the limo, he was cold with her, staring out the window, as Tessa watched him. She was sitting on the seat facing his.

"You've disappointed me," he remarked at last, turning his gaze back to her. There was not one ounce of warmth in his expression, as if she'd done something horribly wrong.

"For hesitating, in the shop?" Tessa inquired.

He didn't answer.

"Then you'll punish me?" Tessa asked.

"In good time," he confirmed, "but not until I'm ready."

The limo stopped again in front of her apartment building, and he opened the door for her.

"Will I see you again?" she asked.

"We've only begun, my dear Tessa." He said no more. He practically pushed her from the limousine, if not physically, certainly with his annoyed voice. He never did hand her back her dress, so she flew up the apartment stairs wearing just her stockings, garter belt, and his suit jacket.

Tessa fell into bed at an early hour, exhausted.

Waking the next morning, she opened her eyes to see Martine staring down at her body. The covers had strayed during the night, and she was naked to the woman's inquisitive eyes.

"Trinkets on your nipples, how lovely," Martine purred like a cat. She leaned down and tugged at one.

"Ouch—they still hurt!" Tessa exclaimed.

"They make you look more like yourself," Martine said.

"How's that?" Tessa asked.

"You're the kind of woman who needs to be some man's sexual trinket," Martine said.

"That's what Miles would say," Tessa replied.

"Then he must know you well," the other woman suggested. She turned and walked out of the room.

CHAPTER FOUR

HE INVITED HER to lunch three days later.

The symbols of his claim to her were more comfortable and less painful each day. With the gold penetrating her nipples, she felt as bound to him as she might feel after being with someone for many years. Even so, Miles remained a mystery to Tessa. She hardly knew him.

The twinges in her breasts, the occasional throbbing, and especially the passing thoughts of him, kept her body at a steamy edge, in anticipation; so much so, that when he called, she was ready to meet him anywhere and to do anything he desired. It was her hope that they would finally have that first sexual interlude between them, even if it was only to satisfy his needs. However Miles saw things differently. Being in control of Tessa was more important to him than hopping into bed for a hasty fuck.

Lunch was at an elegant restaurant, where they were sequestered in a semi-private booth. She was instructed to scoot in next to another man, Arturo. With Miles at her other side, she was wedged closely between them, their combined domineering attitudes overpowering her.

"He wants to see your jewelry," Miles told her, "show him."

She stared from Miles to Arturo's dark Italian face. Although he was acting nonchalant, as if this was something he did everyday, Tessa could see the anxiousness in his eye, as if he doubted Miles' submissive would be so bold as to bare herself in a public place.

To Arturo's delight, Tessa began to unbutton her blouse. Once she had the first buttons undone, he shoved her hand away from her breasts, and reached in himself to pluck a tit from the lacy bra and bring the gold-studded nipple into view. Silently he reached in the other side of her blouse and pulled the second breast from its captivity.

Her face was flushed. Her skin across the creamy white of her neckline was blushing red, as though the whole world was looking on. Arturo tugged at the gold studs. Tessa gasped, but didn't cry out. He leaned down and planted his mouth around one nipple, letting his tongue caress the skin and the gold. She had an immediate reaction between her legs.

"Quite a prize, Miles," Arturo finally commented, sitting up.

A waitress approached their table and served them

their lunch. All the while, Tessa's breasts were nearly bare, her blouse falling open down the center. Though they were still half covered, the shine of the gold could hardly be ignored as it glimmered from beneath the thin material. Tessa had never been so quite so blatant with her exhibition, especially in such a strait-laced place. Yet, she couldn't help but feel a naughty pleasure displaying herself for whoever cared to look.

There was no food ordered for Tessa. Instead, she had bites of Miles' lunch, lovingly presented to her on his fork. She ate with relish, but only a small amount, and only what he offered her. He gave her wine, but not too much of that either. It was clear that while she was in his company, Miles intended to manipulate her every act and dominate her every thought. With each small step of control, she was drawn to him, anticipation grinding at her loins. It made her long for release, but even more, she longed for each new measured step of compliance that brought her closer to him.

Arturo was nothing more than eyes and lips to exhibit for. He left just as they finished eating, and she was alone with Miles again.

His silence was awkward for her. She stared at him, waiting for some clue about what would happen next.

"Had enough to eat?" he finally asked.

"I have other appetites," she replied, teasing him. She stared deliberately at his crotch.

"I'm glad to hear that," Miles replied, "since I have the afternoon free."

She left the restaurant on his arm, wondering what he had in mind. There was a distinct thrill being with him. His reputation made him a curiosity, though it was his dominant bearing that truly had her enthralled.

Miles had a studio in the city: a loft hideaway which was a startling contrast to his formal home in the country. As he showed her the large one-room garret, she was delighted to see that this place had none of the formality she associated with Miles Bryce. She loved this place. It was an artist's garret, with dozens of brashly painted canvases hanging on the walls and leaning against each other on the floor. It was bright and cheery, and erotic in its own unique way.

"I see you like to paint naked women," Tessa said, strolling about the room. It was lit with skylights, and a golden afternoon light streamed through them, casting shadows on the sensuous works of art.

"I do, just as I'll paint you." He watched her as the beams of light hit her golden hair and she squinted because she couldn't see. Her skirt rode up high on her legs, showing off a fine curve. Tessa was unaware of how completely sensuous she was to him.

"You'll paint me, so I can be another picture on your wall?" she suggested, turning toward him.

"Oh! You'll be anything I like."

She smiled at him and turned away.

"Sit down on the bed," he directed. In one corner of the room was a foot-high platform, with a bed waiting for Tessa. It was covered in silky cream-colored sheets, haphazardly tossed over the top. The "just fucked" look aroused her. Around the bed, a rose-colored curtain draped it like a stage, the soft folds descending from the ceiling to the floor. Directly under the skylights, the bed was bathed in the sumptuous sunshine. Tessa was blinded by the light that hit her eyes. She closed them, giving up trying to see his face. She sat on the edge of the bed, prim as a schoolgirl.

Miles pulled out an easel, a sketchbook, and charcoal.

"You're going to sketch me while I sit?" she asked, trying to see what he was doing.

"No," he answered, "while you masturbate."

She moved into a shadow so she could see his expression. Her own blue eyes widened gleefully. "You want me to play with myself?"

"Yes."

It was easy for him to leave her tongue-tied, though it was from excitement, not fear. The idea of posing like a model was intriguing, so she kicked off her shoes and reclined against the pillows that covered one side of the mattress. She pulled up her skirt, pretending to be a magazine model. "You want me to take it off?" she asked, referring to the skirt.

"No, it's much nastier the way it is."

"And that's what you want, a pornographic painting?" she wondered aloud.

"That's all I do," he informed her. "But I'm not painting yet, just sketching. Now play with yourself for me," he insisted.

Tessa pulled aside her panties so she could reach her cunt.

"Take those off," Miles ordered, as if they offended him.

Tessa pushed her hands up under her skirt and pulled the tiny garment down, tossing it aside.

"I don't want you wearing panties," he informed her.

"Never?"

"Never," he affirmed. He went back to his sketch pad and began to work.

The exposed triangle of Tessa's pussy, with her neatly groomed golden brown hair, was moistening. Being observed so closely aroused her. As she saw the charcoal move quickly across the blank sheet of paper, her fingers slipped between her plump labia to find the center of her sex, the cunt and the clit. She used both hands to spread her pussy wide. Two fingers slipped inside her hole, another pressed at her anus below. She closed her eyes, her head falling back against a pillow. Her body seemed to be taking over for her mind, pushing her quickly toward a climax. The sunshine on her opened cunt was as much an aphrodisiac as Miles' eyes, almost as titillating as sunbathing. The heat had her at the edge in minutes.

Miles could see her agitation rise. "Don't come yet," he commanded.

She opened her eyes and flirted with him, her mouth drawing itself into a sensuous pout, her eyes dancing with sexual invitation. Yet he was completely serious about his work, making no comment, or any indication that he enjoyed the picture she created. Did she please him or not? He wouldn't say.

She was driving toward orgasm again when he stopped her altogether.

"I think we need a break," he said.

Like waking from a dream, she jolted to a more conscious state. "Couldn't we finish now?" she countered.

"No," he snapped. He turned away from her and washed his smudged hands in a sink by the wall.

"May I see the picture?" she asked. Rising from the bed, she strolled to his side and pressed herself against him, one leg wrapping around his body.

He shook himself free and turned back to the easel, ignoring her attempts to woo him to bed. Instead, he let her see the picture. It was a remarkable likeness, with her hands in her cunt and her mouth exuding desire.

"This one's finished," he said, wiping his wet hands on a towel. "You are a nasty little tart," he said, admiring his work.

Tessa had to agree that he'd certainly captured the essence of a sexual tease. She'd never seen a picture quite like it. "You plan to do another today?" she asked him.

"Several," he answered. "But I intend to punish you first."

The idea jolted her. "You're fulfilling your promise to me, the one you made the other day?"

"I said I would, and I never renege on a promise."

Her body fluttered with the oddest erotic jolts. The fact that real punishment was imminently upon her sent her into frenzy of feeling. Excitement and fear poured through her in equal volume; half of her wanted to lie down and be consumed by it, the other half wanted to flee as quickly as she could.

She didn't have time to respond, as Miles took her hand and moved her to a steamer trunk at one side of the room. When he opened the lid, Tessa gazed in morbid fascination at the array of whips and paddles and leather thongs. There were chains and clamps and strange devices Tessa had never seen before. Miles removed the first tray of implements, revealing more beneath. Again there were whips and paddles of ruthless design. On top of them all was a collar with a leash attached. She was sure it was for her, but instead, he pulled a strange looking whip from the bottom of the trunk.

"This one," he said, gripping the handle of the wicked-looking thing. It was a bundle of thongs tied together. There must have been two dozen soft leather strips, nearly eighteen inches long. "It's more mild than you might think," he told her.

She viewed it in silence.

When he turned back to the trunk, he pulled out another whip. "And this one," he said. Tessa stared at the nasty thing, at the long lean shaft that ended with a flexible tasseled end. It was a buggy whip.

"The thongs will warm your backside with a slow burning fire, but this will mark you." Tessa shivered, looking from the whip to Miles and back to the whip again. Lifelong fantasies surfaced in her head—woodsheds and razor strops and bending over chairs to submit to punishment. To have this happening to her now made her tremble in ways she never had before. It was more than she'd ever hoped for.

"I've always dreamed of this." She whispered her confession.

"I know," he said.

It was such a foolish thing to say, that she'd dreamed of being whipped. It was a wholly witless admission, but it was so true. The side of her that would protest such an idea was squelched without a prayer. Besides, she knew any protest would be foolish. Miles' intention was clear. Being whipped was unavoidable.

"Go to the podium," he ordered her.

She followed his instructions, finding herself standing on the platform by the bed, waiting. Miles, with both whips hanging from his left hand, stood back and inspected her.

"Remove your blouse," he said. On the surface he was completely restrained and direct, but from his eyes, there was light gleaming with fire, a quickened passion fueling his purpose.

The last button undone, Tessa's blouse slipped from her shoulders to the floor.

"And the bra," Miles said.

Tessa unhooked the lacy piece, and that too landed on the floor at her feet.

Her torso naked, Miles viewed her breasts. They stood out from her chest, so perfectly formed and well rounded; they jiggled erotically when she moved. And her nipples, two hard tight knots of mauve flesh, gleaming with gold. Miles was reminded that he wanted to sketch her bust, just as it was, with its simple statement of lust. He also wanted to add chains to either side of each nipple that would dangle down and tickle her skin. But that was for another time, now he had something far different in mind.

"Remove your skirt," he said.

Tessa unzipped the tiny Lycra garment and pushed it from her hips, leaving only her garter belt and stockings.

"Turn around and crawl up on the bed, on your hands and knees."

She did.

"Part your legs and lower your head and chest to the bed," he snapped.

Tessa complied. The effect was stunning. Miles inspected her open cunt, the puckering rear hole, and her two pert asscheeks waving at him in the tepid air.

He wondered if her fanny would be so brashly beckoning him when it was crimson from a rash of punishing blows.

"Spread your legs wider," Miles ordered, as he carefully considered her pose. Tessa caught a glimpse of his face from the corner of her eye. His eyes were gleaming nastily. He had the thong whip in his hand; the buggy whip was lying across a chair behind him.

When she was exactly as he wanted her, he moved closer, one hand reaching out and massaging her behind. His hand was warm and gentle.

"How often has this flesh been punished?" he asked.

"Never," Tessa replied.

"Never? Never spanked at all?"

"Oh I've been slapped a few times, but not punished," Tessa replied.

"No whip, or belt, or paddle?" he asked.

"A riding crop once, during sex. It was very brief."

"It's too bad you've been denied such pleasures—your psyche and your ass are made for such things."

He didn't stop to play with her cunt this time, though it was damp and pungent; it couldn't have been more ready for sex. Yet even as she wished that he'd quickly prod her with his cock, the need to feel the sting of the whip was overtaking her other desires.

"Your faltering at Maya's salon is costing you today, but be assured my little submissive, I will punish you whenever I like, simply because it pleases me."

She saw his hand draw back, then she saw no more. It happened quickly; in a split second a biting sting suddenly ripped through her rear flesh. She collapsed forward in surprise.

"Get up Tessa, and don't fall again," he advised her sternly.

She struggled to rise, knowing another blast would soon descend on her. But she wanted it, and the pain was not yet difficult to bear. He whipped her again, the blow landing squarely in the center of her waiting asscheeks. The thongs from the whip covered her entire ass, extending themselves around her hips, above to her lower back, and down to the sensitive center of her sex, where it stung most.

"Oh my God," she gasped in a sultry voice. She wiggled her rear, asking for more, and getting it.

He laid on another and another, each with mounting force. He didn't pause or stop, but continued with a measured rhythm, each stroke adding more heat. The effect of the punishment was a warm, dull, pleasing ache that gradually rose in substance, until she felt her backside, from her waist to her knees, was not warm but on fire. As Miles continued, the impact of the two dozen thongs whipped against her rear became more acute, and Tessa's cries became less inviting, more a protest.

"You'll get used to this pain, you'll even grow fond of it," he said. "You'll want it, ask for it, beg for it." She was a breathtaking picture, he thought: a picture so obscene, his body began to quake with lust. His dick was throbbing in his pants. He would have loved to have stopped right there and rammed her until he exploded, but he wasn't the kind of man to deviate from his plans.

He laid on several dozen blows before he finally paused. By then, she was in tears and sobbing, but she was not yet at her limit. She was relieved by the break, but so filled with a rush of warmth that she found herself wishing he'd start again. Her rear made the mistake of taunting him.

"You want more, little bitch?"

"Oh no, no please," she tried pleading.

He unleashed a half dozen quick blows.

"Oh God no, no more please," she wailed. This time, the cuts from the whip began to burn fiercely, especially when one thong would catch her on her cunt, and she would shriek. Miles wouldn't be persuaded one way or another by any exuberant cry, no matter how woeful; after this last blast, he was finished with the thong whip. Knowing he was done, Tessa tried to rise, but he pushed her against the bed again. His hand moved in rapid-fire motion, slapping her where the whip had just made its excursion.

"I didn't tell you to rise," he reminded her.

"Please, no more," she pleaded.

"I'm not finished," he snapped back. "We've hardly scratched the surface of your tolerance for pain."

"Oh, Miles, no," she tried again.

He ignored her and picked up the buggy whip.

She viewed the scene from the corner of her eye, as he descended on her with the implement in hand. Almost like an ancient English cane, it gleamed, the patent finish handle and shaft looking as ominous as Miles' eyes. A sizzle replaced the "swoosh" of the thongs, and the buggy whip cracked against her skin.

"No!" she bellowed, the pain rising in her like knives cutting.

Miles struck her with impassive cool, his frigid eyes fixing on the impressive mark that burned into her skin as a thin red line. He cracked it again.

"No, god, please! Aauuugh!" she blared, her cry resonating in the air.

"Silence!" Miles roared over her protest. The buggy whip sliced the air again twice more. She was rent with searing pain, but her cries quieted into soft sobs, which didn't seem to irritate him the way her screams did. It was difficult to bear this pain in any way, silent or screaming.

After the last nasty cut, her body heaved to one side to escape the next. The next one caught on the side of her thigh, splitting her body in two with its sharp snap.

"Aaaauuugggg, no!"

Miles replied with yet another vicious sizzle and crack.

"That's what you get for trying to avoid them, now quiet yourself!" he ordered, cracking the whip again.

She remained silent, though her tears were bathing the sheets below her eyes. A last cut sliced the air and landed next to the others, and he was finished, with eight distinct stripes rising from the flaming surface of her buttocks. She continued weeping long after he was done, as the pain died away, and even as she realized that some strange satisfaction was filling her. It made no sense at all.

"Tessa, to the mirror," he ordered. She lay collapsed in the comforting cocoon of the silky sheets. Rolling over, she stared at him. He was so peaceful as he looked down at her. She expected him to be enraged, with a florid face, eyes flashing like lightening, but he was calm. He gestured with his hand to the mirror, then turned away. He sat down quietly in an overstuffed easy chair and waited for her to respond. With a freshly opened bottle of dark German beer, he quenched his thirst.

"Quickly, to the mirror," he prompted her. "Hurry, before the marks fade too much, and I have to redo my work."

She bolted from the bed, worried that he'd begin with the buggy whip again. She discovered the full-length freestanding mirror ready to reflect back the picture of her recent anguish in its full technicolor glory. Tessa looked at herself in awe. The glaring red lines on her asscheeks and thighs chronicled her ordeal with exquisite correctness. She winced as she touched them, gawking at them speechless.

"Are you feeling duly admonished?" he asked. His voice, indeed his total bearing, seemed lighter than it had been all day.

"Yes," Tessa replied to his question.

"And it will happen again, whenever I desire it."

She nodded absently, still mesmerized by the stripes.

"It pleases you too, doesn't it?" He waited for a reply. "Be honest."

"Yes." Her voice was faint.

"I'll be marking you again before you sleep tonight."

"I'll be sleeping here?" she inquired.

"For a few days. You need to practice. Submissive though you are, the training will teach you more clearly what you already know about yourself. Now, come here."

She was quickly at his side, dropping to her knees between his legs. He offered her a swollen prick to satisfy, her mouth easily descended over the enormous head, to fondle it with her lips and tongue. He pressed his hands on either side of her head and pushed her down so her mouth was forced to swallow his shaft.

She gagged and choked, then tried again, for a moment allowing nearly seven inches to slide down her throat.

Her mouth began to work his prick, her head rising and falling in his lap. Her hands came up to fondle his sagging mass of balls, her lips and tongue discovering the sensitive places that caused his body to jolt. He leaned back in his chair, letting Tessa be the perfect slave to his rising demands. She was heaven to his cock.

He pulled her up into his lap, where she squatted down over him, inserting his cock into her swollen cunt. Her dark hole was slurping, it was so moist with juice. He insisted that her tongue lick his lips, that it wind its way in and out of his mouth, almost as if she was pleasing a woman's cunt.

His hands grasped her rear cheeks, holding them tightly. He squeezed the bruised flesh with such deliberate force that the pain, somewhat subsided, rose again all through her. She groaned without protesting. Rocking on his cock seemed the perfect thing to quell her discomfort. She bounced on him, half with the strength of her muscled thighs, half on the strength of his arms, which moved her up and down. Her clit was rubbing against him, the strategic place ignited.

He jerked her faster as he came, while her cunt squeezed his spewing prick as tightly as her muscles would allow.

"Auuuuugh! Tessssaaa," he groaned. The groan came from some depth, and rising, it roared through the air, reverberating in her ears.

Tessa ceased her grinding motions for a moment so

Miles could catch his breath. To her delight, he hadn't grown soft at all. Moving against him, the orgasm in her ignited. She squirmed, grinding her pussy with his dick, and he took her on a soft steady ride, with one hand fingering her clit to bring her off.

"Yes, yes, oh yes, Oooo! Ooooh ahummm, yes." Her cunt spasmed. Again and again. Her come shooting through her, she rocked joyously against him, burrowing down on him until every spasm had died away.

She fell on him when she was finished, against a bare chest she'd not yet touched, against a cheek, which, for first time, she pressed against her own. It was heaven!

They remained locked together until Tessa's bent legs ached too much to stay any longer. She pulled away, but Miles stopped her, holding her head in his hands and staring into her eyes.

"Go to the mirror," Miles said softly.

"Now?"

"You know the price of hesitating, Tessa," he warned.

She pulled her limp body from his and stretched enough to get the feeling back into her limbs. She hardly felt like standing in front of the mirror, she was so relaxed. But it was what Miles wanted. Apparently sex inspired his creativity.

For nearly two hours, he sketched her in various poses. He had her model for him, with her arms over her head and then behind her. She looked over her shoulder at the marks on her bottom, and then, bent down in a lewd reprisal of her submissive punishment posture.

When she was forced to gaze at her bottom for nearly a half hour, she confronted the stripes on her ass with curious fascination. For all his fierce work, there were only four that cut into her with enough force to leave distinguishable marks. There was another on the side of her thigh that was particularly noticeable. That was the one he'd laid on when she had tried to get away and had failed. The marks were red, the skin barely broken, but from beneath the surface, a line of bruises was appearing. Running her hands over them produced the most pleasing sensations.

They were not a common sign of affection or devotion, but to her, they were as stunning as the gold studs and as loving as the orgasm that had swept through her. Unlike the studs, these were more personal; unlike the orgasm, they were more lasting.

Later that night, after he was finished with the sketches, he called her close to him again.

"Before I leave, a reminder," he said. The buggy whip had been lying on table with his charcoal and his paints. He picked it up and flicked it against her thigh.

"You said you would, didn't you?" she replied despondently. This time she winced. The prospect of another punishment was not as exciting as before, now that she knew the fierce pain it caused.

"You'll get used to it, you'll beg for it Tessa, trust me," Miles said to reassure her. "This time, I'll be kind, you can bend over the back of the chair."

He led her to the back of his overstuffed chair. The cushion at her pussy was comforting, though this time, the blow of the whip hurt even more. Without the warming thongs first, she wasn't primed for pain. The blazing cuts came out of the blue like arrows shot into her flesh.

There were six of them, but they were sheer torture. Only the brief pause between helped to settle the instantaneous agony that leapt in her unsuspecting body.

"Gaaaawd!" she shrieked.

After each blow, she howled with pain, and this time Miles didn't silence her. By the time he was finished, tears were streaming down her cheeks.

When he pulled her up, he surrounded her with one arm, and cupped the new marks so that he could feel the rising welts. He kissed her on the mouth, her lips so soft, they blended with her tears.

"There's a bed to sleep in and plenty of food, I'll be back tomorrow," he said.

"You won't be here the night?"

"You wouldn't want me to be," he said, shaking his head. He smiled darkly then dressed himself while she watched.

When he left, she was consumed with sadness, empty, as if he'd taken something away she could not have without him. And yet, he'd left something special in return: the stripes. She admired them again in front of the mirror before she laid down to sleep.

CHAPTER FIVE

FOR THREE MORNINGS, he came to the garret with coffee and something from the bakery to eat. When they would finish their breakfast, he'd lay another half-dozen cuts on her ass. Then, for several hours each morning and afternoon she posed for him while he sketched. He kept her naked the entire time, except for a silk wrapper she wore when it was too chilly to wear nothing.

Each morning she waited expectantly for him. Her day didn't begin until he arrived. Sequestered in his artist's garret like a kept woman, she was as selfless as she'd ever been, in a state of bliss she'd dreamed of when she was most sexually aroused.

Her ass was so tender from the buggy whip that she couldn't touch it without feeling jolts of pain shoot through her. She'd peer at her bottom in the mirror for long periods of time, sometimes just to view his recent additions as the stripes increased. At other times, she wondered where he would mark her next.

Miles liked her inspecting the stripes as if they were trophies. He liked it even more when he was watching her in this little ritual. She would become aroused and begin playing with her pussy. She'd rub the spot between her labia where the sensations were the most acute. He watched several times as she brought herself to an orgasmic edge. Sometimes he let her trip over the top, her body jolting against her hands, her eyes half shut, ecstasy written in the finished expression.

More than once he went to her when she was at the edge and stopped her. He took a small crop or diminutive leather paddle from his trunk of tricks and tortured her with it. It wasn't torture of a painful sort, meant to leave the cutting punishment of the buggy whip, but a subtle torment as he pushed her skillful fingers from her cunt just as her orgasm was about to descend and replaced them with a half-dozen sharp whacks on her pussy. The blows stung, and she struggled to get away, though she was bound by his surrounding arms.

"I hate this! Stop!" she pleaded every time.

But he didn't stop.

When she was almost at the edge again, he stopped her orgasm, and beat her with his hand or strap or whatever, until she was dancing wildly to get away. He tortured her this way for as long as it pleased him, usually until she was so raw with energy pouring from her raging cunt that she was beside herself in blissful agony.

Allowed to finish, she would pulse for minutes, pained expression across her brow, her eyes gleaming with carnal passion, her body gyrating with the surging release. She would collapse against his body when she was through, showering him with grateful kisses. Then she satisfied him with her cunt or mouth. Sometimes he didn't come at all, content to let the lust remain for another, better moment.

"I love you, Tessa," he'd say afterwards.

She'd smile at him, the simple words making love to her soul, just as his body had made love to her body.

On the fourth day, Miles surprised her with Gabrielle.

"So here's the little tramp," the woman gushed, rushing to take Tessa's hands in hers. Tessa had been naked at the mirror; she was suddenly embarrassed at someone else seeing her in her natural state.

Gabrielle was a statuesque redhead, with a tender smile and fierce eyes. She was effusive, completely unrestrained, taking Tessa in her arms as if she were a pet. She stroked her body, especially her breasts, painfully flicking the studs with her fingers.

"Cute!" she appraised them.

"Cute?" Miles looked amused by the sight of the two women.

"She'll do for a fine party, is that what you had in mind?"

"Not exactly," Miles said.

"Why not? Such a delicate, pliant one," she went on. Gabrielle turned Tessa around so that she could see the marks on her buttocks. "Ah, what stripes! You've been whipping her hard to leave ones so apparent. They must hurt." The woman pressed her fingers against them, tracing the lines with a firm touch.

Tessa gasped, looking at Miles for some support. He only stared at her, expressionless.

"You going to keep her here forever, as your slave?"

"She's not a slave. She's free to go."

"I like being with him," Tessa said.

"I didn't ask you," Gabrielle said nastily, slapping her face lightly as she spoke.

Tessa would have liked Miles to come to her defense, but he didn't seem interested in directing this confrontation in any particular way. He simply let it unfold, and Tessa was on her own.

"I would think she'd be a fine gift. You have friends that would be delighted with a trinket so charming and refined."

"She's not for giving away," Miles said.

"Really? You're changing your whoring tune, all of a sudden?" Miles ignored the question, disappearing into the kitchenette where the women could hear him rummaging through the refrigerator.

Gabrielle turned to Tessa. "You know he's a devil with women. You see all these canvases around here. How many women are there?" She waltzed around the garret. "Ten? Fifteen? Twenty? Don't you suppose he's had them all on that bed?"

"Why are you telling me this?" Tessa asked, wondering what the brazen hussy's motives were.

"Has he told you about all his conquests?" she asked.

"He doesn't have to," Tessa answered. "They don't matter to me."

"Really, how new age, how generous. I just hope you don't think you're the only place he's getting his cock off."

"It would please me any way he's pleasured," Tessa answered.

"Ah! She's priceless, Miles," Gabrielle exclaimed, as Miles returned with a cold beer in his hand. She turned back to Tessa. "I suppose if you're so open-minded, you'd have no trouble watching me make love to him?"

"If that's what he wants, then it would likely arouse me," Tessa said. She had mettle of her own, more subtle, but more substantial and steady than Gabrielle would ever be. Whether Miles was simply tormenting her with this woman, preparing her with another test of loyalty and submission, or Gabrielle baiting her was just a fluke, she wasn't about to turn into a jealous nag. Besides, she would be aroused by sex between the two of them, so what would there be to worry about? This woman was certainly no competition for her, she was sure of that.

"Shall we make love and let her watch?" Gabrielle said, sashaying to Miles, as he sat peacefully in his chair. Gabrielle dropped to her knees and began running her hands along his thighs.

"I haven't had you in a couple years, can you still keep up with me?" he asked.

"Can I keep up with you! You brute! Just remember, no hard stuff, you hear." She was coy like a cat.

"I don't know, Gabby, you've never complained when I laid a strap across your butt," Miles said, leaning forward and taking the woman's face in his hands. He forced his mouth on hers, and she opened wide for a wet kiss. Miles dropped his hand inside the woman's blouse, and fondled her at will. Then he dispensed with her blouse, so that her voluptuous tits were naked for his eyes to see.

Gabrielle gasped and grunted in response to his massage.

"God! You are a devil, Miles Bryce," she exclaimed.

The sex was fitful and raucous. He took what he wanted of Gabrielle's generous breasts, kneading them like dough and slapping them with harsh pelts so that her flesh reddened quickly. She purred, and wailed, then purred some more.

Tessa, from the other side of the room, watched in wonder, never having witnessed the sight of a man and woman making love like this. It was much like the way Miles made love to her, though it seemed the care she felt from him was missing in his sex with Gabrielle.

"Stop it!" the woman pleaded when the pain became too much. Her protests were meaningless. Miles refused to alter his style for her. He was as in control of Gabrielle as he was of Tessa.

After some time, Miles pushed the woman from his lap and pulled her toward the bed. He leveled his eyes at Tessa, still sitting before the mirror. Tessa was no longer looking at herself, but intently staring at the other two. Miles flashed her a steely cold glare, that seemed to say, "Obey me without question, or you'll pay the price."

"Don't move, little slut," he said aloud. "Perhaps you can learn something." His attention returned to Gabrielle, who was already reclining, legs open on his bed like a whore in heat. Miles' prick entered her quickly, as Gabrielle pulled him to her. Her legs wrapped around his body, and he humped her fiercely.

"Ah, ah, ah yes, you bastard, fuck me!"

He pounded her vigorously, while she ground her cunt into his groin.

"Fuck me, yes!" she screamed.

Miles threw the woman's legs up over his shoulders, so he could penetrate her deeper still.

"Ah, yes! You ass! Fuck me, yes, fuck fuck fuck it in." She groaned as deeply as Miles groaned, and roared as he roared. The two climaxed almost simultaneously, their cries deafening.

As Tessa watched, she found herself wiggling her pussy against her legs, wishing that her cunt could be filled the way that Gabrielle's was.

When Miles pulled himself from the woman's sloppy cunt, he collapsed on the bed beside her, letting the last of his spasms jolt his body with pleasant sensations.

"Goddamn, I hate you Miles Bryce, look what you've done scratching my tits," Gabrielle declared, looking down at the mounds of flesh that she cupped in her hands.

"They look better that way," Miles said, slapping at one of them again.

"Stop that!" she seethed.

There was no soft meandering quiet after their fuck. That seemed curious to Tessa, especially when it was those moments of tranquillity after sex that she treasured most.

"I wish I could slap that smile from your cocky face," Gabrielle seethed, as she pulled herself from the bed and looked down at a chipper Miles.

"Didn't you have a good time? Didn't you do exactly what you wanted to do?"

"Well, of course, I showed the little trollop what a nasty ass you are."

"I think she already knew."

"Of course she knows you're a brute, but perhaps she didn't know that you're also the world's most accomplished Lothario." She said that with a heavy degree of scorn.

"Well now she knows, thanks to you," Miles said. He stood up and walked to Tessa, pulling her to her feet.

"So am I a worthless Lothario?" he asked Tessa, the hint of a smirk on his face.

"Probably," Tessa replied with a smile.

"I don't understand you two," Gabrielle said, shaking her head. She had a stocking in her hands, and was trying to put it on. "Oh damn, I've ruined these. You've ruined these," she charged. Her eyes flashed sharply at Miles.

"Then I'll buy you another pair," he said in a gallant gesture. "It's the least I can do for such a fine fuck."

"Don't bother, dear, just take care of this little plaything, and if you want to share her around, I'd love to know."

"In good time, just don't hold your breath."

"Maybe you'll have her ready for Damien's Ball."

"Why, that's a thought."

"Don't use that mocking tone on me," she informed him.

"I'd never mock you, Gabrielle, I think too much of you." His voice dripped with sarcasm that the woman chose to ignore.

Miles led her to the door, while she gathered her clothes and her purse. She tossed her wide cape around her shoulders with a flourish, completely ignoring Tessa, except for one brief sidelong glance.

"Good-bye, darling," she purred at Miles, and kissed him softly on his lips.

Miles turned from the door, leaning against it. The playful version of his eyes met Tessa's amused ones.

"So what did you think?" he asked.

"Of Gabrielle?"

"Of course," Miles said.

"I think she's deluding herself," Tessa said.

"Oh? How so?"

"I think she'd love to be submissive to you," Tessa said. "Bound, whipped, and loved."

"You did learn something then," Miles said, a smile of satisfaction breaking out on his face.

"What about this ball she talked about?" Tessa asked. She'd heard of Damien's Ball—just the thought of it sent a sinister shiver though her.

"What about it?" he asked.

"Would you take me?"

"Would you want to go?"

"It sounds fascinating."

"It is," Miles said. She watched him walk to the kitchen and return with a glass of juice for each of them.

"So would you take me?"

"Maybe. When you're ready to go the way I want you."

Tessa wondered what that meant, but she didn't ask. "Would I wear a mask of feathers?" she asked, remembering the infamous costumes she had heard so much about.

"That's possible, but you're not going, Cinderella, until you've paid your dues to the wicked stepmother and her sisters." She looked at him puzzled. He flashed her another beguiling grin. "You'll just have to wait and see, won't you? Now go on and get cleaned up. Now!"

She was about to follow his order, when she turned back to him. "Just one thing?" she inquired.

"Yes?"

"She orgasms with you fucking her."

"So?"

"I don't like that."

"I like the way you come, I'm in control," Miles said.

"But perhaps we could climax together, sometime?"

"We will Tessa. But remember, our arrangement isn't about romance and fine artistry, it's about sex."

CHAPTER SIX

MILES THREW TESSA an old cutoff sweatshirt.

"Here put this on," he told her.

It fell lewdly off one shoulder.

"These should do," he added.

He handed her a pair of biker shorts that fit skintight around her. The Lycra rubbed against her sore stripes, and with each move she made, the discomfort reminded her they were there. She was certain Miles had planned it that way.

"Where are we going?" she asked, when they were in the car. With the top of the small sports car down, the wind blew through her hair. Such sumptuous freedom.

"I'm taking you home."

"To my apartment?"

"Is that not home?"

"Yes." She was disappointed.

They didn't talk while they drove; the sound of the wind made it too difficult to hear each other. Miles was typically silent anyway, and Tessa, realizing that her extended "date" with Miles was over, didn't want to talk. She was already missing him, and the garret, and his unbridled imagination.

When they arrived in front of her apartment, Miles got out with her and followed her into the building, across the lobby to the elevators. They waited in a fitful silence for the elevator to reach ground level.

When the behemoth machine ground to a stop, the doors pulled apart. An impatient Martine ran into them as she was exiting. Her brisk departure interrupted, she looked at the two in amazement.

"Well, where the hell have you been?" Martine asked.

"This is Miles," Tessa said, introducing the two. As usual, Martine was wearing black from head to toe. Sometimes she looked like a witch, taking her somber air to the extreme, but today she was quite attractive, in a filmy black skirt and blouse that draped around her small firm frame. Her long hair was tied atop her head like a Gibson girl. The little wisps falling around her face softened the effect of her stern eyes and tight-set jaw.

"Ah! The dominant," Martine remarked, taking Miles' hand in hers, looking him squarely in the eye. She smiled as if she were impressed. So little impressed Martine.

"You've been whipping her butt?" she asked. "She likes that you know." The three strolled together toward the front door, talking as casually as if conversing about the weather.

"I've been taking good care of her," Miles said, pleasantly. He couldn't take his eyes off Martine.

It frightened Tessa seeing the two of them standing side by side, though she wasn't sure yet why the jolt of trepidation flew through her like a Halloween bat.

"You do that, Miles Bryce, you take good care of her," Martine said. "Perhaps you'll discover what I've known about her all along."

"And what is that, Martine?" Miles inquired.

"Her sexual greed. There's nothing she won't do for her cunt."

Miles nodded as if he understood. Not once did he take his eyes off the irrepressible woman. "Thank you for your appraisal, I'll keep that in mind," he told her. They reached out to shake hands again.

"Glad to have met you," Martine said, and she briskly walked out of the building.

"Are you two lovers?" Miles inquired, once Tessa's roommate had disappeared.

"Sometimes," Tessa replied.

"She seems to know your sexual tastes. You told me you were never whipped," he said.

"I wasn't, until you. Martine just knows me, or so she thinks. She does enjoy taking advantage of me whenever she likes."

"Takes advantage of you—you're telling me you don't like making love to her?"

"It's rarely what you'd call making love."

"So it's sex. Do you like it?"

"Of course," Tessa answered, remembering what turned her on about Martine. "I like that her body is different from a man's. I like the way she touches me, the way she licks my cunt and scratches me with her fingernails. It's just sometimes her attitude..." She was reluctant to say everything she was thinking.

"Her attitude is what?"

"Overbearing."

Miles eyes lightened mischievously, "You mean dominant."

"Yeah, I suppose so," Tessa admitted.

"I'm surprised that bothers you."

"I know. It doesn't seem reasonable, considering the way I love you to control me. But you're different." She didn't want to discuss the matter more, but Miles pressed her as they started back toward the elevators.

"I'd like to see her whip you sometime. And I *will* fuck her."

Tessa stopped in her tracks.

"That bothers you?" Miles asked, noticing Tessa's hesitation.

"Are you going up with me?" Tessa asked, avoiding the interrogation.

"No, I'm not going up," Miles said. "Now answer my question."

She turned to him, pouting like a schoolgirl. "You know, you can have any woman you want, why would you suddenly want Martine?" Tessa asked.

"Yes, I can have any woman I want. But that's not what I asked. Tell me, does it bother you that I want Martine?" He was eager for an answer.

"Yes, it does," she admitted.

"Good," Miles said, "that's all the more reason for me to have her." His words were laced with an arrogance that she didn't like.

"Where does she work?" he asked.

"At the museum."

"With you?"

"No, in acquisitions," Tessa told him.

The elevator, creeping like a ponderous dinosaur, came to a rattling halt once again. As the doors jerked open, Tessa saw it rescuing her from a conversation she wanted ended. Though as she waved good-bye, she feared that more than just the conversation was finished. It seemed a time of innocence with Miles was ending too. She watched a strangely winsome grin flash across his face before he disappeared from view. She shivered, suddenly ice cold.

Two days later, Martine came barging into the apartment after work, ready for a major proclamation. She loved the drama of outrageous pronouncement, and this one was high drama indeed. Tessa could tell before she said a word.

"He came to see me today," Martine said. Like two darts meant to hurt, her eyes shot through Tessa.

"Who?"

"Your boyfriend," she answered sarcastically.

"And what did he want?" Tessa asked.

"To take me out."

"When?"

"Tonight."

"Are you going?"

"Of course." She took off her shoes and threw them in a corner. "He's fascinating, but you already know that, don't you? The man captivates my roommate, sometime lover, for days, and then turns around and asks me out like it's no big deal. I love it. He's a real scoundrel." Martine retreated to her bedroom. Tessa could hear her tearing through her closet. "You got yourself a real bad one this time. I'm really surprised, Tessa, that you're handling this so calmly." Martine said this with complete admiration.

Tessa could see that Miles and Martine had a common temperament. And strangely, the idea of the two of them together turned her on. She didn't like that fact. But she couldn't deny the pleasant churnings that were beginning to rise in her.

Martine returned to the room, wearing a pair of leather pants. She was buttoning a red leather bustier around her. "Besides," she went on, "the idea of your sitting at home pining for him all night, while we dance the night away—I find that a perfectly shameful, but fitting thing to do. It'll piss you off, won't it?"

"You're really dreadful," Tessa exclaimed.

"Oh, I am, I know it." She suddenly changed her look, staring right at Tessa's crotch with a bewildered expression. "Where'd you get those shorts?"

"Why do you ask?"

"Because I know they aren't yours."

"Maybe I bought them," Tessa said.

"Did you?"

"No," she admitted, "Miles gave them to me." She looked down at the shorts as if she'd forgotten she had them on.

"Take them off," Martine ordered.

"Why?"

"Take them off, I want to see your ass," Martine pressed.

Tessa looked at her, knowing that she could refuse her demand, but as usual, it didn't seem important to deny Martine her wishes. The command could easily have come from Miles. Perhaps he'd told her to inspect her ass. Then, the demand would be as much Miles' as Martine's.

Deciding to comply, Tessa tugged at the waistband of the snug shorts and pushed them down over her hips, so they dropped to her ankles. The silky hairs of her pussy gleamed for Martine to see. She'd seen her pussy a hundred times; this was nothing new.

"Take off that shirt, so I can see you better. I want to see what he's done to you."

Tessa obeyed. Her nakedness was exciting them both.

"Turn around," Martine ordered.

Tessa turned around, showing off her buttocks and what was left of the bruising cuts. There were still at least a dozen clear spots where the nasty buggy whip had marked her skin. Martine gazed at her ass, while Tessa waited for some typically critical remark, though she found Martine's inspection was having an unexpectedly titillating effect on her.

"He got you good, didn't he?" she finally said. Tessa nodded. She was becoming juicy between her legs, she couldn't help herself. Whether it was the memory of the punishments, or revealing them to someone else, the careful examination was provoking in her a gnawing desire to fuck.

Tessa's arousal must have been obvious. Martine wasted little time taking her roommate by her hand and leading her to the couch. She pushed Tessa down, belly first, so that her bruised butt was available for her to play with.

"I like this Tessa—perhaps I should have done this

to you a long time ago. Such vivid stripes, they must have been welts to begin with."

Martine continued to move her hand about the punished bottom, only to find Tessa beginning to churn her groin into the couch.

"You little slut, this turns you on, doesn't it?" Her hand continued to stroke Tessa's bottom. She pinched it where it looked most sore.

"Ooooo, ouch," Tessa seethed quietly, though her bottom continued to gyrate. She wasn't looking for Martine to stop.

Grabbing a pillow, Martine shoved it under Tessa's groin so that her rear was bobbing high in the air. The woman's finger slipped between her asscheeks, deep into her rear cleft. Tessa responded, parting her legs and raising her ass so that Martine could better explore. A finger pushed against her asshole.

"Did he fuck you here?"

"No."

"I bet he will."

Tessa didn't reply; the answers were all too obvious.

"Anyone been inside your ass?" Martine probed.

"No," Tessa answered.

The deeper the woman's finger prodded her, the more her whole sex ached. She wiggled against the invading probe, letting it slip even deeper.

"You want more of this, don't you, you vile little tramp!"

From a cabinet nearby, Martine pulled out a jar of cream and a dildo: an eight-inch-long prick, three inches around. They'd used it inside their cunts many times, but never in an ass.

"No! Not that one, it's too big," Tessa protested, as

she saw Martine grease the thing so it would easily slip inside her anus.

"It's as big as he'll be, I bet. You'll handle him, he'll make you. So you can handle this."

"Please, Martine."

"Just relax little tramp, you owe me this. After all, you were mine first."

"I was never yours," Tessa answered back nastily. She tried to wiggle away.

"Oh, no you don't." The stronger woman, Martine, planted an arm around Tessa's waist and held her firmly. With the other hand, she pried apart Tessa's clenched asscheeks. "You'd better open up, you slut, or I'll shove it in you and it'll hurt like hell."

Tessa relinquished her claim on her rear. There was no point in fighting Martine, especially when her own body was screaming to have her rear channel filled. The peculiar feelings were too splendid to give up, the way they made her body explode with one bright burst of energy after another. Parting her legs again, she let Martine's hand open her wide enough so that the thick shaft of the dildo pressed against her anus. The sphincter released slowly, as the head of the dildo, shaped just like the head of a cock, pushed open the tight barrier. It wasn't easy.

"Ouch, that hurts."

"Because you're too tense," Martine purred in her ear. She rolled Tessa on to her side, the dildo just half in. "Play with your cunt and relax. You know you want this in all the way."

Tessa's hand went between her legs, finding the place she loved most to rub. She played with herself, while Martine pushed the fat prick deeper into her rear channel. The tight place finally gave way completely, so that the eight long inches nestled inside her. Tessa sighed with relief and began to grind her rear against the invading prick.

"Ooooo yes, this is...," her voice trailed off softly.

Martine began to pump the thick cock in and out.

"Oh God yes." Tessa humped her rear. "Oh God yes, do it more," she screamed. The dildo went in and out of her, with sharp vigorous thrusts, even as Tessa's hand played with her clit and juicing hole.

"Damn yes...please more, yes, yes more, I love it, please Martine, don't stop...."

"Ah, yes, take it, you little whore," Martine purred, hammering Tessa as hard as she could.

Tessa was weeping, tears of pleasure running down her cheeks, her orgasm rising inside like one fierce clap of thunder rolling through her.

"Aaaarughhhhh, yeeeeesss, yeesssss." She clenched against the dildo and her own hand, once, twice, a half dozen times more. Then she went limp.

Tessa was aware of nothing until she felt Martine stroking her bottom: her stripes, bruises, and violated rear hole. Martine turned Tessa over on her back and smiled down on her with a familiar cunning smile of celebration. "You're so easy Tessa, the only thing you care about is your cunt, and now of course, your ass." She laughed. "I was right, wasn't I, you could take it all. Next time, I'll strap it on and ram you like a man."

Tessa's eyes were glassy, tearing still. She was still enjoying the last of the prickly sensations that had driven her mad, and she couldn't think of anything to say.

"Now," Martine smirked. She slapped Tessa's thigh with a firm whack. "If he asks, you can tell him that I had you in the ass first." She shrugged her off and walked away, getting ready for her date, while Tessa remained on the couch, watching.

CHAPTER SEVEN

SHE WAS BEHIND glass, the window display in the museum nearly done. Watching her bent-over position, Miles could see almost everything he wanted to see—the tops of her stockings, the rear garters, and the delicious swell of her upper thighs that would meet at her pussy. Did she know how she looked? He watched her for some time, until she became uneasy. A little voice inside told her to turn around.

"You bastard!" she mouthed to him, when she saw him on the other side of the glass. She motioned him to a side door, behind the display, to a storeroom filled with mannequins, props, drapes, and novelties not being shown to the public at the time.

"Are you finished?" he asked.

"Very close. I can stop for tonight," she told him.

"I want you to pose again."

"You mean more time away from the museum?"

"Can you arrange it?"

"Not until these are displays are finished."

"How long will that take?"

"Three days?" she guessed. Her eyebrows drew up in consternation, then relaxed. "Well, I'm not really sure." She shrugged, not wanting to displease him.

"Three days should do," Miles said, "I can be ready then."

"Three days for what?"

"For the preparations."

"And what are those?"

He didn't answer. Instead he gazed around the storeroom. There were dozens of useful things he could use right there to provoke his subject. He grabbed a length of rope.

"Stand still and put your hands behind you."

"Here?" she questioned him.

"Here," he confirmed. "No one's going to see us. Though I think you'd like that, wouldn't you?"

She hadn't thought about an audience before. It would be startling—but certainly not now, not here!

He bound her hands behind her.

"I bet you've been waving this nasty backside of yours all day, bending over like that. I wonder who else got to see that fine view?"

"No one but you," she assured him.

"Well, I'm not going to waste a perfect opportunity," he said. From out of nowhere, she saw a leather spanker in his hand.

"What if someone hears?" she asked.

"You won't make a sound, Tessa. Besides this doesn't strike that loudly, that's why I picked it."

He reached out and opened her blouse. Her breasts with their gold studs stood out lewdly. She'd worn no bra, and he liked that.

The spanker came down on the left breast and then the right.

"Ooooo…no…," she gasped. It was not a cry of pain, far from it. It had been days since she'd seen him, and she missed his attention to her submissive training. With Martine coming home two nights in a row, after dates with Miles—dates she wouldn't breath a word about—Tessa had wondered if he still wanted her. This was a sign that he still cared, at least enough to punish her.

The spanker snapped against her tits a half dozen more times on each side, until the white flesh was glowing red. Then he came down with the leather right at the very tips, where the skin was most tender, and the studs poked through her nipples. It stung like crazy to have them nipped by the edge of the leather.

"God, no more Miles," she cried, her face screwing up into a frightful scowl.

His left hand came up to slap her face.

"You'll take what I give you, Tessa. Be careful how you protest," he warned.

He continued tormenting her tits until they burned, then he whipped her around and thrust her over a sawhorse that was conveniently standing just behind her.

"I should have come here before—it's inspiring what you have to work with." He pushed her short skirt to her waist; she was wearing a thong panty and her garter belt. He pulled at the thong. "Panties?" he growled. He pulled the thong so hard it hurt, cutting her along the soft flesh it was meant to cover.

"Please," she whimpered.

"Where did these come from? I thought I told you to keep this cunt of yours naked?"

She said nothing.

He cracked the leather against her ass angrily. "Is that not what I told you?" he said, demanding an answer.

"Yes, Miles."

"Too bad. I was planning to fuck you, spank you a little, and then fuck you. Now I'll have to punish you. I'm afraid you'll regret this blunder."

It didn't surprise her that he would spank her ass, since the leather had already heated her breasts. But now she'd angered him. She had no idea what might result.

He let the leather fly ferociously. With one smack after another, the leather came down on her rear flesh. Methodically, he made his way from the top of her thighs to the top of her asscheeks.

She wanted to cry out, but there was the sound to worry about, sound that might bring the janitor or the curator from out of nowhere. She compromised, groaning deeply. She struggled with her hands—the bonds hurt—but the more she struggled with them, the tighter they got.

"Please, Miles, please stop, I'm so sorry."

He ignored her, the blows continuing.

Her unfortunate position over the wooden sawhorse was painful, and she had to spread her legs wide to steady herself, so she wouldn't topple forward. This only spread her more openly, so that the leather was able to strike the places between her rear cheeks where the cuts blistered her.

She wanted to let loose with a frantic howl, but she suppressed it.

Miles stopped for a moment. She thought it was to admire his work, but he was looking for something.

"This should do," he finally said.

From the corner of her eye she saw the bamboo rod in his hand. It had come from an old display. Tossed in a corner, it was of no use to the museum anymore. If she'd known what it would do to her rear, she would have begged him to find something else.

It produced a sizzling zing in the air, landing with a snap across both asscheeks.

"Eeeaw..." She couldn't help the cry that surfaced, splitting the air with her instantaneous woe.

"It hurts, doesn't it, Tessa?" Miles chortled, satisfied that he was cutting her more deeply than he ever had before. He landed another in the same place. She fought to squelch the pain and the scream about to blare out into the cold, dank storeroom. Another two, with the same fierce action, and sobs spilled from her. Soft as her cries were by necessity, they were as impassioned as a bloodcurdling scream. "No more please," she wailed at Miles with a savage whisper.

"No more what?" he said, as if he were laughing at her. Another two stripes devastated her rear. She would have fallen forward on her head, just to get away from another, but that wasn't necessary. He pulled her up by her bound hands and held her around the waist, while whispering in her ear.

"A good submissive anticipates her dominant's will, and she never, ever, fails to do as she's told."

Her sobbing made her body heave, made tears spill

onto Miles' arm. He waited until she had quieted, body and soul, holding her, letting his forceful command consume her.

Though calmer, her bottom still burned, a fierce fire tearing through it.

At last, he let go of her waist and pushed her back against the sawhorse to view the damage. All six cuts had left cruel welts, and in two places he'd broken the skin. He removed his handkerchief to dab the specks of blood away.

"How lovely," he exclaimed, "these will last some time. You'd better watch yourself, Tessa, or you may never heal this tender place." He pulled her to her feet again.

"I'm sorry about the panties, I wasn't thinking," she apologized.

"Don't waste your apology. Following my wishes, that's what matters."

"I wasn't certain if you still wanted me."

"Why would you think that?" he asked, both annoyed and surprised by the admission.

"Martine."

"Really? Martine thought otherwise, that you were actually aroused by my screwing her."

"I am, but I don't think I should be."

"Why's that?"

"I want you totally devoted to me," she said innocently.

"And I am. Completely." He was totally sincere. "Remember Martine's not you."

"I know that." Tessa tried to smile.

"Then trust what we have together, little captive." He patted her on her bare rear.

"I wish I had," Tessa confessed.

"I would think so. And it's too bad. Now, you'll just have to wait for another time."

"Another time?"

"For sex," he explained. He looked down at her exposed womanhood.

With her skirt still around her waist, Tessa gazed down at her cunt, at the curly hair and the soft swell where it made a mound full enough for Miles to grab with his hand. He looked as if he wanted to change his mind about the sex. And for an instant, she was sure he'd screw her. Instead, he simply ran his hands through her pubic hair.

"I think I'll have you shave this soon," he informed her. "It'll become an obstruction to other things. As soft as it is to touch, what's underneath is even softer." He pulled at her hair as he made his point.

"You want me shave it for next time?" Tessa asked.

"No, not yet. When I tell you. It'll be something to think about. Before I'm finished with you love, your body will tell all the world what you are."

The very idea was mind-boggling. Tessa couldn't even guess what he had in mind. But she was very curious about his comment, "You're planning to 'finish' with me, as if I'm some project?" she asked.

He smiled at her. "No, my darling, there's no real finishing, you can be certain of that. If nothing else, whipping your delicious body will keep me well satisfied for a very long time. And on that account, we've only begun to discover your limits."

His implications scared her, but he was also reassuring. She couldn't imagine losing him to Martine, or anyone else for that matter. She couldn't imagine losing the wildness and the fine freedom he gave her each time they were together.

"Think!" he said again. He pulled at her pubic hair with a fierce tug, as if he were going to pull it off at that very moment. "Imagine how it might feel to have your naked cunt take the whip."

She cringed. Yet her eyes were fixed on him, and his adoring gaze kept her from letting the horror of his designs unnerve her. Wrapped in his embrace, she could only feel protected and cared for.

He yanked at the thong panties, still drawn up inside her, the material burning into her the way the cuts had burned. He pulled a pocket knife from his pants and cut them free, then pocketed the useless piece of cloth, as if she might be tempted to restore them.

"Three days," he said nodding to her. "The car will come by for you after work."

Then, he was quickly gone.

Her bottom ached. These stripes were the worst he'd laid on her. Her skirt rubbed against them, and with every step she wanted to wince. What could he possibly do more, except wield his passions across her more tender places?

CHAPTER EIGHT

TESSA WAS DROPPED at the door of Miles' garret on Friday night. His limousine and driver had been in front of the museum waiting for her when she left work that afternoon. No Miles, just his aide, ready to whisk her away.

Tessa wondered how long this interlude from the real world would last. She wondered if she wouldn't rather this be her entire world, this reveling in bondage, this surrendering to Miles' capricious whims. His odd carnival feast of lust made her tremble so. She'd never been so satisfied with sex or her life.

For three days after his surprise visit to the museum, dizzying expectations had wracked her brain. Her body was constantly hot, though there was little place to put her raging urges, since Miles still seemed more enamored with Martine than he was with her—at least when it came to having his own sexual needs satisfied. Martine had been out with him two more times. She'd left the apartment each time dressed like a whore, her clothes barely covering her body. Her ass had a splendid swish inside the tight skirts, her breasts bobbed softly against the fabric of her stretchy tops.

"Do you think he'll like it?" she asked Tessa. Her wicked make-up and tousled hair were straight from the pages of a pornographic magazine.

"I'm sure he will," Tessa answered evenly.

"He likes my ass. He squeezes it hard."

"That should suit you—you're a closet submissive, we both know that," Tessa observed.

"Jealous, are we?"

"No." It was only half a lie.

Martine looked down at her with sultry eyes. "You know you're very good, being this coy. I'd be pissed as hell, if it were me."

"Well, you're not me," Tessa reminded her.

"I know," she replied triumphantly. "And I'll be on his arm tonight, I'll be in his bed, and I'll eat breakfast from his plate in the morning," she said, waving her ass near Tessa's face. "Have a nice night." She swaggered out the door, leaving traces of her spicy perfume in the air.

The bitch returned in the morning with her face beaming, though she said little about her escapade. Tessa couldn't be sure if that was because sex with Miles was indescribable or disappointing. She decided that she would rather not know. It would only turn her on. Especially since her body was screaming for some completion, besides what she gave herself with her own hand.

Now, as Tessa climbed the long stairway toward Miles' garret on the third floor, the only thing she could think about was how much she wanted to be spirited away into this lost world, where nothing made sense, nothing was normal, and nothing was logical, where everything was a function of pure carnal satisfaction. She liked thumbing her nose at rules that condemned her for her inborn desires. "Let them have their morality and have no fun," she would say to herself. While the straight world was busy being desperate and unsatisfied, she was having the time of her life in the bosom of decadence.

When Tessa reached the top of the stairs, she was almost out of breath. Seeing the door to the garret ajar, she pushed it open. She was surprised to see that the scene inside had changed, in much the same way that a theater set changes with the new act of a play.

There was a darker hue about the large room. The drapes had been changed from soft white to deep cranberry. The bed on the platform, once draped in white, was now also covered by a darker shade of cloth; a bedspread with a muted paisley design completed the picture. The day was overcast, so the light that entered through the massive skylights was gloomy at best. And there was one distinct addition to the room: A strange apparatus was hanging from the ceiling, a rope dangling from a heavy hook, with leather straps hanging down from that. A quiet comforting beauty accompanied the new arrangement. Tessa marveled at the changes, knowing the atmosphere suited Miles' purposes, mystical and enigmatic like Miles himself. Her body responded with a gentle erotic rush, even though there was something ominous about the transformation.

Hearing a shuffling sound behind her, Tessa turned to see a strange man. Across the room, opposite the bed, he was setting up a video camera and a bank of lights.

"Hello?" she said. She approached him cautiously.

"Tessa?" he guessed.

"Yes," she confirmed.

"I'm Hector," he introduced himself, politely holding out his hand for a conventional handshake.

Tessa nodded, still puzzled by his presence. She looked around the room. "The place looks so different," she said.

"Do you like the changes?" he asked.

"I do," she said, perusing the room one more time. Returning her attention to the stranger and his video camera, she concluded only one thing. "You're going to film me?"

"Yes, he is." Tessa heard Miles' voice answer, coming from behind her in the direction of the bathroom. She turned to see him walking toward her, beaming broadly. He was wearing black, a black silk shirt and pair of black pants. His hair was tied back in a ponytail, and the ring in his ear gleamed. He was stunning. Oh! How she'd missed him and this garret!

"Are you still going to sketch me?" she asked.

"Of course."

"But this?" She gestured to the lights and the video camera.

"Hector's going to record what we do...when I want him to." He wrapped an arm around Tessa's waist and walked with her to the bed.

"But why?"

"To excite you, among other things," he replied.

She wanted to laugh, a little snicker crossing her face. She wondered if he was joking. "Just to excite me?" she asked.

"It'll be fun," Miles assured her. "Then, I can watch the video and have you any time I want."

"But you *can* have me anytime you want now," she said.

"I know, but I want other people to see you too. There's a decent market for such films, for porn of a genuine sadistic-masochistic flavor."

"My God, I never thought of us that way," Tessa remarked.

"But the rest of world would, and that's no shame, is it now?"

"No. I'm not ashamed at all, but you'll sell these? To strangers?"

"Or give them away. Don't worry, the demand is limited; you won't be in theaters across the country. Though I should think you'd make a perfect subject for a feature film, instead of some of the drivel that's passed off as art these days."

Tessa had thought she could accept anything that Miles offered in their relationship, but she wondered at accepting this. Did he own her that completely? Did he have the right to display her body for all the world to see? It was a frightening thought.

"Get out of your mind and into your cunt, my dear," he told her, whispering in her ear. His warm breath aroused her. "I can feel your body heat, and so can you. The very thought of making a porno movie is provoking all your immoral desires." His hand pushed its way up under her skirt and grabbed at her pussy.

She breathed deeply, realizing that he was right.

"This is as obscene as anything I've ever done," she said quietly.

"Good, then you'll love it. Don't try to deny what you feel because I know what it is. You can't escape anything with me."

Sometimes he knew her better than she knew herself.

Miles sat down on the bed and brought her close to him. Raising her skirt, he pushed away her silky hair and began to finger her carefully. He pulled her to him and began to lick her, parting her labia so her clit was exposed. The hard bud protruded provocatively. It was so tender to touch, the way he held it open, that even the air passing over it made it sting. Miles' tongue made it sting all the more. She jerked back, though he held her fast to his face with a firm hand planted on her sore behind. He ran his tongue about the soft flesh above her clit. She was quivering from head to toe. It would take little to start her body toward a crashing finish.

But it was just a tease.

Miles backed her off and pulled down her skirt.

"I have things to do," he said. "Be good while Hector finishes getting ready." He gave her a few patronizing pats on her bottom.

Minutes later, he was gone, leaving her still standing by the side of the bed in stunned silence.

"Perhaps you'd be more comfortable if you sat down," Hector suggested, after the photographer noticed her still standing stock-still.

"Ah, yes, I guess I would," Tessa said, blushing.

She sat down on the dark bed, on the velvety paisley cloth that was so smooth to touch. She felt it against her legs, almost like satin would feel, soft and inviting. She sat as a child might sit, with her legs hanging over the edge of the bed. They didn't quite touch the floor. She put her hands in her lap politely, thinking that with all the sordid things that she'd already done in this place, she was feeling rather pristine, almost holy, like a virgin waiting to be violated by her husband for the first time. Then again, wasn't every sex act a virgin experience, wasn't every escapade an awakening to something new?

"Relax, Tessa," Hector said. He'd been staring at her while she waited in her virtuous repose.

Hector was the kind of man Tessa used to fuck—the playful eyes, the sparkling smile, the risqué Latin swagger in his hips. He'd be the kind to dance with her hips to hips, crotch to crotch, in a lusty unison. Her cunt would likely get off just swaying against his protruding pouch. She would feel his dick rising beneath his pants to meet her aroused mound, and they'd move on each other like lovers in bed.

Once, when she was in the cafe where she'd met Miles, a man like Hector, with the Hector kind of smile, unzipped his fly; while the two were pressed together, surrounded by a crowd of frenzied dancers, he pulled her up enough to force his way inside her cunt. They'd fucked on the dance floor until she came and he had shot his load inside her. He left her after he was fully spent, without even telling her his name. But the memory of their scandalous liaison was one she'd never forget. The only thing that might have made it better would have been a crowd that watched—so Tessa imagined. As it was, only Martine had noticed.

"Was he screwing you?" she'd asked her afterward.

"He came in me," Tessa answered.

"You little whore!" Martine said.

Tessa wasn't sure why Martine thought it so obscene. It was something she would have done herself. Maybe she was jealous.

Hector would have screwed her in public. He was the kind who wouldn't care who saw what, pleasure was pleasure. Tessa read that in his dancing eyes.

But now, the only man that really turned her on was Miles. His essence was so much more formidable than that of any affable gentleman. She needed his rough, wicked sense of deviance to bring out her own. The Hectors of the world were for the novices in sex, for women who like to be wooed. Miles would never woo her, not in any traditional way.

"So why do you do this?" Tessa asked him.

Hector smiled, eyes far away for just an instant, as if he were gazing on some pleasant memory. Looking back at her, he said, "I suppose I do it because I don't have the guts to do what Miles is going to do to you."

"And what's he going to do?" she asked.

"I'm not sure, I'm never sure."

"Have you videoed him with other women?"

"Half a dozen, maybe."

"So I'm just another in a long string?"

"I wouldn't say that."

"Why not? Am I special?" she inquired coyly.

He shrugged. "Perhaps. You seem to have a lot of the qualities he's looking for."

"And what are those?"

"Miles wants the perfect submissive. He's had a lot of women, but few match up to his demands."

"And do you think I will?"

"That's up to you," Hector answered carefully. He'd never think of speaking for Miles, especially regarding his women.

"So what was the last woman like?" Tessa asked.

Hector looked at her for a moment, wondering if he should even be having this conversation. Tessa was a charming diversion. And since Miles was gone, and he had no idea when he'd return, he had to pass the time some way. Fucking her had crossed his mind from the start, but he never would. Not without Miles' okay. He couldn't risk pissing the boss off and losing the job. Miles paid too well for him to be that foolish.

Tessa Cotille had the perfect body for a good screw. She had matchless curves, and a swell to her hips that made him want to grasp them in his hands and fondle them at will. And her tits—he couldn't wait to see the studs pierced through her nipples.

It didn't take long for him to decide that he'd have her naked before Miles returned. That wouldn't upset him. In fact, Miles would probably enjoy the picture of his submissive being photographed.

"The last woman he screwed for the camera?" Hector remembered aloud. "Meg."

"Meg." Tessa repeated the name to herself. "What was she like?"

Hector laughed. "A prudish bitch. Actually she looked a little like you. Miles must like blondes. She had a perfect body, enormous tits, not better than yours, just bigger. And full lips. She probably shot them up with collagen."

"Were her tits real?"

"Yeah, they were real, real big." Hector obviously liked Meg's breasts, in a BIG way.

"What else? You said she was a prude?"

"First-class bitch. She liked looking good, but she was as cold as a whore when the money's run out." He chuckled to himself.

"So what happened?"

"I took about an hour's worth of video, and Miles suddenly looks at me, and shrugs. He was whipping her with a mild thong, and she was oooooing and ahhhhing, to a point. Then she'd scream bloody murder whenever he tried to make it hurt. Damn, what a bitch! She wasn't submissive; she was like a Greek warrior coming from the Trojan horse, ready to cut his throat. When she left, Miles was practically rolling on the floor, laughing like a hyena."

"A Greek coming from the Trojan horse? Miles was so vulnerable that he'd succumb to that kind of woman? I can't imagine him laughing like a hyena."

"He hardly succumbed to her—but hey, I've said too much. Take off your top," Hector suddenly ordered.

She hesitated, surprised by his command.

"Take it off, bitch," he ordered again when she didn't respond.

She was sorry she hadn't complied right away—she really wanted to please him, almost as much as she wanted to please Miles. She reached for the bottom of her black T-shirt and pulled it over her head. She pretended she was an erotic dancer doing special favors on command.

With the shirt off, her gold studs winked at him. He was ashamed of himself for being so familiar with Miles' slut. But she was so appealing, not like Meg, and not like any of the others he'd filmed. Except perhaps for Penny—she would have been perfect, but she bolted right in the middle of a damn good scene. This Tessa just might pass Miles' thousand tests. He hoped she would. She would make them both a good bit of cash with the movies, not to mention the way she would likely screw his cock. Of one thing Hector was glad: He wasn't as picky with his love life as Miles. He could never be that patient!

Behind the video camera, Hector focused on the gold studs, as Tessa showed off her voluptuous torso like a pro. She was a natural in front of the camera, not at all shy, and not as reluctant as her earlier conversation with Miles might have indicated. Perhaps she just had to get used to the idea.

After several minutes of good footage, Hector was ready for more. "Remove your skirt," he ordered.

She stood up and looked into the camera as she tugged at her mini-skirt. Pushing it from her hips, she dropped it to the floor at her feet. She was naked.

"Beautiful," Hector said. The camera whirred again. Tessa played the exotic dancer, gyrating her hips and forming a seductive pout with her lips. "Keep going...let me see your rear..." The camera rolled as he watched through the viewer.

Tessa turned her back to him while looking over her shoulder, a provocative gesture to say the least. Hector's dick was stiff inside his jeans.

He admired the stripes on her butt, though he almost winced himself, knowing that they were there only after some painful episode with Miles' whip. He could never wield the thing the way Miles did. That aspect of his friend fascinated him. In fact, that was why he liked to work with Miles, recording the masterful way the man tamed this compliant kind of woman into an obedient slave. He watched Miles challenge a woman like Tessa, who was at the edge of compliance and defiance at the same time. The man feasted on that kind of confrontation, he and his submissive like two beasts facing off in the wild. It took a very special kind of woman to be his lover.

Hector sensed that Tessa was that kind of woman, little jewel that she was. She'd be in pain, wrenching pain before the night was over, and loving it.

Hector filmed the little tart and her gyrations for some minutes, until he couldn't stand it any longer. He'd either have to ignore the "hands-off" arrangement with Miles and fuck her silly, or he'd have to quit the video and take a break. Knowing that he'd get laid sometime before he was finished that night, he decided to stop filming and wait for the main event.

"Let's take a break," he said.

She looked disappointed. But obedient to his order, she sat back down on the bed. She was naked, her clothes strewn across the floor, sitting demurely with her hands in her lap, feeling strangely self-conscious.

"I'm going for a Coke, you want something?" Hector asked.

"No. Nothing," Tessa replied, and she watched Hector move off to the kitchen.

When the photographer didn't come back for some time, Tessa fell back on the bed and pulled a sheet over her. She grew sleepy, finally dozing, as she wondered when Miles would return.

"Tessa!" She heard her name from Miles' tongue. His voice was sharp, piercing her sleep. "Tessa!" Hearing it again, she finally pulled up on one elbow, a languid sultry look in her eyes, as she gazed at her lover. He was looking down on her impassively.

"Sleeping?" he inquired.

"It was refreshing. It's been a long week."

"That's good, it's likely to be a long night," Miles said. He sat down on the bed, looking a bit more amicable. "Hector tells me you're quite a tease for the camera," Miles said.

"Oh, we were just having some fun," she explained.

"Did you want him to fuck you?" Miles asked.

"I suppose so," she answered. She hadn't thought about it, even though the sexual heat between her and Hector had been building steadily, as he filmed her. She'd only planned to fuck Miles. His question made her think that she'd like them both. It certainly wasn't an unpleasant idea, if that's what Miles wanted.

Miles pulled the blanket away from her body, seeing her nude, seeing the wet juices of her cunt beginning to form on the inside of her legs. He reached between them and began to stroke her thighs. A finger quickly penetrated her vagina, pounding her briskly. She leaned back against a pillow and let him have her. With the languid warmth in the room, sleep still clouding her mind, and Miles' earnest probing of her cunt, she was ripe for orgasm.

But before she could climax, he ripped his hand away from her, rose from the bed, and walked to the back of the room.

Tessa gazed around, adjusting her eyes to the light. The room appeared even smaller to her now that the sun had set and there was nothing but starlight coming in through the skylight. While she'd slept, there had been more changes. Oriental screens had been placed around the platform, her bed even more a stage than it had been before.

When Miles returned, he had a key in hand and was reaching overhead to where the apparatus was hanging. Tessa watched him unlock the wrist cuffs. Grasping her wrists, he placed them inside the cuffs and locked them so that only the key would free her. She was more a captive, in a literal sense, than she'd ever been. The effect was frightening, but at the same time her cunt was juicing. Her breasts protruded from her chest like ornaments. Her nipples stood on end, a hint of a chill in the room, making them knot up into tight hard buds.

Hearing a humming sound from somewhere in the room, she fought to recognize it, until it dawned on her that Hector was running the camera again. She turned toward him, seeing the lens focused directly on her breasts, on the nipples, and the gold studs.

"Think of the eyes that will be watching you, Tessa," Miles whispered in her ear very gently. He referred to the movie being made of her. It felt strange to think that Miles would show these intimacies to other people.

"What do you think, Hector?" Miles asked. "Another set of studs to match these? Her tits are so large they could handle more."

"I prefer rings myself," Hector commented.

"Rings, of course," Miles said. "Two sets perhaps, different sizes, more to pull at." Miles tweaked her nipples with his fingers and watched the pained response. It was pain, but it was so much more.

He backed off to the side and admired her torso with her arms stretched out above her. She was so beautiful he could have gazed at her for hours, thinking of ways he could mark her and of the trinkets that would decorate her body.

Grabbing the pulley that was attached to her bonds, he tugged at the ropes so that she was forced to rise from the bed. He allowed her time to move, though not too much time. She had to scamper to the edge where her feet landed on the floor. She was quickly pulled up tighter still, her hands and arms high above her, standing on tiptoe. The camera recorded it all, the way she wanted to tug against the bonds, the way she was stretched taut, the way Miles didn't stop pulling until she was exactly as he wanted her.

Seeing Tessa restrained excited both men, their pricks rising jubilantly. They gazed at her for several minutes, seeing the look of frightened anguish cross her face as she wondered what would happen next.

"Spread your legs," Miles ordered her. He tied off the ropes, to secure her confinement, while Tessa struggled to part her legs.

"I can't!" she pleaded, wiggling against the bonds.

"You're not trying, my dear," Miles countered calmly.

Her struggling made it worse, the savage stretch and the weight on her arms. Relaxing, she found it less painful, as if the leather and ropes stretched to accommodate her need.

"You might try getting used to this pose, love. I like it so much, I'll likely keep you here as long as you can tolerate it."

"Perhaps the spreader bar, Miles?" Hector interjected.

"Maybe, let's see how well she holds up. She seems a little more compliant now. If she behaves, I won't need to use it."

For some minutes the camera whirred, and Miles' sketch pen flew across a sheet of paper at his easel. Both men captured Tessa's taut and yielding body. Her head was bowed to one side. Miles thought it was a perfect act of resignation.

Of course she was resigned. Tessa had no choice but to relent. And after some moments, she began to do so with her body as well as her mind. As she relaxed, a full flood of warmth begin to flow through her. Her cunt moistened readily. She knew, after Miles was finished with his sketching, that she'd feel some sort of lash against her skin, but she could wait. Getting used to this level of submission took some time. She was thankful he was so absorbed with his work, since it gave her time to adjust.

Miles didn't take long creating the black and white sketch.

"There," he announced. His voice shook her back to reality, and she opened her eyes to see a lovely picture of herself. The lines of her body were drawn with bold angular motions, the pout on her lips was seductive. She wondered to herself if she looked that aroused or if Miles had read into his vision of her that much sexual animation.

Finished, Miles picked up the easel and took it to an out of the way corner of the room, where it would remain. Then, putting his pencils away and wiping his hands, he proceeded to the trunk. He stood for some seconds looking down on his chest full of wicked implements, finally reaching down to withdraw the ones he'd use this night. He chose two, as he had before, one to warm her and one to cut.

This time, both implements were longer than the ones he'd used before, since he intended to stand some distance away when he punished her. It was a dramatic distance he had in mind, particularly suited for the videotape.

As he approached her, a savage scowl crossed his face, as though he was angry with her. Was he punishing her, as he had in the museum days before? It was the same nasty scowl on his face, the same wrinkled brow, the same gleam in his dark eyes. It was clear that Miles had entered into his role of Dominant, letting his darkest passions rule.

"So soft and delicate," he said. His hand tenderly touched her cunt. He massaged her there, lovingly. "So juicy." He smeared the juice all over her, then he felt her from front to back, parting her labia, and moving a finger along the moistened cleft. "You really love this, don't you?" he asked.

"Yes," she whispered.

"What was that you said?" he asked, as if he hadn't heard her.

"Yes, I love it," she replied.

Tessa gasped as he fingered her, each small touch sending spasms through her. It would have taken little to make her come; but Tessa was not so naive to think that he'd allow her to orgasm so soon.

Miles backed away and took a whip in hand. Its three-foot long thongs dangled from the large handle. He dropped the other implement out of sight, so that all Tessa could focus on was this one and the anticipation of that first blow.

The sounds, the whooshing noise of the leather against air filled Tessa's ears, and her body jolted with the first blow hitting her waist level. The thongs reached across her entire abdomen to the top of her thighs.

"Ah!" she gasped. Her body tingled, but without pain.

The next blow was higher, across her breasts.

"Oh, oh oooo," she whimpered softly.

Miles flogged her with blow after blow, from her breasts to her thighs and back again. Lashes covered her everywhere, the thongs reaching around to bite against her tender sides, then hitting her breasts and cunt straight on.

"Oh, please, please!" she gasped. The thongs lapped around her body like waves lapping on the shore.

"Oh, oh my…ah yes."

It was seduction, and pleasure, and a biting sting, and then just the most perfect rush of sensation. Her belly and breasts were blushing in response.

But oh! What a fine sweet pain it was!

The camera whirred unemotionally, at its measured distance, capturing every blow with its unfailing accuracy. Neither Tessa nor Miles paid any attention, both too enthralled with each other, and Tessa with the whip that struck her, and Miles with the ecstatic rush that ripped through him.

When he had her entire front side blushing a fine shade of pink, he turned her around, and began in earnest on her back.

"Oooooo ouch, oh my," her sultry voice answered each stroke. Each blow was a little piece of lightning against her skin. Just a hare's breath from painful.

"Oh God, no, no, yes."

She tingled deep inside. The flogging warmed her with a luscious fire that spread throughout her body. She could go on forever with this shameless bliss.

But Miles was not about to leave her without a more remarkable reminder of her submission. He'd thought about it for days, the way he'd finally mark her abdomen and her thighs. He'd imagined it, especially when he would gaze at the sketches he'd drawn of her. He could see the marks in his mind so clearly. His cock had been stiff each time he'd thought of it.

"Ah, ah yes, ooooo yes," she purred like a cat, her eyes glimmering when he looked at her. There were demons shining there. It was time to turn pleasure to agony.

He laid down the whip, and let her wriggling body rest, then turned her around so that he could inspect her chest and belly. Already the pink blush had faded away, and there was little trace of the whip's blows. He stroked her as she jerked.

"Oh God, I could come," she purred.

"I'm sure you could, but not yet."

"Aaaahhh yes, oh yes."

He stroked her thighs. "You won't even have to look in the mirror to see your stripes. When I'm finished, all you'll need to do is look at your belly to see the impressions."

She looked down at her creamy white skin, wondering what it would look like to wear marks of his dominance in such an obvious place. Would it thrill her the way the ones on her rear had?

"These." He was stroking her breasts, admiring the soft round orbs and the studs at her nipples. "Perhaps

I'll mark these too. Then when I'm finished, we'll find some appropriate way to show them off."

She was simmering on the edge of fear, but not so frightened that she didn't want him to go on.

Miles backed off and picked up the second implement that had been lying on the floor. Tessa knew when she saw it that it would be nothing like the teasing thongs that had seduced her. The crop was three feet long, of pliable leather. The shaft was firm, though it would bend when it was unleashed. The last few inches were quite soft, but only in looks. Two separate thin thongs dangled off the end and were tied together at the tip. With the proper snap of the crop, they would land with a ferocious cruel cut against the skin.

"You'll be happy to know Tessa...this building is empty, except for us three. Your screams will be heard by no one but Hector and me."

It was a chilling piece of trivia.

Like the bamboo days before, and the buggy whip before that, Miles' instrument split the air with an unnerving hiss. It landed against Tessa's belly just at the top of her pubic hair.

"God no!" she screamed, when the pain from the savage cut registered in her head. She went limp against her bonds; the next cut landed at the top of her thigh, the tassel snapping nastily against her outer labia.

"God no!" she shrieked again. She tried to turn away.

"Stand up Tessa! Turn to me!" Miles demanded. He waited for her to comply.

She was so frightened of the next cut that she could hardly move, managing to turn back only just the slightest bit.

"Look at me!" Miles ordered.

She pulled herself up and looked Miles in the eye. She was trembling.

Suddenly he turned away from her, looking at Hector, still poised at the camera behind him.

"You see the look on her face?" he asked the photographer.

"Terror," Hector said. He'd seen it before, in other submissive targets of Miles' dominance, but never was it so breathtaking to behold. There was a fire in Tessa's eyes, in spite of the pain. She matched Miles' fierce persona. He admired her.

"Can you record that?" Miles asked.

"Perfectly," Hector answered.

Miles turned, taking Tessa off guard. He let the whip fly, its sharp edge catching her abdomen, extending its punishment down to the softer places on her cunt.

"Yeeeeoooooo!" Her cry of woe lifted into the air, the only reply she could fashion. There was no way to get away from the lash and its cutting tassel. She didn't dare look below, for fear of seeing blood where he'd cut the skin.

Another three devastating cuts sizzled on the night breeze, landing in erratic form against the most tender places on her body. There was only one place more tender, and that was dangerously close to this target, though yet tucked away and unavailable for Miles to reach.

"Aaaauuugh, nooooooooo, aaaaaaaaaugghhh!" she screamed.

The pain went through her like arrows shot from a bow, penetrating deeper than her skin. The sound of her voice was the only sweet relief she could savor.

It was an eerie quiet when he stopped. Tessa waited for another blow, eyes closed, not realizing that Miles had already put down the implement and was simply staring at her.

"How beautiful," he murmured, gazing at the deep red stripes.

Tessa opened her eyes and looked down, to see the same red stripes that he saw. To her surprise, the skin was not broken, though the marks were as distinct and raw as anything he'd laid across her backside. The two waited while Hector moved closer to film the mesmerizing streaks of red in all their colorful glory.

When Miles reached out to touch them, Tessa winced.

"Ah, ooooo ouch!" she gasped, though she was not in pain anymore. The heat from the wounds was firing her, just as it had those times before. "Ooooo, ooo, yes."

Miles' fingers traced each thin red line. She jolted. Her cunt pulsed.

His hand slowly moved from her abdomen to between her legs. He fingered her between her labia where her clit was rock-hard, engorged and painful.

"Oh my, yes, please," she cried. Joy swept through her body with wildly brilliant spasms. "Oh yes, please, Miles!" She threw her head back—even her blonde curls tickling her back were erotic playthings. Every little pore of her body seemed to come alive.

When Miles' hand began to penetrate her cunt, she panted. He spread her legs wider still. The juice from her cunt cascaded around his hand, letting him slide his fingers easily inside her warm hole. He began with three, and then four, and continued until he was forcing his whole fist at her opening.

"Oh yes, do it!" she begged. She couldn't imagine that he'd fit his whole hand inside her, but she wanted it there. She opened her legs wider still, and her cunt expand to receive him.

His full fist was at the door, about to push its way over the threshold, when he pulled out. His hand moved further back along her cleft and smeared her juices against her hole. Just as he'd done with her cunt, he began prodding one finger after another at her anus. She took a deep breath, scared, but still wanting him to penetrate her dark channel.

"Relax, my love," he murmured in her ear.

"Oh yes, please, please go on," she encouraged him.

"You've been taken here before?" he asked.

She remembered well that day with her roommate. "Yes, once," Tessa replied, not wanting to explain Martine's rape of her ass.

"By whom?" Miles asked.

"Oh, yes, please," she purred for him, trying to dissuade his question.

"By whom?" Miles insisted.

"Martine," Tessa replied, rocking against his penetrating hand. "Oh, please more."

"Ah, the bitch has had you here, I'd like to see that."

Tessa twisted against his hand, wondering how far his hand would go inside her ass.

"Yes, I'd like to see that," Miles repeated. "Wouldn't you like to capture that on film?" He turned, addressing Hector.

"Perhaps a strap-on dildo," Hector suggested.

Miles nodded his head, inspired by Hector's

suggestion. "I'll just have to have her here so we can watch." His hand pushed further, Tessa's sphincter releasing a little more with each thrust.

"I'm sure she'd accommodate you," Tessa replied sarcastically. She couldn't help herself, even though she knew the flippant retort was ill-advised. It seemed her lot in life to be perpetually annoyed by Martine.

Miles didn't appreciate her tone of voice. "Perhaps she will," Miles replied. He took her chin in his free hand and forced her to look him in the eye. What had started as a lighthearted probing was turning more intense, both physically and verbally. His fingers pushed harder into her anus, as his eyes darkened even more fiercely. "Aaaugh!" she cried out.

"If I allow her to have you, she'll have you Tessa, whether you like it or not!" he informed her. "Do you understand?" He punctuated his message with a vicious thrust of his hand as his four fingers, forced their way beyond her tight sphincter. The chastisement elicited another guttural cry.

"Do you understand?" he repeated himself.

"Yes, sir!" Tessa answered back. A searing pain from the penetration made her eyes well with tears.

Miles backed off.

Resuming a more pleasurable probing of her backside with one hand, he began playing with her cunt with his other. It was almost as if she had two cocks inside her. So full, she was teeming with the need to release, though she was quick to realize that any orgasm Miles might allow was still a long way off.

He had other things in mind.

Confident that she was ready for his shaft, Miles

withdrew his hands. Then he turned her around so that the camera would have a clear shot, recording the anal entry. Hector lay on the floor to get just the right angle.

"It would be better, Miles, if you were to let her down from there and take her on the bed," the photographer suggested.

"Of course it would, but then it wouldn't be much of a challenge for any of us," Miles answered as if it were all a game.

Hector was used to Miles' demands, just "a submissive photographer slut" he called himself when he was pressed to do the job that Miles wanted. But it was worth it; it was an unparalleled experience, photographing this nasty smut. Besides, he could sense his own participation would soon be required. His dick was getting hard in anticipation.

Hector moved his camera, capturing the slow deliberate entry. For a moment Miles' cock remained poised at the brink of Tessa's anus, and then with a steady push, he began to force his way inside.

Tessa squirmed and held her breath.

"Relax my dear, and it won't hurt a bit."

Miles pressed himself against her back. He had stripped himself of his clothes, and feeling her silky skin against his, he knew he had a most succulent prize in this one.

"Relax, dear one, it won't hurt," he said again.

She knew that was true—even though the idea of his cock planted deep inside her seemed impossible. It was different than Martine's fake prick. It was alive and pulsing—she could feel that before it even entered.

His hands reached around and grabbed her loins,

and as the head of his penis pushed harder, she released and allowed more of his thick shaft inside her ass. There was not a whimper, not a cry at all. He was proud of her, so proud that he toyed with her clit as a reward. The two in unison bucked and churned against each other.

"Augh!" she seethed quietly.

"Such a good slut," Miles answered her.

Hector followed them in every position with his camera, from the penetration, to the gradual building thrusts and jerks, to the expressions of half pain, half pleasure on their faces. He'd never a made a video quite like it. He couldn't wait to see the results.

"Hector, now," Miles said at last.

With his cock still planted in her ass, Miles lifted Tessa so she could relax her limbs.

"Uncuff her," he ordered.

Hector responded quickly. He didn't like seeing her strung up that long. Her poor arms must ache like crazy, he thought. He loosened the pulleys to let her arms rest. Then he unlocked the cuffs, so that Miles could carry her to the bed.

When Miles withdrew from her ass, it was torture. She wanted him to orgasm. She couldn't wait to have him pound her hard, as hard as she'd ever been pounded, harder than Martine had with the dildo, harder than she'd been pummeled in her cunt.

"On the bottom, man, you get her cunt," Miles told the photographer.

Hector returned the camera to the tripod and scampered to the bed.

Pushing his pants from his hips, his stiff dick was ready. Tessa grabbed it lustily. She wasn't thinking of the pain anymore, only of the way another cock would make her feel. She could fuck both men all night long, she could have taken a dozen and have been in heaven. She only cared about being filled, everywhere.

She sucked Hector's swollen prick, taking his enormous purple head into her mouth.

"God, yes, you slutty little whore!" he gasped.

Her expert tongue circled the head, running along the sensitive rim.

"Damn yes!"

Miles pulled the two apart, pushing Hector to the bed. Tessa climbed on top of him. Her breasts dangled down on his chest and then on his face, where he buried his nose between them, smelling the sweet smells of sweat and perfume that lingered there. He kissed her, his mouth devouring the surfaces of her skin as if they were delicacies from some king's banquet.

His cock quickly thrust up and forward, finding the succulent opening of her cunt. She relaxed down on him, wiggling against his groin with a little girl giggle.

"Oooo, so big," she purred. She was wet and pulsing.

He thrust deeper still. "You'll see just how big," he warned her. "Ooooo, ooo yes, keep that up!" Tessa exclaimed.

He was beginning to rock against the bed, slamming himself into her. In seconds, the two were frantically screwing to a crashing end.

But Miles interrupted them again. "Not yet," he told them.

"Ah, Miles, you're torturing me," Tessa wailed. She eased off for a moment, churning softly against

Hector's prick, while Miles climbed on the bed, positioning himself with his prick against the opening of her anus.

"My God, it won't fit!" she exclaimed.

But he proved her wrong, his dick sliding into her well-worked hole.

"Yeeeeahhhhhh!" she groaned. It was not so much painful, as it was overwhelming, split in two—not like she'd been split by the whip or the bamboo—but spilt in the deepest part of her body. Filled so full, impaled, ripped, as if she'd break in two.

The two cocks moved inside her in a cautious unison. It was a fragile entry for them both, the wrong move and one would be suddenly withdrawn. But Tessa managed them as if she'd been fucked this way a hundred times.

"Aaaaaahhhhhh yes," she began to moan as they both settled in.

It was becoming the best erotic ride she'd ever had. She thought she would explode, the surging in her was indescribable. She moved faster, and so did they.

"Goddamn, fuck meeeee! Fuck, dammit fuck!"

They were quickly on the brink of orgasm.

First Hector began to climax. His cock seemed to detonate within her, expanding exuberantly. He moved briskly, while Miles held off, waiting. The friction of the two inside her made her squeeze and grind on Hector all the more.

"Goddamn, you nasty bitch, fuck me!" he screamed.

He exploded. Tessa squeezed him. He grabbed her tightly as pain and ecstasy leapt across his face in an impassioned scowl.

A sassy look of gaiety filled Tessa's face as she saw

Hector's grimace. She reveled in the wails of pleasure that rose to greet her ears with an unending stream of four letter exclamations.

"Damn fuck meeeee!" he ordered her one more time. And she bore down even harder on his prick, until his body finally went limp beneath her.

She wasn't happy that he was done so soon. But his penis wasn't soft, not yet. He remained where he was, enjoying the sensuous aftermath of orgasm, as Miles began to pound his cock deeper into Tessa's ass.

"Ahhhhhh!" This was something else altogether. "Ah, ah, ah!" she panted. This was like nothing she'd ever felt before. Raped in the rear, with a cock in her cunt, she thought her body would break.

It was astonishing!

"God, yes, you ass!" she screamed.

Like Hector, Miles came quickly.

"Gawwwwwdd auuuuugh!" he groaned from the pit of his stomach. His cock moved with incredible ease inside her rear. She would never have thought she'd be so open, accepting, willing to push against him the way she did. As he spasmed, the tight channel milked him dry in seconds, and he collapsed heavily against her.

For an instant, there was an strange quiet in the garret. No moans, no cries, no pleasured exclamations.

In Tessa's cunt, one pulse after another echoed through her body. She moved her hips as best she could. The two cocks spasmed. Aftershocks.

She jerked and jerked again. And a dozen times more on the way to her climax. She was someplace else besides this room. Where? On her way to heaven perhaps. But lost, only the pleasure mattered. Only the cocks in her crotch. Only the delicate and savage sensations that alternated there.

She might have passed out, but Miles withdrew from her.

She felt his absence as pain and a nasty interruption of her finish.

"Oh no! Please don't leave," she exclaimed, though she was already collapsing into the dark sheets next to Hector's hairy body.

The photographer reached for her cunt and began to play, while Miles reached deep with his fingers to where his cock had been. They knew she had not yet peaked herself. Her body was clamoring against the sheets, against anything that would finally bring her off. And within seconds it began: a long rolling finish. Tessa tightened and released, tightened and released again and again, until she fell into a gentle unthinking calm.

She came to when Miles began lapping at her earlobes.

Her body ached. For a time she couldn't understand why her arms and chest were so terribly sore. But as Miles began to massage her upper body, she recalled with vivid accuracy that she'd been strung up nearly an hour, maybe more, she couldn't be certain, since she'd lost track of time.

"I want to film you again," Hector told her. His face beamed at her lovingly. For a man she hardly knew, she felt incredibly close to him. He played with her nipples affectionately, without pinching, pulling, or twisting the studs. Tessa was grateful. She wasn't prepared for any more pain.

As Tessa moved, she was beset with sharp pains.

"The marks," she thought to herself. They aroused her. After all the penetration, after a smashing climax, she was aroused again.

Hector rose from the bed and took the camera from the tripod. He began filming again, close up. He aimed the camera directly on Tessa and Miles for several minutes, recording the quiet ending to an unquiet venture.

"I could do her often," Miles said, still pushing his finger at her asshole.

"Ouch no!" She was quickly filled with a burning sensation, that wasn't arousing.

"No more for now, Tessa, you can recuperate. In fact, I think you need a bath." He slapped her ass playfully, sending her on her way.

Tessa listened while the two talked about her. It was apparent by their conversation that she would be the object of more video work and that pleased her. It meant that, at least to some degree, her relationship with Miles would continue. Strangely, it seemed so tenuous, as intricate and fragile as a spider's web. Caught in Miles dark lair, she was worried that the winds would blow too strong, and she would land elsewhere, without him.

CHAPTER NINE

IN THE TRANQUIL aftermath of her hot bath, Tessa watched Miles as he sent Hector away, then fiddled with the leather apparatus hanging limp near the bed. He returned and looked down on her, while she played a game of possum, pretending to have suddenly fallen asleep.

He stared at her abdomen, seeing how well the stripes showed up on the background of her white skin.

"They'll be gone too soon," he said.

"Hummm?" Tessa murmured as if she hadn't heard him.

"You heard me. I know you're awake."

She opened her eyes and smiled. "You said they'll be gone too soon?" Tessa questioned.

"You shouldn't be without a sign of your devotion to me," he said.

Tessa wanted to make love to him a second time, without Hector, just the two of them rocking together in impassioned embrace. He must have read her secret thoughts. Perhaps they weren't secret at all, but written all over her face.

"Not now, Tessa," he said.

She looked disappointed.

"But...perhaps a friend, to keep you company for the night?" he posed. "To remind you of tonight?"

"I don't think I'll ever forget tonight," she said.

"Well this will be a particularly fine reminder."

He walked to the trunk and pulled out a belt, straps, and a flexible dildo. On closer inspection she could see it was a double dildo.

"You think you can handle it all night?" he said. There was a whimsical expression on his face.

She stared at the dildos, petrified of them.

"Let's try."

He pulled her to her feet and fixed the belt around her waist. Then with a slow steady push he shoved the twin-pronged dildo inside her cunt and ass, so that they sunk deep inside the well-worked holes. She was as full as she'd been earlier.

The dildos were attached with straps to the belt, and thus lodged inside her, where they would remain until Miles chose to pull them from her. To secure her captive loins, Miles locked the straps to the belt with a tiny gold lock that fastened behind her. He pocketed the key.

"Perhaps after a night impaled, you'll have had enough of such things?" he speculated. He was amused by her flustered expression. As he walked out the door, Tessa sat back on the bed, bewildered by her captivity. She wanted Miles, not the dildos, but apparently that was all she'd have of him, at least for now. She wondered what she had to do to keep the man with her for an entire night.

The straps and dildos were only a burden to her for a short time. The worst was the leather that cut across her belly, rubbing against the raw stripes. But a little cold cream that she found in the bathroom soothed the skin so that she could relax. Then with memory of the extraordinary night still fresh in her mind, she drifted off to sleep.

"Don't move!"

Tessa opened her eyes to see Miles staring down at her. It was morning, the sun streaming through the skylight. He pulled back the sheet, so he could see her with the dildos still tightly inside her.

Tessa stared up at him, saying nothing.

He began to sketch her.

Once begun, she couldn't move. It was horrendous. She ached everywhere, her arms, her chest, her wrists, her belly where the whip had cut her, and even her thighs, which were, as everything else, stretched to the limit the night before. To add to her woe, she had to pee and found it almost impossible to hold back the call of nature while Miles worked.

She spent at least twenty minutes of agony before he finally pushed the easel away.

"Come here, Tessa," he said.

She negotiated the distance between them awkwardly. Then Miles undid the lock and Tessa scampered to the bathroom, to alleviate the pressure bearing down on her. Unfortunately, the sweet relief of peeing did nothing to alleviate the pressure deep between her legs where an immense sexual longing begged for release.

When she returned to him, he made her wash the dildos in hot soapy water. She wiped the leather straps clean, till the surface shone. Bringing them to her nose, she smelled the fragrance of cowhide and female cunt mingling in a strange aromatic blend.

Miles took them from her and began the binding ritual again, replacing the straps and the dildos where they'd made their home. "Think of these as my cock, and remember, there's not a place I cannot penetrate you," Miles told her. "You'll feel my presence everywhere inside you. You don't have to seek me, I'm here every moment. Trust me, the more you make these your lover, the more I will have conquered you." His eyes were fired with the dark aspect that she loved so much.

He made her sit primly on a high stool with her feet dangling, not touching the floor. The dildos pressed into her as tightly as they could go. There was no relief from the sensations, like she'd been able to secure when she was lying on her side, sleeping.

He sketched her, creating another perfect rendering of her body, adding to the several dozen sketches that he'd already done. It was quite a collection of artistic pornography.

"What are you going to do with these?" Tessa asked, as he helped her from the stool to a blanket lying on the floor.

"I've done several books of such sketches, though never just one subject. This will be of you alone."

"Really?" That pleased her. "And someone will buy it?"

"Connoisseurs of smut revel in these. Just think, your pictures might end up on the private walls of some great decadent palace. You, my Tessa, my little slave." His eyes twinkled. "Now lie down on your back," he instructed her.

Following his instructions, Tessa waited for him as he gathered some straps from a closet on the wall. Returning to her, he lifted her feet to her hands, and tied them to each other. Then he attached them to the pulley with a large hook. He didn't lift her completely from the floor—her back continued to rest there. He certainly could have strung her up like so much raw meat, but he was being kind to her.

Miles stood back and inspected his work. Satisfied, he sketched her again. In this position, the dildos shifted uncomfortably within her. When she squirmed, it only made it worse, and she moaned to indicate her discomfort. But Miles was unconcerned with her plight. He was completely fascinated by the beautiful line of her extended legs and the curious rods that opened wide her holes, stretching the skin to its maximum degree.

When he was finished, he let her down. Her already sore legs and arms ached even more. When he showed her the sketch, she gasped, surprised by what she saw. Miles had drawn her as if she was suspended in the air. Her head was flung back and her mouth filled full with some ball gag or dildo, just as her other orifices were still filled.

"Your imagination?" she queried him. "Why didn't you just bind me this way?"

"Some things in our imaginations are more possible than others," he told her. "I did consider the dildo in your mouth, except that you were so good at being quiet, I decided that I could easily imagine one there. What do you think of it?"

"It's amazing, almost surreal. But it's me!" she said, still shocked by the bizarre sketch.

"Are you uncomfortable?" he asked.

"Not really, I'm much better than I was while I was suspended."

"Good, then you can remain this way until I get back. Just remember, this is me, these are my cocks." He pressed his hand between her legs, and pushed up on the double rods, so that they jerked higher inside her.

Once Miles had left, Tessa collapsed on the bed, and slept a long time. She hadn't realized how tired this kind of play was making her. Every bit of her ached mightily, yet it was a soothing kind of ache. Her submission had become a cocoon of joy that colored her life with satisfaction straight from her finest dream. If only there was something to satisfy the ever present aching deep in her cunt, she would have been content. Like this, however, with the ache still gnawing at her, she could not rest as peacefully as she would have liked.

When Tessa woke from her nap, she was still alone. There was no clock in the garret, no radio or TV, but she assumed from the angle of the sunlight coming in through the skylights that it was afternoon. She would have loved to orgasm—the ache inside her had changed to a vibrant pulsing. She was wet between her legs, with the sticky juice of sex pouring around the implanted dildo. Unfortunately, there was no way to finger herself with the tight leather straps covering her cunt.

It was no use trying to push the straps to the side; her fingers had no room to play, her cunt no way to respond. She rubbed against the leather, but it was drawn too tightly against her to allow room for her fingers to play.

She might have gotten off just focusing on the brightly fired places in her loins. But Miles had told her weeks before to anticipate his desires. Certainly this careful binding had been for a purpose. Perhaps Miles wanted her aroused this way, with no way to find release.

Rather than torture herself more, Tessa rose from the bed and wandered around the garret.

Curious about his artwork, she viewed the several groups of paintings that were stacked against the walls. She was careful only to look, not to disturb their order. Each painting was erotic to some degree. Even those that looked like flowers or fruit oddly resembled some part of female sexual anatomy or male genitalia. Miles was an artistically clever painter. Tessa was amused by his imagination.

He was a successful painter too. She knew his buyers to be some of the most well-known people in the city. He was known to be a raunchy bohemian with tastes so obscure and out of the ordinary as to shock people, though he'd developed such a reputation that his offbeat proclivities were taken as eccentric, to the point he'd become a celebrity to be courted, not shunned.

To be his most recent trinket was a distinction not to be taken lightly.

Tessa could see from his paintings and the numerous sketch pads filled with his visions of naked women that no one had been sketched by him in quite the ways that she was being rendered. One particular painting did catch her eye: a woman bound. If the painting told the truth, the woman was a voluptuous redhead, with magnificent breasts, a bold hairy red cunt, and a willingness to have her portrait painted while her arms were bound above her. Her plump flesh was further tied with ropes at her thighs, so that they were marked indentations in her flesh. Perhaps the ropes were just Miles' imagination, the way the gag in Tessa's mouth had been. Tessa hoped otherwise; at least the redhead would have been a sister to her in bondage. She looked so beautiful, so graceful and content.

Tessa wondered if *she* looked so content when she was bound. Remembering the sketches that Miles had made of her, she recalled raw lust, not serenity. Did this make the redhead a better subject than she was? Or was Tessa's erotic chaos as worthy as the redhead's peace?

She ran her hand along the surface of the canvas. Why had Miles not yet painted her in oils? Maybe he had sketched the redhead a couple of hundred times too, before he began this more permanent piece.

And why, she wondered, was this painting buried here, her canvas lost amid some half-finished others and ones no doubt ready for the junk heap? Was the redhead as forgotten in Miles' mind as the painting of her was?

She wondered if the two had made love. Was she a passing fancy or a submissive like herself who spent hours in captivity, prisoner in this garret? Was she nothing more than his "trinket of the month"? Was she, when the excitement had faded and Miles' inspiration had gone, sent away, the beauty of her captured in this picture the only reminder that she was ever here? Did she matter so little that even this portrait of her was now abandoned, cast in a corner of a garret filled with other past faded flings?

Tessa quit her explorations after her moment with the redhead. The woman made her feel so sad, she didn't want to think about it. She reminded Tessa that she too might become little more than an image on canvas, or worse yet just a smudged sketch on wrinkled newsprint.

Tessa had planned to look through the sketches of herself when she was finished with the others, but she changed her mind. Instead, she wandered toward the kitchen, the dildos making her journey uncomfortable but not impossible. With every step she took, both rods massaged her deep inside, as if Miles himself were pumping her with them. She was reminded of Martine's crude assault days before, reminded that she thrived on this horrendous kind of pleasure. Certainly she was as wicked and deviant as Miles himself.

Finding the small kitchen, Tessa pulled an apple from a basket of fruit and took an enormous bite. She hadn't realized how hungry she was; she hadn't eaten in hours. Hunger would certainly be an enemy. With no way to relieve herself, she didn't want to fill up on food and drink. But the apple tasted so good, she polished it off quickly, then returned to the bed.

CHAPTER TEN

THE SUN HAD nearly set by the time Hector arrived. Tessa had wrapped herself in thoughts of things to come with Miles, her imagination taking flight in strange twisted ways. She knew her fate with Miles was to go deeper into his web and the outrageous acts that testified of her submission to him. Each place he'd taken her had made her feel all the more his, like she was his property.

When Hector popped in the door, he interrupted her disquieting reverie. He had another camera bag flung over his shoulder. Was it another night of videos?

She was glad for the company. Seeing his face, hers lit up. Sometimes it was difficult being by herself with her thoughts; her imagination took her into such wild places. Hector brought her back to reality.

Unfortunately, Hector wasn't in his usual cheerful

mood. At least to begin with, he didn't want to talk, grunting his way through the innocuous conversation, much like Miles might have done.

He did let her have some time in the bathroom without the dildos. But when she finished, he dutifully replaced them as they had been, and left her to begin working on his video equipment.

"Miles is coming soon," Tessa said, hoping he would tell her when she might expect her lover. She stood near him, watching his careful preparations.

"Perhaps," Hector replied.

"Doesn't he tell you these things?" she asked.

"He tells me what I need to know," Hector said.

"Hummmm. You seem as much at his beck and call as I am," Tessa observed. She wondered if this was why he was so moody.

"Sometimes I feel that way, but then again I'm free to go, you…well?" Hector stared at her naked body, clothed in the garments of bondage, and said no more.

Tessa blushed. "I suppose there is a difference," she admitted.

"Yes, there's a difference. And he pays me, does he pay you?"

"Of course not! That would make me a whore."

"Yes, it would," he said, raising his eyebrows. His visage still glowered darkly. "But tell me, Tessa, don't you feel like one anyway, the way he violates you at will?"

"I don't know how a whore feels," Tessa said. "And I've never made the comparison."

"Used, whores feel used, at least the ones I've met," Hector informed her. He was carefully attaching the camera to the tripod. This time he also had a smaller one that looked more suited to the close-up shots he was doing the night before rather than the cumbersome one he'd been using.

"I don't feel used," she said.

"Really? That surprises me, usually women in your position thrive on feeling used. When they make a choice like you've made, they tell me that's their greatest thrill."

Tessa had to consider his assertion. He might well be right. "I think it's more like being selfless," Tessa said. "At least for me. You see I do get a great deal back, if you'll remember last night?"

"He was being easy on you. But then, maybe that's because you were performing so well. You made one hell of a video, I looked at it this morning. Not much editing required. Should bring a hefty price from a collector. He was even talking about selling it to a distributor."

"So you know he'll sell it?"

"He has every other one I've made."

"You've made a lot of these?"

"Six, maybe seven."

"And were they like mine?"

"No, not exactly, each one's different."

"So was I the best?" Tessa was intensely curious.

Hector laughed at her. "You sluts are all alike." He shook his head. "I suppose it depends on what you want. For pure SM, this was pretty good. But you know it's not as hard-line as some of the private collectors want. If he gets inspired to do something like that, I'd be careful. It might take you weeks to get over it."

Tessa realized what he meant. "I don't think he'd be that cruel to me," she replied.

Hector eyed her thoughtfully. "No, you're probably right about that."

"May I see the one you made last night?" she asked.

"That's up to Miles."

Tessa was disappointed.

She stood back for some time and watched Hector complete his preparations. He was very fussy about camera angles and the light in the room. He took a half dozen test shots of the bed, without Tessa there, and then checked them on the viewer. Tessa wasn't allow to see, but then what she really wanted to see pictures of herself.

"Do you think he'll sell my movies to a private collector?"

"He could."

"Do you know these people?"

"Sure, they're friends of Miles."

Tessa wandered to the bed and sat down. The camera was aimed at her, so she began to pose, moving around erotically for Hector's benefit. The photographer continued doing test shots; this time of her, since she made it so available.

"What are they like, his friends?"

Hector chuckled. His dour mood seemed to be fading. "They aren't monsters with horns and tails, if that's what you think. Some of them are names you'd know, others you wouldn't. They're just people that share the same passion for whips and chains and all that goes with them."

"You don't seem to be one of them," Tessa suggested.

"Only in a passing way. I find SM fascinating, but

then, I find filming any sex act fascinating. What I like about Miles is that he pays me well, and...he gives me a piece of the action."

"A very pleasant piece," Tessa suggested, flirting with him. She was on her hands and knees on the bed, her ass end waving in the air, dildos and all. She looked over her shoulder and smiled at him seductively.

"You must have had quite a time after I left last night," Hector commented. He left the camera running while he adjusted Tessa's body in the position he wanted. She liked the warm feel of his hands on her flesh. For good measure, Hector pressed his hand against the dildos and pushed them in still further.

"Oooo, that's awfully deep," she replied.

"You like these?" he asked, pressing them again several times, so that they pulsed inside her. His tone of voice was changing; he was becoming aroused. Tessa was certain that if she'd looked at his crotch, she'd see his dick rising nicely inside his pants.

She wished he'd act on his urges. Just the touch of his hand on her ass reminded her that she was horny beyond belief. The past hours of subdued tranquillity hadn't squelched the flames, they'd only masked them enough to survive. Now, she was wiggling her hips in the air, in an amorous dance for Hector's eyes. Would that he'd just take her, unlock the straps and dildos, and jam that delicious cock inside her cunt.

Her fantasy was cut short.

As her provocative rear swayed before Hector and his camera, Miles, with Martine clinging to his arm, burst through the door.

Tessa caught sight of the two and fell to her side on

the bed. She wasn't certain if Miles would approve of the impromptu performance. But to her relief, they took no notice of her or Hector. The two were all over each other, already in the throes of a sexual moment.

"Ooooo, Miles, keep going," Martine purred at him. His hands were traveling over the bitch's body, her blouse practically off her naked torso. One hand was up under Martine's short skirt, squeezing her ass with a firm grasp, grabbing at her flesh like it was bread dough to be kneaded. Martine loved every minute of it, cooing and purring, and ooooing and aaahing in his ears.

Tessa could tell that she was about to come—the sounds she made were all too familiar.

Miles pressed Martine against the wall and fondled her, then took off her blouse and skirt, leaving her naked except for stockings and garters. He pressed his mouth to hers, his hands roved her responsive body, finally settling in on her juicing cunt.

"Oh God, yes, you bastard, rub me harder."

He grunted, then lowered his pants, showing off his hard purple-headed prick. He had to lift her up, to penetrate her, but with Martine's slight build, and Miles' massive one, she was light as a feather to hold in his hands.

Martine wrapped her legs around Miles' waist as he thrust his dick into her sloshy cunt. Hector and Tessa looked on, keeping their silence. The scene was so mesmerizing that neither one could say a word. They watched the two pound against each other with brazen force, like two animals in heat with only one intention—to get to the end.

"Aaaaaaaaugghhh!" They creamed in tandem—

their fucking language could hardly be told apart, as it came from the same deep source.

"Damnnn, asshole, fuck me!" Martine's voice rose on its own.

"Damn, damn, fuuuucck," Miles bellowed.

Somewhere in the middle of their screams, the two released. Only then did Hector and Tessa sigh with relief, as if they'd held their breath the whole time.

Martine remained pressed against the wall, Miles' body holding her there. They didn't move for several minutes, until Martine finally found her voice again. "Damn, my back, put me down," she ordered.

Miles backed off and set the woman down with her feet on the floor. They collapsed together in each other's arms.

When they finally broke apart, Miles and Martine were suddenly laughing uproariously, as if the whole thing had been a fine joke. When they turned toward Hector and Tessa, Martine sported a cunning smile. So collected, so abruptly cold and stern, she looked like her most conniving self as she gazed at Tessa sitting on the bed. She noted the double dildo with curious fascination.

The two women stared at each other some moments before Martine walked toward her. Miles had excused himself to go to the bathroom.

"So what have we here?" the bitch said. On reaching Tessa, she pulled on one of the straps that was attached to the dildo below and the leather belt above.

"Good evening, Martine," Tessa said. She was trying to be polite for Miles' benefit, certainly not her roommate's. She couldn't think of anyone she least wanted to see in this garret, let alone fucking her dom.

"He wears me out, you know?" Martine said, as if she were exhausted, though she didn't look exhausted at all.

"I guess so, too bad Hector didn't record your show."

"Oh that's right! you're making a porno film!" Martine turned to Hector, "And my old friend, how are you?" She stared at the photographer with a broad pleased smile.

"I don't change much Martine," Hector replied evenly.

"You're charming as ever," Martine observed.

"Is that a compliment?" Hector asked.

"Of course."

"I never know with you," Hector replied pointedly. "So what keeps you busy, beside screwing the boss? Any more movies?" Hector asked.

"Not for a couple of years, not since the little tramp and I have been together." She turned to Tessa. "You did know that I did some porn of my own a few years ago?"

"No, I didn't know that," Tessa said. She couldn't mask the sarcasm in her voice. The scene minutes ago had raised her hackles as well as her sexual heat. Tessa would have given anything to have been in Martine's place against the wall.

"Hector here did quite a job," she said. She joined the photographer at the camera and began fondling him. "Damn, you're hard down here, did we make you that hot?"

"I suppose," Hector conceded. "Of course, Tessa already had me hard before you showed up."

Tessa watched the two, noticing that it was not a pleasant reunion. She wondered what story they'd written together. No doubt, Martine had used her typical ball-busting tactics on Hector, and he'd gotten pissed. No man could put up with her for long.

"Can I help you out?" Martine purred at him, running her hands along his pants. "Tessa hasn't taken very good care of you." She laughed. "But then, how could she, all locked up?"

"You like her bondage?" Miles asked. He'd returned to the room, listening to the strained babble between his "house guests."

"I think it's lovely, wish I'd thought of it." Martine pulled away from Hector and focused her attention on Tessa. She strode to the bed and began pulling at one of the straps. She pulled hard enough for the leather to cut into the sensitive creases of her flesh, constricting the already tight bonds even more. She tried to twist the leather strap in her hand.

"Stop it, damn you!" Tessa seethed at her.

Miles whipped around and glared at his insubordinate submissive.

"What was that?" he asked, moving to the bed.

"The bitch is cutting me!" Tessa protested.

He slapped her face. "Don't argue with my guest," he blared at her.

It was the one moment she could have spit in Miles' eyes, but she didn't dare do it.

He slapped her again. "Wipe that look off your face or I'll string you up, like I didn't do yesterday."

Two pairs of eyes smoldered, just one spark away from a full blown conflagration. Tessa backed down. Taking a deep breath, she relaxed.

Martine let go her hold on Tessa's straps with a triumphant grin. "These are quite clever," she said, fingering them lightly. "How long have they been there?" Miles nodded for Tessa to answer.

"Nearly twenty-four hours," Tessa replied, "except for when they give me a break."

"She looks good in them," Martine commented. "And I see you haven't forgotten her ass."

"I understand you fucked her there," Miles remarked.

"Yes. She should have been violated there a long time ago—it makes her more compliant. Something in her spirit really takes to this kind of surrender. In the ass is so demeaning, don't you think?"

"She seemed to enjoy it last night," Miles said.

"Oh, of course she did. That's what's so perfect about Tessa. The little tramp would have done anything when I shoved that dildo in her."

Miles observed his accomplice carefully.

He appreciated her crafty manipulative disposition. He had plans for it. He couldn't think of a more perfect fem dom for his slave. The animosity between them was sparked with such desire. Miles had realized that the first time he saw the two together. He knew they'd make a vintage piece of pornography, as long as the bitch remembered who was in control.

Listening to their conversation, Tessa pulled back, frightened.

"Don't worry my dear, there's only one person in charge here," he told her. "She's as much under my thumb as you are." Martine was fondling him again while Miles' hands enjoyed a brisk journey around her breasts.

"Yes, that's what he thinks," Martine said.

Miles pinched the bitch's tit with a nasty twist.

"Stop that!" She winced and pulled away.

Miles chuckled, then walked to a closet, where he retrieved a robe. "Here," he said throwing it at Martine. She put it on, while Miles slumped down in his overstuffed chair, with a glass of dark German beer in his hand. Martine joined him at his side, pulling up a creaky rocking chair, as the two stared at Tessa.

Hector was busy with the camera on the other side of the room. He'd recorded part of the scene between the three, just to see how it would turn out, though he was far more interested in what was to follow.

Martine was an unpleasant surprise, even though he still found himself aroused by her. Five years before, she'd been one of the most nauseating models he'd ever used. She was crass and crude. His biggest problem was getting her to shut up. He didn't see much change in her. But she was perfect for the scene that Miles had planned. Her heartless glacial cunning would offset Tessa's soft compliance.

"So what do you want to do to her?" Miles asked Martine, as they eyed their captive.

"I've been thinking about that," Martine mused. "You've filled her so well, it's impressive, inspiring even."

"Thank you," Miles answered.

"But what really inspires me are those stripes on her belly."

Miles' eyes danced delighted as he read Martine's thoughts.

"You know what I've always wanted to do?" she continued.

"What?"

"Whip her cunt."

Tessa, hearing her, trembled.

"I want to mark her right between her legs, while she's spread wide. I want to wield a wicked lash against all that feminine charm."

"You're worse than I am," Miles exclaimed.

"Maybe I am," Martine considered. "It's been a very potent fantasy. Ever since I read *The Story of O*, where O is whipped by the woman while she's tied to the pillars—I always knew which part I wanted to play. And Tessa? Well, she's been the center of that fantasy for years. What do you think of that?" Martine called to her roommate.

Tessa didn't reply.

"What do you think of yourself being laid open, your pussy being whipped?" Miles demanded an answer.

Tessa fidgeted with the leather bindings, trying to put off her answer. She found no words to authorize such brutality on her own body, even though the idea had been one that had often appeared from out of nowhere in her mind. In any event, Tessa knew the die had been cast. The only thing she wondered...had it been an spontaneous suggestion or had they planned it? Was it a flash of inspiration or part of a larger devious plot?

"Answer me, Tessa," Miles said. His eyes were brimming with darkness. In fact, it seemed at that very moment that the lights in the garret dimmed appreciably. Tessa was amazed by the strange coincidence, even though it could be easily explained, with Hector standing next to the switches on the wall, adjusting the lighting.

Suddenly, there were but two lights lit in the room, and both were glaring at Tessa, blinding her vision. She could still make out the glimmer on Miles' face, but it was as shadowy as if he were a ghost just materializing.

"Answer me," he repeated.

"It would be another sign of my enslavement to you," she finally replied.

Miles nodded. "How true. But how would it make you feel to have you have your pussy whipped?"

"I imagine it would excite me."

"Eventually," Miles said, "and before that?"

Tessa's eyes flashed angrily. "It would make me scream in agony. Is that what you want me to say?"

"I only want you to admit the truth," he said.

"If you want me in agony now, be assured I'm there."

"And no doubt wet between your legs," Martine guessed.

"No doubt," she reluctantly conceded.

"And, if it's Martine that wields the lash against your pussy?"

"I'd hate it," she snapped, before Miles finished the question.

He smiled. "That's good. This way, with Martine brandishing the implement, you won't have the advantage of some affection getting in the way."

"I'm sure I wouldn't," Tessa declared.

"You two must think I'm a totally ruthless bitch," Martine objected, though her objection was only in fun. She had every intention of being a ruthless bitch with Tessa. She couldn't wait to have free reign on the poor little tramp—it was a dream come true.

Miles took Martine's hand in his, affectionately stroking it. "Your temperament is perfect for what I have in mind. It's perfect for what Tessa needs. I told her I'd give her an exquisite ride into her nastiest passions and that is exactly what I intend to do."

Martine admired him. She didn't like admiring any man, but this one was so much like herself, she couldn't help it. She knew one day she'd hate him, probably because he'd chosen Tessa over her, but she was used to that. She didn't really want a man the way most women do. She wanted challenge, a good contest, risk, intrigue. And he was certainly giving her that.

"Besides, this is going to be one helluva videotape," Miles said. "I know several collectors and dealers that will pay dearly to own it. Each little jerk of the female cunt in abject pain makes some dicks crazy."

"Then I'll really make the lash sizzle for you," Martine said. Her eyes gleamed darkly; her voice had grown husky. She was ready to begin.

Tessa cowered on the bed. She wanted to run away. Their conversation had made her a nonperson—flesh, limbs, cunt, nothing more. Used. She was reminded of the word that Hector had applied to submission. Like a whore. He'd said that too. Was she just a commodity, an unpaid one at that, allowing herself to be used by Miles to make money and an impression on his friends?

Tessa was fuming, boiling mad. The straps cut into her, and they hurt like hell. All the pulling and the posing had made the dildos almost too much to bear. And...there was the ever present gnawing sensation in her groin. She knew it was lust, and she hated that fact.

God, if they'd only get on with it, she brooded to herself. Do anything you want with me, just do it! she wanted to scream. Her body was crawling with anxiety, prickly with sexual heat churning through her with dark designs and nowhere to go.

Yet she could say nothing to them. She waited, looking a bit like a little trapped lamb, waiting for the lion to pounce.

CHAPTER ELEVEN

MILES PULLED TESSA to her feet, then turned her around and unfastened the lock that held her bonds. When the dildos were released, she almost flooded the floor with pee.

"Go the bathroom and clean yourself, quickly," he ordered. Tessa padded away, feeling ever so naked without her rods and straps.

In the bathroom relieving herself, she felt empty. She realized the same noxious passions that had ignited her all day long were returning with a fierce zeal. Her mind was consumed by what would happen next. The whip. Martine. Her pussy flogged like O, in that classic tale of surrender. Could she handle it that well, she wondered?

Tessa finished her brief bathing and returned to the room. Both Martine and Miles were standing, waiting for her.

"I have just one thought before we begin," Martine said.

"What's that?" Miles asked.

"Her pussy, I'd like it shaved." The woman looked down at the silky hairs still glistening with water.

"She'll be more vulnerable to the pain that way," Miles observed. "With no protection, that pretty cunt will be as striped as her belly and ass."

"That's the idea." Martine was utterly without compassion. The very worst in her seemed to have surfaced.

"She's your slave now," Miles told her, "do whatever you want with her."

"You have a razor in the bathroom?" Martine asked.

"With a fresh blade," he answered.

Martine reached out and took a fistful of Tessa's pussy hair and yanked it hard.

"Ouch, stop!" Tessa cried.

Martine slapped her face. "Take care of it, slut," she barked, "the more naked you are, the more it will hurt, the more you'll get the message that you're nothing but a slutty little whore to be used."

Tessa's eyes spat out enmity so deep that even Miles shuddered.

"Do what you're told," Miles told her. There was no room for questioning him, his voice was icy cold.

Without another word, Tessa turned away from the three pairs of watchful eyes, and trotted to the bathroom.

"Hurry up, slut," Martine called after her; the celebration in her voice did not go unnoticed.

Tessa remembered Miles talking of shaving her pussy. She had thought the act would be a dutiful gesture of surrender. She had imagined baring herself this way as another milestone in her training. She had imagined it as a ritual performed lovingly for him.

But now the act was tarnished. All the pretty pictures vanished.

"Don't take too long, Tessa," she heard Martine's voice again.

Tessa grabbed the razor from the medicine cabinet. Then splashing warm water against her pussy, she applied a generous amount of shaving cream and began a hurried excursion about her pussy with the fresh blade.

It didn't take long to have the obvious hair removed. As the razor cut each lock away, she could see more of her bare skin beneath. She didn't stop with the outer hair, but opened wide her pussy lips and ran the razor along the tender flesh on either side of her clit. She reached back even further still, as far as she could go, and shaved away the hair from her entire cleft, to the few remaining wisps around her rear hole.

As the hair disappeared, her fingers felt the softness. It was arousing in a most peculiar way; she could have brought about a lively orgasm in seconds, but there was not time. She heard Martine's raspy voice bark at her again.

Splashing herself with the warm water, she watched in the mirror as the shaving cream disappeared to reveal her Venus mound in its breathtaking naked glory. The opening between her labia looked so childlike and innocent, even though the purpose for it was not. She had only seconds to wonder what horror would greet her before she was compelled to move on. She shivered head to toe as she replaced the razor in the cabinet and then returned to the others.

"Ooooo my, how nice," Martine purred. She admired the clean bare skin. The woman pried apart her labia and felt her from her vagina to her asshole, impressed by how well Tessa had completed the task. For a moment, she stuck a finger into her cunt and prodded her. Pulling away, Martine put her soaked finger in Tessa's mouth.

"Lick it, slut," she ordered.

Tessa tasted her juices, recognizing the musky smell of her own sex.

"If I were you Miles? I wouldn't let her grow it back. It's very fitting for a slut like her." Martine smiled, with the tiniest hint of affection, but that was quickly dispensed with; she had other things immediately on her mind. "So let's get on with it," she announced.

Miles pulled Tessa away and led her to the large wardrobe at the side of the room, while Martine moved off to one corner behind an oriental screen. She would change her clothes to something suitable for the camera and her task.

"She needs to look the part, and so do you," Miles explained to Tessa. He spoke to her quietly. He opened the wardrobe, showing her a bevy of lacy lingerie, costumes, and exotic-looking dresses. "Let's see, we need something soft and compliant like yourself." He looked down at her, taking notice of her bare cunt. She wished he would fondle it, even with rough gestures like Martine's; instead, he appeared to be deliberately avoiding it.

As he rummaged through the closet, he looked at several things, then went on to others. He seemed to be searching the wardrobe for something in particular.

Gazing at all the finery, she wondered who had worn these interesting garments. And how had Miles come to collect such a selection of women's clothes? These were nothing like the things that he'd wanted her to wear for him before.

What he pulled out surprised her. It was an old-fashioned corset, in a deep mauve, like the color of the skin between her labia.

"You want me to wear this?" she questioned him.

"Yes. It will be perfect," he said. He didn't explain more.

She looked at it warily, thinking how she'd expected some nasty leather piece, instead of this more traditional symbol of submission. A whimsical expression flashed across her face. "Reminds me of something a harlot would wear in a brothel."

"Then it's very fitting," Miles retorted.

"And just think, I'll look so pretty with the lace matching the stripes on my privates." Tessa laced her words with a surprising degree of sarcasm. She was still angry about Martine wielding the whip on her cunt.

"Watch yourself, don't get too testy. Don't make me punish you now, Tessa dear," Miles warned. "That would be very foolish, since it would only double your agony tonight."

She gave him a sassy pout, but said no more.

He pushed her toward the mirror, "Go put it on, and be sure to lace it tightly."

Tessa padded to the full-length mirror to begin dressing.

"Hector," Miles called to the photographer, "begin the filming."

Tessa's first look in the mirror was shocking. She'd almost forgotten the nakedness between her legs. For several moments, she just stared in wonder, thinking how virtuous she looked without the symbol of her womanhood, the silky hairs that would glisten with her female dew. But then she saw something more, a strange seductive quality, as if her bare pussy was winking at her naughtily, reminding her of its feminine power. The message was mixed, but the eroticism potent. Her reverie almost made her forget her anger.

The corset fit perfectly around her waist, as if Miles had designed it expressly for her. The corset had heavy stays at the sides to hold her torso firmly, and it was joined at the front with crisscrossing laces. As Tessa tugged on the ribbons, she could feel it constrict her, each tug imprisoning her in its firm grasp.

"Tighter love," Miles called to her as he watched.

Tessa worked at the ribbons, pulling them up tighter still. She had to hold her breath to make the two sides of lace and satin pull together so that the edges almost touched. Breathing was becoming difficult, and she could go no further on her own.

To her surprise, Hector walked to her side to assist. His strong hands grabbed the laces firmly and gave them a hearty yank.

"Yikes! I can't breathe," she cried.

"Relax, of course you can," he said gently. He pulled on the ribbons with a steady tug until they were so tight she thought she would surely burst. "It will take some time to get used to, but I think you'll like the effect. Now look at yourself."

Tessa turned back to the mirror and admired herself. Feeling a little like Scarlett O'Hara trying to pull her self into a tiny-waisted ball gown, she found the hourglass of her figure a surprise. And a pleasant one at that. She was instantly transported into another time and place, that Victorian era of cruel discipline and high-spirited antics of schoolgirl-like erotic trainings. She had a half dozen books of such adventures hidden under her mattress, for lonely nights by herself with her raging loins and her imagination flying.

Seeing her breasts spilling over the edges of the corset, she viewed herself as the voluptuous innocent, being instructed and disciplined in the fine art of submissive behavior. Seeing her hips swell at the bottom of the garment, and her cunt framed by the dangling garters, she knew how it might feel to be the pure young maiden, about to be raped by the cruel but deliciously inventive renegade and his accomplices. It was proving to be a fun excursion into fantasyland—until the reality of the moment descended on her.

"Here, your stockings," Miles said, handing them to her.

She could hardly bend over to put them on, the corset was so restricting. But she had no choice. Miles and Hector stood just off to the side, watching her in her awkward task, ready to pounce on her if she faltered. She managed to pull the first rose-colored stocking over her leg and attach it to the garters front and back. Taking the second, she put it on and turned back to the mirror to get another look at herself. The impression of those old Victorian novels hadn't faded away; it only seemed to become more vivid in her mind.

Turning away from the mirror, she looked at the rest of the room, noticing that the furnishings had been transformed once again—this time into the period that she recalled in her mind. Certainly Miles and Hector deliberately planned it that way. The dark drapery and the old Oriental screens made perfect sense. A glowing old-fashioned lamp added just the right touch of period authenticity. Had it not been her who was the center of attention, she might have been fascinated by the scene that the two artists were creating.

Tessa had a flippant remark about that fact just on the tip of her tongue, but it fluttered away with the appearance of Martine, coming out from behind the screen.

Tessa stood stock-still, marveling at what she saw. She'd never seen Martine so ravishing!

She was dressed in what looked liked a Victorian ball gown: a flowing garment, with a bodice so low that her pinched-up breasts were nearly naked. Indeed, Tessa could see the edges of her aureoles peeking out, though her full nipples were pressed tightly into place.

In turn, Martine looked at Tessa taking note of her attire. "This is quite a mood you're setting, Miles," she observed. It was a noncommittal statement, no one knowing if she was happy with his choice of clothes or annoyed.

To Tessa, it seemed an unusual choice. Martine was the kind of woman she always envisioned in tight-fitting leather—probably because she often wore tight-fitting leather. She looked so perfect in modern mistress garb that this seemed a little too genteel and refined. But then, what a contrast it would be! Perhaps that was why the Victorian period was such an interesting background for such ruthless designs. On the one hand, it appeared on the surface so elegant and civilized, while underneath, there was a simmering debauchery to shock even the most practiced modern-day sadomasochistic devotees.

Martine looked at herself in Tessa's full-length mirror. Tessa turned back around to look. Seeing both dominant and submissive side by side in the glass was a stunning picture of opposites, a delight to behold.

On further inspection, Tessa could tell that Martine's dress was a period "fake." No doubt it was specifically designed for this occasion, no other. It was lace from the bodice to the hem, with no concealing sheath underneath. As it flowed to Martine's ankles, her bare skin peeked through, so that it concealed but did not conceal. It would tease the untrained eye and be a pleasant revelation to the astute observer. On one side of the dress, there was a deep slit, and when she walked, the dress opened, so everything below her waist was dangerously close to being exposed.

To add to the drama, Martine wore long black gloves on her hands and a pair of shiny patent leather ankle boots. Her generous brunette hair was piled atop her head in a bun, completing the picture of some mistress from another place and time.

"The first day I met Martine, in the lobby of your building," Miles said, "I decided then, that she would look perfect in this dress. I knew she would be perfect for this initiation. You remember? Her hair was fixed like this, like a genteel nineteenth-century lady. It was a perfect clue to her true nature." Miles had stepped behind the two women, his form appearing in the mirror towering ominously over theirs.

Hector aimed his camera at the scene. He had been

filming the entire show, the preparations, the banter, everything. And now this, this shot of the trio would be a perfect transition to the next dramatic scene.

"Her true nature?" Tessa whipped around to look at both Miles and Martine. "You knew that day? Why you hardly talked!"

"I knew instantaneously she was right for the part," he said.

Tessa was speechless.

"Shall we get on with things?" he said.

Moving out of their way, he ushered the two women past him, on their way to the platform in the corner. By some silent order from Miles, Martine was given command, and Tessa was powerless to change anything, captive to a woman she hated more than loved.

"Lie down, Tessa, on your back," Martine instructed her, in the same dark sultry tones she often used when making love to her. It was not what Tessa expected, but these welcome niceties soothed her. She wondered why Martine suddenly was so kind. Perhaps the dress and the surroundings had altered her disposition? Or perhaps she was just taking her time, before she would pounce with her catlike claws.

As Tessa approached the platform, she saw that instead of the bed—which had been pushed into another corner of the room—there was a antique lounging settee in its place. The ancient piece of furniture was covered in a paisley brocade to match the period of their reenactment. Sitting down on the edge of the couch, Tessa lay back against the cool smooth surface, shivering with a chill so deep, she wondered if any warmth would return to her at all. She was deathly afraid of what was to follow, of a Martine that scared her, and the lash the woman was about to wield in a more harrowing form than she'd ever experienced.

"Her hands, bind her hands," Martine ordered and Miles responded willingly.

He drew her hands above her head and pulled them tight, binding them with ropes that he then fastened to some unseen device behind her. Tessa's rear was at the edge of the couch, her legs dangling down to touch the floor.

Martine stood over her with cold eyes flashing. The terms of endearment that she'd uttered before did not appear in her next speech. For that she became the heartless bitch that Tessa expected.

"I'm going to whip your pussy," Martine informed her. "You should count yourself lucky to have my attention. Every submissive like yourself should revel in this bliss at least once. You deserve this kind of satisfaction. You deserve the bite and sting against the most sensitive places of your body. You deserve your cunt abused this way. And it will show Miles that you're willing to do anything for him, to suffer any kind of correction, no matter how severe."

Martine walked around the bound Tessa, inspecting her. There was a severe scowl on her face, as if she despised her submissive. Tessa stared at her with eyes wide and frightened, watching as Martine dropped to one knee at her side. Taking Tessa's chin in her hand, Martine's eyes bore into the slave with a scorching heat.

"I'm going to whip you, Tessa, because sometimes it's all that I can think about. With your lithe little figure traipsing about the apartment, flirting with me, sometimes I want to brutalize this fragrant thing of yours." She grabbed Tessa's cunt with her free hand. "You're a shameless tramp, a brazen shameless tramp."

Tessa breathed deeply, trying to hold back the vile things she was thinking. How could Martine talk to her this way? What had she possibly done to deserve so much malice? Had they not made love dozens of times? Had she not given herself to Martine, almost without question? Had they not called each other friend?

"And you know, my little tramp?" Martine continued, "I believe you've wanted me to take you like this, but you were too cowardly to ask. Isn't that true?"

"No!" Tessa couldn't help but shout her reply.

Martine laughed. "I knew you'd say that, you little floozy. But guess what?" Tessa tried to pull away from her grasp, but the bitch held her tight. "You will admit it to me before I'm finished with you."

Tessa wanted to shout, "*never!*" But it was a dangerous assertion that she was smart enough to keep to herself.

Martine let go of her chin and stood up. She glared contemptuously at her bound slave.

"A pillow under her ass," Martine said, then she turned away.

Miles found a pillow on the bed, and shoved it under Tessa's hips, lifting her cunt to the precise height that suited her dom.

"That's perfect," the bitch cooed.

Tessa's exposed cunt now dangled over the edge of the settee so that nothing was bared from view and nothing would be protected from the whip.

"Tie her legs open," Martine ordered. "I don't want her squirming away from this."

"Please, no," Tessa pleaded.

Miles ignored the plea and followed Martine's instruction. Taking several lengths of rope, he tied her feet to the legs of the couch and then wrapped other ropes at her knees so he could fasten them open as well.

Finished, he leaned over her bound body and kissed her cheek gently. "You may think you're doing this for me," he said quietly, "but remember, you're doing it for yourself."

He backed away.

Tessa's attention was quickly diverted to Martine again. The bitch stood to one side of her with a witch-like face and a triumphant grin. Behind the mockery in her eye, there was an hypnotic beauty about her haughty appearance. It was something Tessa had seen before, something that attracted her to the woman in ways that mystified her. Seeing it now made her less afraid, as if she was acknowledging a bond between the two of them that she hadn't wanted to accept before. Accepting it now, this surrender to Martine, was like fate catching up with her.

Martine held the buggy whip in her hand. It was the same one Miles had used on her rear end, the one that had marked her there a dozen times before.

"Remember, Tessa," Martine whispered softly. "Remember what I said. You'll confess this desire before I'm through."

Martine stepped off the platform and took her place in front of Tessa. With no further comment, she began.

Thwack! The whip cut through the air and landed on Tessa's inner thigh, high up next to her labia.

"Yeow!!" Tessa shrieked.

Thwack! The next cut sizzled exactly as the first, though this one landed on a plump pink labia.

"Gaaaawwwd noooooo!" She tried to buck her hips away from the next, but the bonds held her fast.

Thwack! Thwack! Martine picked up speed. There was no time between cuts for Tessa to relax. She howled in pain, each cut adding such a horrid sensation, she feared she would pass out from the pain. Martine, seeing Tessa's agony, abruptly stopped the beating. But just for a moment.

"Calm yourself, little one, I've only begun. You'll take much more of this before you're through," she said. She waltzed around Tessa's recuperating body, then returning to her place in front of her. She began again.

Thwack, thwack, thwack. She peeled off a steady stream of cuts, one after another. She aimed at the centerpiece of Tessa's life, her cunt, not particularly planning any specific assault, but letting each blow land at will on the tender inner thighs, on the reddening labia, and even on the tip of a clit that peeked out between the protective flaps of flesh.

"Oh gawwwwwd, nooooooo, pleassssssssse, nooooo-oooooo, aaaaauuuuugggggggg!" Tessa tried to twist away, with no success; she squirmed, but barely moved an inch. There was no getting anyway from anything. The pain continued to mount, even though Martine paused now and again to allow her submissive a moment to get used to the next level of intensity.

"Let it take you away tramp, that's what you want," Martine asserted.

Thwack! Thwack!

"Oh gawwwwwwd, nooooooo." She wailed frantically, but to no avail.

Pain began to swim over her, a hellish aphrodisiac. As much as each cut hurt her to the core, she was becoming resigned to its ruthless result, and resigned to the way its force was arousing her. She felt herself rising to each new burning bite, as if she wanted it. And each cruel cut of the buggy whip imprinted her with the message that she craved the pain it would give her.

Thwack, thwack. Her cries became moans, gasps of willingness. The "oh pleeeese," in her voice was not for Martine to stop, but for her to continue.

Martine, whose dominance had suddenly burst forth in such overt fashion, was possessed. The power she wielded charged her body with such passion, she thought she would come, simply from the act.

And yet, to her surprise, there was an unexpected feeling running in tandem with her lust. By some bizarre twist of fate, she discovered herself respecting Tessa and her submissiveness. Seeing her at the mercy of the whip, she was in awe of her.

Martine found herself striking the swollen cunt, not to hurt her lover, as she thought she would, but to pleasure both of them. Each lashing cut descended on the vulnerable cunt to entice her. Some cuts were softer, some more harsh, but behind them all was the clear understanding that at some point she would have to stop. She, Martine, would have to judge that moment when Tessa had reached her limit. And she, Martine, would have to demonstrate the grace required to end it.

Martine's cunt was burning hot; with each cut, the

fire in her own loins seemed to burn brighter. Finally, she could take no more. She could not endure another scream, or the sight of Tessa's muscles clenching, or the way her own cunt responded so joyously to Tessa's torture—even if the submissive woman was in her own ecstasy.

Martine dropped the buggy whip, and flew to the bound maiden, flinging her legs over the settee, so that her own bare cunt was at Tessa's face.

"Lick me now, love," she ordered.

Tessa responded quickly, her tongue reaching out to fondle the moistened cunt. She sucked the dear bud of the clitoris she knew so well, with a tenderness Martine had never shown her. It was a pleasure to hear Martine sob with joy, as a crashing orgasm claimed her and her juices spilled out all over Tessa's face.

When she was finished, the bitch looked down on Tessa.

"Was I right? You wanted me to do this, didn't you?" She wasn't as haughty as she usually was, just matter-of-fact.

Feeling the throbbing in her loins, like a cannon going off, Tessa murmured, "Yes." She hadn't wanted to admit it, but it was true. Everyone present heard her admission.

Now, all Tessa needed was a moment of her own. Her body clamored for release. To accommodate her, Martine dropped down between her legs, and began to lick the raw aching flesh of Tessa's cunt. She began to shudder. The bonds, though still holding her fast, could not hold back the thunderous earthquake that rocked straight through her.

CHAPTER TWELVE

IT WAS SO QUIET in the morning, Tessa could hear birds singing outside Miles' loft. She hadn't expected their song ringing in her ears, not in the middle of the city.

When Tessa rose from the bed, she realized that she was alone. Miles didn't respond when she called out, so she assumed that he'd left some time in the night. She remembered being exhausted after the punishment. She remembered being freed from the bonds and carried in Miles' arms from the settee to the bed. She remembered drifting off to dreams on the gentleness of his touch and his soft words spoken in her ear. Apparently, she had given him everything he wanted, because he asked no more of her, not a blowjob, or a quick fuck, or anything. Even Hector didn't have her. Poor Hector, he likely had to satisfy himself with Martine, or with nothing at all. She wondered to herself which it was.

Now the garret was bright with sunlight. Tessa could see the blue sky beyond the windows. Grabbing a robe that had been thrown at the bottom of the bed, she tossed it over her shoulders and walked along an unexplored corridor, to find a door she'd not seen before. Opening it, she discovered a rooftop patio bathed in sunshine. And there, as if it had been waiting for her, was a lounge, the perfect place to sit for her morning coffee. She scooted back inside, made herself a quick cup, and grabbed a plum.

As she made her plans to sunbathe outside, Tessa knew she was avoiding the freestanding mirror. She was avoiding even touching the soreness between her legs. She'd winced from the pain before she'd even opened her eyes, and she winced a little now as she walked. But she wasn't yet ready to face the damage or the feelings that had been brought up the night before. In the clear bright morning, it was easy to forget darker things.

Lying back on the chaise lounge, she let the robe fall around her, the sun's rays hitting her with its generous cheerful warmth. She was refreshed and smiling to herself, even though she was frequently reminded of the scars and wounds between her legs.

Her mind traveled back and forth on an easy path between the night before and the present. She felt herself become juicy, though the sticky dampness evaporated in the sun's heat. Her hand, finding her cunt deliciously aroused, began to pull her labia apart, so that the hard bud between them was as heated as the rest of her. She churned against her hands, despite the pain. Indeed, the little pains from the wounds made her flinch, but only for an instant as the sharp sensations blended with every other vibrant feeling of sexual heat taking over her body.

Her cunt roared quickly, climaxing, with her juice pouring out over her hands.

When she relaxed, the sun did its bidding again, almost instantaneously, a rush of tingling sensations surfacing once more. She didn't have time to come down from the first climax before a second was on its way. She bucked against her hands. Her thighs burned. Her groin reached toward the heavens, as if getting closer would bring her to a heavenly end, all the more easily.

She gasped. The tiny moans, petal-soft, rose into the wisp of a breeze that teased her body.

Tessa might have delighted in herself for hours, but this time when her eyes fluttered open, she was looking into Miles' eyes. He was standing over her. She jerked up in surprise.

"Having your morning's pleasure without me?"

"Oh, *with* you Miles, you're in my thoughts constantly," she flirted with him shamelessly to head off any displeasure.

But he wasn't displeased.

"How long have you been here?" he asked, sitting down on a small sliver of the lounge next to her.

"A half hour perhaps. How long have you been looking at me?"

"I saw you climax."

"Just the second one, or the first as well?"

"Two?" he queried, impressed.

"I'm often like this after a night like last night."

"Ah, I see. You mean that was a commonplace adventure for you?"

"Oh no! But when I've been so filled with sexual energy like last night, sometimes it doesn't get completely spent."

"Then perhaps you should continue," he suggested. His hand traced its way along her thighs, bringing back the same feelings that had claimed her twice before. She pushed herself toward his wandering fingers, asking for more. He teased her, and she reached even harder with her thrusting cunt. She opened herself with her hands, for him to touch her sensitive clit.

"Pleeeese, my love, please," she agonized, "bring me off."

"Bring yourself off, slut, you do it so well."

She bucked wildly, the slightest sensation, even the slightest breeze tickling her mercilessly.

"Ah, yes, please," she moaned.

"Reach for it, Tessa."

She jerked, almost mad with need, as if she hadn't come in weeks. His presence was like a booster rocket attached to the burning in her abdomen.

"Ah! Ah! Yes." She panted in oblivious staccato gasps, until she screamed, letting her voice rise loudly.

She jerked toward his hand as it came down on her cunt, his fingers instantly penetrating both her holes. She squeezed against them, and he drew from her all the longing need as heaving spasms crashed through her.

When she finally relaxed, her body stopped its incessant twitching. Miles was still looking down on her, his expression questioning. Was she finished yet?

"I get off so much more vividly when you're here," she said.

"That's the way it's supposed to be," he said. "So, can you stop long enough for me to take you home?"

"Home, my God, why?" She abruptly turned into a brazen vamp, her lips and eyes pouting coyly, her hands reaching to find where he was hard between his legs.

He pushed her away.

"I think you might want to get back to your life?" he said.

"Isn't this my life?" she said.

"I'd hoped you'd feel that way, but I have obligations and so do you."

"But I have more time, you asked for several days. You're reneging? Haven't I pleased you?"

"I don't think you have that to worry about—I was referring to other obligations you have to me."

"Oh. And what are those?"

"You'll see. Right now you need to get dressed."

Miles looked down at her legs, this time noticing the welts that Martine had left the night before.

"How nice," he observed. "Just as I had hoped."

"I haven't seen them," Tessa admitted.

"Ignoring them?"

"I suppose."

"Then you'd better get your ass inside and see what your roommate thinks of you."

Reminded of Martine, Tessa shivered coldly, the sun choosing that very instant to find a cloud to hide behind, as if that impassioned orb could read her thoughts. Tessa pulled herself reluctantly from the lounge and hastily rushed toward the garret with Miles following closely on her tail.

Tessa looked to see the lines of pain between her legs. She was surprised at how remarkably lovely they looked to her. They appeared to have been put there by a tender lover, helping her seek some rare ecstasy through the refining fire of pain. She had never thought of Martine as that kind of lover, but there was no escaping the memory of the night before, when the bitch had reached inside her soul with the buggy whip, finding a level of submission so unexpected that it had taken her by surprise. To be that willing with a woman she sometimes loved, sometimes despised, astonished her. Yet the fact remained that she had willingly allowed herself to be punished by Martine, her own body encouraging the act.

"Martine punished you thoroughly and with remarkable affection," Miles observed.

"I know," Tessa admitted.

"So perhaps you two can take off your guns and holsters and enjoy each other?"

"We did last night…eventually," Tessa smirked.

"It was good for your souls," Miles ventured, "and mine."

Tessa nodded, agreeing.

"Now get dressed, love, we have places to go."

In his car, they wound about the city streets, stopping for a brief moment at a small deli, where Miles picked up bagels and juice for breakfast. They ate in the car, chatting about normal things, like a normal couple, until he pulled up in front of Maya's shop.

The moment Tessa saw the place, she knew what was going to happen. "I've earned more?" she asked.

The memory of his words weeks before made her heart pound rapidly, though she wasn't surprised that she was returning for more gold jewelry.

"Your willingness last night, the whipping, your yielding, yes, you've earned more."

"This is going to hurt, isn't it?" Tessa asked nervously.

"It could. But less so if you're relaxed, let's not have a repeat of the past." His reply sounded more like a threat than assurance. She would have preferred that he phrase the thought in a more soothing vein.

It was clear from the outset however, that this would not be a repeat of her initial session with Maya. First, Tessa felt very different. Just walking in the door, she noticed that she'd changed; she was hardly the innocent initiate any more, and that realization comforted her. The very idea of having her nether regions pierced as her nipples had been made her cunt juice instantly. Taking something that was once just fantasy into the real world was much less threatening than it had been in the past.

Besides her internal changes, there were other differences between this time and the first. While the shop itself was much as it had been before, upon entering, Miles immediately took her to a back room behind the outer salon. The atmosphere in this closed dark place was almost sinister; with incense burning and candles glowing, there was a heavy, mysterious feel all around her.

It was more intriguing, but also more frightening.

Even Miles changed. His once friendly demeanor vanished, replaced by a coldness Tessa knew well. He brusquely placed her in Maya's hands, as if she was so much merchandise to be dispensed with.

"Pierce her cunt, above her clitoris," he said, "and place rings through her inner labia. I want them to hang down noticeably."

"A little showpiece," Maya suggested, quite delighted with the prospect of Miles proposal.

"Will Vincent be here to do her?" Miles asked.

"Soon. I expect him back shortly. You don't plan to watch?"

"No, I have an appointment. When you're finished, let her rest. I'll pick her up when I'm ready. And Maya, don't make it too painful for her, remember how delicate she is." He was being sarcastic.

Tessa wondered if his quick mood change was a show for Maya, or for her. Or whether it might be his former exasperation with her in the salon, suddenly surfacing again. Either way, he left without saying anything to her, making her feel even more like a piece of clothing left for alterations.

"Vincent will like the color of her pussy," Maya reminded Miles, as he was almost out the door.

Miles turned, expressionless. "Then let him have it," he said. Without another word, he was gone.

"Well, my little trinket, we'll be adorning your cunt." She tugged the short skirt Tessa was wearing until it was bunched around her waist. "A little glitter will do this pale skin good. Ah! Look at those stripes!" She inspected them carefully. "Only a good whip would do them so deeply." She ran a long black finger against the sensitive skin. "I like this, no hair. The gold will show better."

Tessa remained silent, while the black woman pawed her. She pulled down the shirt Tessa was wearing to see the studs at her nipples.

"Ah!" she exclaimed delighted. "I'll give you another pair. Nice rings, just above these," she said, tugging at one of the studs.

"He didn't say that," Tessa protested.

"But he won't object, will he?"

The woman was in control. It was pointless to argue with her. Maya was as sure of her plans as Miles was of his.

"Who's Vincent?" Tessa asked.

"My husband. He does pussy, it's his specialty." Tessa wasn't sure she was referring to fucking her or piercing; probably both she decided, witnessing the smiling expression on Maya's face. "You'll have to wait until he comes."

"When will that be?"

"Hour or two, you'll wait here, I have things to do." Maya shoved her into the small cubicle and proceeded to affix cuffs to her wrists, then attached them to a hook above her head, making her strain. She'd spent too many hours in the last forty-eight stretched out this way, and her arms were instantly aching. And then, as if that were not enough, Maya pulled her legs apart and tied them. Her cunt was forced by the awkward position into the rough fabric of the upholstery, where it scratched her already tender flesh.

"Please, anything, just not above my head," Tessa pleaded.

Maya flashed her a reprimanding glance, then finished her work. Once done, she left Tessa by herself, closing the door after her.

As it turned out, what might have seemed like hours to Tessa was only a few minutes, though each aching moment with her arms suspended only enhanced the fear floating through her.

When the door snapped opened, a blaring light hit her eyes. She was blinded for a moment, unable to see who was staring at her from the doorway. She craned her neck to get a better glance. But only when the intruder moved inside the room could she see who was eyeing her so carefully.

He was a pale-skinned black man. He must have been nearly six feet, five inches the way he appeared to tower over her. She'd often pictured Miles looming ominously above her the way this man did. But the black man was even more imposing, no doubt because he didn't have the tender sensibilities that Miles had for her. There was no affection in his eyes, no smile on his face.

"I'm Vincent," he said, once he shut the door.

Tessa said nothing.

Thankfully, he wasn't interested in conversation. The man proceeded to lower her arms, letting them fold naturally in her lap. They were still bound with the cloth Maya had used, but at least there was no aching in her shoulders.

"Maya goes to extremes," he said coldly, as if that was an explanation for his untying her.

"Thank you for lowering them, they were very sore."

He said nothing, but he sat down on a black stool with wheels, one just like in a doctor's examining room. He moved up close to her, now nearly at the same eye level.

"So we're piercing you today?" he said. He even sounded like a doctor.

"As Miles wishes."

"Ah, you belong to Miles," he said, as if he hadn't known. His mouth broadened momentarily into a smile, then quickly returned to the blank expression he'd worn before.

Turning on a spotlight lamp behind him, Vincent shined the light on Tessa's breasts. He examined her nipples with a physician's gentle care, then pulled down further on her top. With her hands still tied and in her lap, he couldn't remove the shirt without cutting it. So finding scissors in a small credenza behind him, he clipped the shoulders straps and pushed the material down and out of his way.

"These too, Maya says," the black man remarked, referring to her nipples.

"Miles didn't ask for that," Tessa informed him. She wasn't sure why it was important that he knew. If it had been Miles' wish, it wouldn't have mattered to her, having another set of holes pierced through her hardening nipples. As it was, she thought Vincent should know that it was Maya's idea, these extra ones.

Vincent ignored her comment. "Let's see you below," he said almost gently. "Lean back." Tessa allowed the man to ease her back so that she was lying on the bench. She couldn't help but think that his easy professional manner suggested that Vincent must really be a doctor, a man who performed such simple rituals with patients every day.

To make it easier for her, he untied her feet, though he quickly pulled stirrups from the corners of the table and secured her legs so that they were spread wide.

The table raised and lowered with the touch of a button, and she was rapidly raised to just the height he wanted.

He shined the light on her spread-out cunt and examined it.

"He's whipped you, I'd guess last night, these are fresh."

"Yes."

"Miles?"

"No."

"Who?"

"A woman."

"Humph! It's a fallacy that women crack a meaner whip than men, though this one must have given you quite a wealth of pain—these are deep."

"She did."

His fingers played with her, with the folds and her clit and the inner labia that were to be pierced. He did it under the guise of examination, but there was more to it than that. He watched carefully as she jolted each time he touched a spot that ached with either pain or pleasure. Tessa realized that her wild rushes of the morning had not yet subsided; in fact, she was close to exploding once again, even with this cold stranger.

"You're aroused?" he asked.

She didn't respond.

"Answer me!" he raised his voice.

"Yes."

When Vincent stood up, Tessa could see that she was level to his waist. She was certain that he was about to fuck her, and her intuition wasn't wrong. He fingered her hole and labia more, as he was letting down his own zipper. Then he pulled his cock from his pants and thrust it deep between her legs into her waiting hole. He spread her wide; he must have been gigantic. She grunted, trying to contain the pain of his hitting her rock bottom.

He screwed her with a passionate grace, as if it were in time to some music he was hearing in his ear. He pulled her ass up from the bench, lifting it into his groin, where he pounded her again and again and again.

"Ahhhhhhhhhh! Gawwwwwd," she gasped. Her voice pierced the air. In the tiny room, it seemed too loud. Yet it was not as loud as the fierce groan that rippled behind her's: the one that came from Vincent as he smashed himself into her.

Tessa thought he was about to come. She was about to come herself. But he pulled out of her, and came to her head, pushing his dripping cock in her face. He was at the perfect height to push it down her throat. Picking up where he left off, he pumped himself into her mouth with rigorous strokes, then pulled out just enough to let the come spew across her face, down her cheeks, in her mouth, and down her chin.

He tapped the side of her face with his cock, letting the last of his come dribble about her neck. Then finding a towel on the credenza, he cleaned himself and restored his cock inside his pants.

"You didn't come," he suggested, when he finally turned back to her.

"No," she whispered. She wanted it, but she held her breath, afraid he wouldn't let her release.

To her relief, he played with her briefly. She was easily over the edge with soft rippling surges making her tremble gratefully.

Except that her face was still covered with his come, the scene was restored to the task at hand, Vincent again becoming the detached professional he'd earlier been.

"Miles wants one here," he said, tugging gently at the hood of her clit. As if he knew what he was doing, he played with the one place in all her sex that was the most sensitive of all. She shrank back, just having his fingers on it again.

"I'll have to tie you down, Tessa," he said. "I can't have you jumping like a fish out of water."

He used leather straps across her waist and abdomen to hold her torso in place, then lowered her legs in the stirrups, enough so he could tie them to the edge of the bench. For good measure, he pulled her arms above her again, though this time they didn't dangle in the air; they were merely tied over her head, so that her hands wouldn't get in the way.

He swabbed her cunt with something cold. It smelled medicinal, like alcohol.

"You've been through this before," he said matter-of-factly. "Keep it clean, especially here, where you're likely to be wet all the time."

Perhaps not seeing him at his work was better for her, because the quick pokes of the needle didn't hurt as much as she expected them to. There was only a sharp sting and it was over. What she felt more than anything was a heaviness at the top of her clit. The ring. It was lush feeling.

That done, Vincent proceeded to the labia, so they too were pierced. As he did each side, Tessa could feel him pulling on the strange flaps of flesh. A similar sensation of heaviness accompanied the finish. She wanted to touch herself between her legs. She wanted to feel the jewelry for herself. Most of all she wanted to gaze in the mirror at the result. They were like small bonds, each one tying her all the more to Miles.

"That's done," Vincent announced, "now the nipples."

Vincent rose from the stool, towering over her

again. At her side, he showed her two small rings in his hand. "These will go above the studs. You know you really have perfect nipples for this kind of jewelry, I can think of all kinds of decorations you could wear. Perhaps we'll improvise, something out of the ordinary," he suggested.

Tessa had no idea what he meant, though she acknowledged his comment with a wide-eyed look of apprehension. Her main concern was right now, not the future. The other piercings hadn't hurt. Why would these? Perhaps it was the memory of Maya and the horrid fear that passed through her that first time in the salon. Perhaps the more she was afraid, the more it hurt. It seemed that way when she was punished. When she wasn't so afraid, it was never the same agony as when she was terrified and cringing.

Still, she couldn't help herself. She was cringing. Perhaps she shouldn't look.

"I hear you faltered last time," Vincent said. Maya must have told him. "Don't be that foolish with me," he warned. "I'm not as naturally kind as Maya." Tessa didn't believe that. Already he had displayed more kindness in his cold manner than she'd experienced from Maya. But he obviously had a reason for his warning.

Swabbing her nipples with the cold disinfectant, he then took needle and rings in hand and had her pierced once again, in a matter of seconds.

Her nipples burned as he performed the task, but by that time, Tessa had transported herself to an altered state, her mind tripped out almost as if she was stoned. She was swimming in sexual lust, wishing Vincent would plant his cock in either her mouth or cunt again, just to allow her to let go some of the mounting pressure that was making her drunk.

He didn't accommodate her this time.

Instead, the man finished with her in the same style that he'd begun. Except for the wild rude fuck, he'd been perfectly decorous in his attitude, the exemplary professional. Tessa would have to ask Miles about him. She couldn't imagine that he wasn't schooled in this precise bedside manner.

He released her from all her bonds, removing the straps and untying her hands.

"You'll want to rub your wrists when they are bound like that, get the circulation going. I'll have to talk to Maya, she tied them too tightly." He stood over her, making eye contact one last time, then lowered the bench to the height it first was. He left the room.

When Miles came to pick her up, Maya gave her a long scarf to tie around her bodice, to replace the torn blouse. To Tessa's surprise, Miles didn't bother to examine her new jewelry. Apparently he was too busy to rush through what she hoped had would be a thorough examination.

As he promised earlier, he took her home.

CHAPTER THIRTEEN

MILES CALLED TESSA several days later. She was to accompany him to a luncheon.

"Wear the scarf that Maya gave you," he told her.

"Tied as it was?"

"I like the way it looks on you, and wear the black leather skirt. By the way, how's the jewelry?" he asked.

In the days since Vincent pierced her, the tenderness in her cunt had diminished, but not the crude sensations of pleasure that accompanied every move she made.

"Trite though it may sound, I can't get you out of my mind," Tessa replied. "The little chains you attached to the labia rings tickle my thighs almost constantly, and the ring on the hood of my clitoris hangs there heavily."

"Goading you?" Miles asked.

"That's a good way to put it."

She could almost hear a chuckle issue from him. "Then my purpose is fulfilled. You can test yourself in public tomorrow. That's something we can both look forward to."

"What kind of gathering did you say this was?"

"Something casual, a new exhibit opening. Lots of notable people who like to be seen with artists, no matter how obscene we are."

"I heard one patron at the museum describe one of your nudes as filth," Tessa said.

"Really? That's good," Miles replied. "I wouldn't want to slander my reputation with anything wholesome."

"Then I suppose that me, in gold, leather, and silk, will certainly maintain your notoriety," Tessa said.

"I'm glad you think the way I do," Miles replied. "You'll have quite a time this afternoon."

By the time they arrived at the luncheon, there were already at least a hundred people in the room, milling about. They were having cocktails before the sit-down luncheon. Tessa's expectations of the event were quickly shattered as she looked about the crowd of people chattering gaily.

"I think I'm under-dressed," she whispered in Miles' ear, as she peered at dozens of women in pastel business suits with long skirts and baggy slacks and high-collared blouses, dripping gold, their noses high in the air, ready to look down in well-practiced amazement at any slut like her.

"You look ravishing," Miles whispered back. "That

scarf's worth a few hundred dollars, you're hardly dressing down to anyone. Besides, if you looked like one of the bitches here, I wouldn't have you." He eyed the prudish matrons around him with contempt.

"Why are we here?" Tessa continued to whisper.

"Politics, good politics."

"Politics?" That was a word she hadn't expected to hear from his lips.

"Sometimes I have to make an appearance, especially if it's my own opening."

"Your own opening? You didn't tell me that," Tessa said.

"It's not all that important, but I do have to be here. There's a positioning in the art world—you have to be in the right place at the right time."

"I didn't think that things like that would influence you," Tessa said innocently. It seemed odd to her that Miles would let anyone dictate what he should or shouldn't do.

"I may not like this kind of event, but I do want to sell my work. If nothing else, it's a necessity from a financial perspective." The two were strolling about, Miles nodding to acquaintances, while he whispered to Tessa. "Besides, we'll have some fun with this." He had a devilish look in his eye.

Tessa hated this kind of ostentatious show. Fully resolved that she wouldn't put herself in this kind of milieu for any reason, after many such occasions for the museum, she was displeased to find herself in the middle of another congregation of arrogance. The only thing that didn't displease her were the infrequent glances at her bosom. People, mostly men, noticed the bumps about her breasts where the jewelry pierced her. The silk did little to hide the obvious. The women were especially interesting, the way they gave her sidelong glances, and whispered to each other like Siamese cats.

It didn't take long before Tessa felt like nothing more than a trinket for Miles to show off. She was as much a part of the exhibit as his paintings on the wall. To her surprise, there was even one painting of her, one she wasn't aware that Miles had done. It shocked her to see the image of her rounded buttocks, asshole included, shimmering in oils. The blonde mop of hair was a dead giveaway, though there was likely not enough of her own physique to make the identity of the model obvious to anyone but Tessa and Miles. Still, she moved away from it quickly, not sure how she'd handle curious comparisons.

Miles came and left her side several times, while the two drank iced tea laced with some liquor. It was delicious and made her head just fuzzy enough to appreciate the finer points of sticking out so blatantly in the crowd. Usually, she did her exhibiting among friends with sentiments and tastes in clothes similar to her own. With just a little help from the potion in her hand, this exhibition was becoming most intriguing.

It was clearly fascinating to Miles too.

When he went off to chat with some notable person, he'd gaze back at her, and draw the patron's attention to her. She was greeted with appreciative smiles and waves several times. She wondered to herself why he didn't just put her on a pedestal for all to see, a living model. Take the clothes from her body and let everyone see what was underneath her clothes, what lovely gold dripped from her pierced places.

"Tessa, I want you to meet Damien," Miles said, escorting a gentleman and lady to her side. "This is Adelle, his wife."

She shook their hands graciously. Was this *the* Damien, of Damien's Ball? she wondered to herself.

"This is the girl you told me about?" Damien was a graying man, likely in his early sixties, though his robust manner suggested that he would be a virile Cary Grant type for many years yet. A fine charm glimmered in his eyes, along with a kindness that Tessa hadn't seen before that day.

"Yes, she's the one," Miles said.

"Dear, this is the girl in the movie," Damien told his wife. The woman was a carbon copy of all the other woman at the luncheon. Her nose was so pinched, it looked as if she'd just removed a clothes-pin from it. Her nostrils flared slightly when she spoke. She reminded Tessa of some cartoon character, but she couldn't quite figure out which one.

"Really?" the woman said, her eyebrows raised in glee, as if she couldn't wait to get on her gossipy way, telling the rest of the manicured crones, who Miles' slut really was. "Such an interesting work of art that movie," she said. "Not my taste—Damien has such depraved inclinations—though I figure that's his prerogative at his age."

What a strange thing to say, Tessa thought.

The woman smiled obliquely. "You're quite charming my dear," the woman continued. "But I do have to run now."

"I'd like to see *her* butt whipped," Tessa said under her breath.

"Please don't mind her, my dear, she appreciates

your art, she just doesn't quite understand it," Damien said.

"Maybe she's afraid of it," Tessa said. "Seeing all these ridiculously groomed bitches here, I wonder why any of them are feasting on Miles' porn, if it weren't for their own secret fascination with it."

"You have a point, but even try to get one of these woman naked, and you'll have a fight on your hands," Damien informed her.

Tessa shook her head. "Then why bother with them—if they're frigid in bed, what good are they?"

Damien didn't reply, though he noted Tessa's spunk with a slight smile.

"Really Tessa, you might want to suck up to Damien just a little—he has paid me well for the videos," Miles told her.

"I didn't know you already sold them."

"Actually, they were commissioned."

"Commissioned?" This was new to Tessa.

"Damien has an ever increasing interest in SM."

"Unusual and very original SM," the man qualified. "I'm not looking for mindless flagellation and heartless dominance. Miles manages to provide something more."

"I'm glad you like what we did," Tessa replied. She was suspicious of the man. To add to her misgivings, there was something guarded in both men's manner, something they were not telling her. "I didn't realize that Miles had done other films like mine."

"I haven't, Tessa," Miles answered.

"No, not to the depths you two traversed in the last one, the one with the dark-haired vamp," Damien agreed.

"That was hardly a week ago," Tessa said.

"Humph! Then your stripes have probably not faded," Damien surmised.

"Most have, but not all," Tessa said.

"I'd like to have her now." Damien turned to Miles, his softness vanishing with the turn of his head, replaced by the a familiar darkness that she'd seen often in Miles.

"By all means," Miles told him. Miles turned to her, the air of command pervading his voice. "Damien needs to handle some things with you in private, please accommodate him."

This twist in the plot was ominous, Tessa could tell by the way she shivered at the sound of Miles words and the way her nether jewelry suddenly felt heavier than it felt before.

With a sly smile on his face, Damien led Tessa away through the halls of the aging Victorian mansion, turned art gallery. They stopped inside a round drawing room, where the older man looked very much the master. "You don't mind, do you Tessa?" Damien said. "You'll likely miss the poached salmon and crepe suzettes."

"I don't mind missing lunch," Tessa replied warily, still unsure of what he had in mind.

"Good, that's very good." His charm returned with a smile, but the smile was not as breezy as it had been when Miles introduced them. There was something devious in the works. Tessa wondered if she was looking into the eyes of the devil, the way the man's expression changed in a twinkling, back and forth from sly to sweet, from sweet to chilling. It was hard to get any kind of reading of his intentions.

"Take off your scarf," he ordered her.

Not used to taking orders from someone other than Miles, she hesitated. She shouldn't have been surprised by the request, but still the whole thing was incongruous with her expectations for the day.

"Your hesitation is unacceptable," Damien snapped. He glared at her and tugged at her scarf.

Tessa finished the job, pushing it to her waist. Released from the binding, her breasts jiggled, her flesh almost glad for a breath of fresh air. The double-pierced nipples glowed in the dim lights of the room.

From out of nowhere, the man drew what looked like a conductor's baton. With it, he prodded at her tits, and raising them from underneath, he viewed them with a judgmental eye, as if he were inspecting something he intended to purchase.

"He told me they were even more exquisite with the second piercing," Damien commented. The man eyed them with an incredible coldness, so like Miles, just in an older form. "You know, the movies hardly do you justice, though Miles has captured you quite well in some of the sketches."

Tessa didn't see any need for conversation. She let his comments remain unanswered, though his careful inspection of her was arousing. "Raise your skirt," he ordered next.

As they stood in the midst of the elegant room, they were like two divergent views of life. Tessa was the one out of place. She began to feel like the used woman, like the whore that Hector spoke of, the common whore, in this house for only one purpose—she wouldn't have dared deny this man whatever pleasure he wanted, she was fulfilling Miles' wishes.

But it was a nasty business being such a slut, allowing the whole world to see her exactly as she was. Though as Miles' trinket to give away, his pleasure became hers; doing his bidding was like a soothing ride down the territory of her own desires. She couldn't imagine being anything but what she was.

Unfortunately, events like the luncheon today jolted her consciousness back to the weird reality that the rest of the world wasn't like her at all. Indeed this *normal* world judged her harshly. It was a fact she'd have to get used to.

Tessa raised her skirt, almost as a statement of defiance to the gathering down the hall. Wouldn't it have been lovely to have flaunted her naked bottom before them? Miles wouldn't have minded, in fact she wouldn't put it past him to parade her this way in front of a crowd of tittering onlookers, who could only watch but never really enjoy the fine aspects of their sexual joining.

"Open your thighs," Damien commanded.

As the man stared at her groin, Tessa complied. He wanted to see her pussy with its glittering jewelry. His gaze was pure admiration, a wave of utter satisfaction crossed his face as he saw her cunt appearing with its treasures dangling before his eyes.

He reached down and pulled at the ring over her clitoris. "It hurts, doesn't it?"

"Yes," she admitted.

"I like to see what depths of pain women can take. I should like to whip your body until you scream. The agony would make me mad with joy." The man was mad, crazy mad, Tessa thought. His face made another of its unexpected shifts, almost glaring with a phosphorescent glow. Then the chilling visage turned to loathing, a scowl walking across his brow, chin, and cheeks. The man seemed to change masks in seconds. He did it so easily. Tessa had never seen anything like this last expression on any man's face. For all the mesmerizing, demonic, lusty, wicked faces that had been cast at her, never had this one appeared.

She was about to panic, when the baton came down wickedly against her naked tits. She was too scared to cry out, though she might have wailed on another occasion, the blow was so fierce. Yet the punishing cut calmed her, forced her away from her fears. She was staring at the slice against her white breast where a thin red line was rising. Damien brought the baton down another three times across her tits. Each time the same result occurred: Her breasts instantly reflected the unleashed passion with a red line etched in her skin.

"Some things, my dear Tessa, I like to see for myself firsthand," he explained as he finished.

Tessa remained silent. She liked this less than she had liked the scene with Martine. But again she was foiled by her own physical response. Like some brazen whore, she was juicing between her legs.

"Miles said your passions for perversion were limitless," he said, pressing his hand to her cunt. His expression had changed again, to admiration. Tessa wondered now if there had been any reason to be frightened of him at all. She could handle hard cocks and lust with little effort.

Bending her over the back of a chair, Damien spread wide her legs and pushed his cock deep into her cunt. She squeezed down on him instinctively, and he groaned delightedly. And while snapping the baton against her naked bottom, he pummeled her cunt with deep quick thrusts.

She moaned in reply, though not so loudly that their fucking could be heard outside the room. Then, right in the middle of their screw, the door opened noisily and two women from the luncheon walked inside the room.

"It's Miles' slut and Damien," a coiffured woman announced to her escort. The two stood stock-still in the doorway ogling the scene before them with ecstatic expressions.

"Do you see that! She's pierced!"

The two didn't bother to leave, they didn't even bother to close the door. Instead, they watched the fucking as if it were a performance.

"I wish he'd take her in the ass," one woman said.

Tessa was glad that Damien didn't pay any attention to her. Nonetheless, her round rump was soon being pummeled, not only for the eyes of the two party crashers, but for a dribble of other guests that happened down the corridor, unsuspecting.

Damien, lost in the pleasure of his mounting climax, didn't seem to care that anyone watched. He didn't even take notice of the audience, he just kept on fucking, too hot and wet to worry about embarrassment.

As he orgasmed with a truncated bellow issuing from his mouth, the door slowly closed. For some curious reason, the audience retreated. Perhaps the voyeurs were too embarrassed by the intimacy of the final act and the awkwardness that would no doubt follow.

When Damien pulled out, he was stone-cold dominant. His sperm dripped out on Tessa's behind and down her leg.

"Don't wipe it up," he told her. "Let it dry. Let Miles see it. He'll appreciate the gift."

Tessa was glad to see that Damien's face didn't change, now that the fuck was over. Maybe it was the lust that had made him appear so crazy, for he wasn't crazy now. She could count on the ruthless passions he displayed, she was used to them.

"Don't rise," he ordered. He brought the baton down on her asscheeks, first the right, then the left, then in the center along the crease of her ass. She wanted to scream, just as she wanted to scream when he laid the baton across her breasts, but she remained as silent as a mouse to keep her agony from being discovered. It occurred to her, in one brief respite from the blows, that anyone from the luncheon could open the door and find her being whipped. Especially if the ones that had watched her earlier shared their discovery with the other guests. Yet as Damien commenced with his nasty cuts, they remained alone.

"Stand up!" he ordered, as he finished off with the baton.

She was shaky at first. So much had happened so quickly she could hardly get her bearings. An empty stomach, a strange concoction of liquor, an audience, a punishment, a rabid fucking, and more punishment. She almost collapsed, her knees weak.

"Stand up, Tessa, and behave yourself." Tessa was surprised to hear Miles' voice behind her. She stumbled and turned around, catching herself on the chair.

There were three women behind him in the doorway, watching too.

"This is the woman in the paintings," he told them. There she stood with the silk scarf and leather skirt both bunched around her waist, realizing that all her fine attributes were there to behold. The women stared at her in wonder. Their complementary pastel knit suits—looking so like they'd come from the same designer salon of Saks—made Tessa feel smutty and torn in comparison.

"Has she given you any trouble?" Miles asked.

"She's testing well," Damien said.

"Use the baton on her pussy—that faltering shouldn't go unpunished," he said coldly.

"Can we watch?" one of the women asked.

"I'm afraid not," Miles told them, turning around to usher them out. "Perhaps another time."

Tessa was relieved, though not for long. When the door was closed again, Damien pulled out a stool and made her lie back with her legs open.

"The cuts the bitch gave you hardly show," he observed, looking down at her exposed pussy.

He slashed her hard against her pierced labia.

"Auuuuggggg," she whimpered quietly into the air.

The baton sizzled again and hit her on the other side, just catching the side of her clit, where the ring appeared to protect her this time.

Another cut was laid directly in crease of her groin, the flesh so tender, she couldn't help the biting cry that rose from her mouth.

"Oh gaaaawwwwwwd, nooooooo!" she exclaimed aloud. He protest was, at the very worst, a dainty cry that tittered in the air; it wouldn't be heard much farther than the next room, if at all.

Another cut found its target, the tip of her clit.

This time she shrieked more vociferously. Her hips bucked angrily against the stool, wriggling to get away. She wanted nothing more than to bolt from the room and Damien's nasty baton, but she knew that would bring Miles' wrath on her in ways far worse than this thrashing. "I'm doing this for Miles. I'm doing this for my love," she told herself a dozen times. There was no reason she would do it for herself; the pain and humiliation were far too cruel to ignite her lust.

The final cut from the baton landed viciously across her tits. Surprising her, she tumbled off the stool, landing clumsily on the floor. She felt like a fool, forgetting all her submissive training. She looked up at Damien wondering what reaction would ensue. But he didn't seem bothered by her deportment. Perhaps he knew how much he hurt her, and that was excuse enough.

Damien stared at Tessa with cold eyes.

"I'm sure Miles will want you in the dining room," he finally said. "I'd suggest you not tarry with your primping. There's a private bath through that door." He pointed to a door at the side of the room, then nodded to her as he collapsed the baton and replaced it in his suit pocket. Without so much as a another glance, he left the room.

Before Tessa had a chance to rise, Miles entered, this time alone. He looked at her trembling miserably on the floor.

"My, look at this. He's replaced Martine's faded cuts," he said.

"It hurts like hell," she said, her annoyance surfacing.

"You do look a bit worse for wear, Tessa," Miles

remarked. It was actually a friendly comment, though Tessa wasn't in a friendly mood.

"And I should be," she blurted out nastily.

"Rattled?" he asked.

"This is the most absurd thing I've ever seen," she charged at him. "These people are like ghouls, watching as if I were some sort of bauble being brutalized for art's sake and their perverted pleasures. Is this what I am?" she asked angrily.

"Is it? You tell me. What are you today that you weren't yesterday?"

"I didn't like it at all, Miles," Tessa said, ignoring his implication. "Your friend is creepy."

"Creepy!" he laughed.

"Odd, strange, bizarre," she fought for another adjective.

"Bizarre? Yes. But he's harmless."

"Not with those eyes, or with that baton."

"There are women who would have given anything for the pleasure you had from Damien today."

"And what makes him so special?"

"Only what you believe makes him special. If temporal power is important to you, he owns a great deal of that."

"I don't give a shit about *who* he is," Tessa said. Her anger was only beginning to diminish. "Besides it wasn't just him, it was those fiendish women. I'd rather have Martine dominating me any day than those bitches hovering around me like some little pet."

"I wasn't asking you to like it, Tessa."

"Then what purpose?" she asked.

He looked at her with a comical grin. "To shock them."

"That you certainly did," she agreed.

"Ah. Not as much as I would have liked." He almost sounded disappointed. "Some were expecting to see more of your antics."

"Antics! My punishment, my defilement is a simple antic for your company's pleasure? Is that all I am, entertainment, a trinket for whatever you desire?"

"Sometimes that's all you are, and you know it," Miles spoke truthfully. "Because," he explained, "that's all you want to be." He looked at her with a wise expression. His knowledge of her was so complete that she couldn't dismiss anything he had to say. "So now, Tessa, you tell me. Why are you so angry?"

She pouted for a moment. "I don't know, I'll have to think about it."

He came to her. She still in complete disarray, with her skirt and silk still askew about her middle. He gently placed his hand on her cunt and felt the softness there, and the jewelry, and the wetness she couldn't deny. "Frankly Tessa, I think you're lying to me."

"Lying, never," she asserted.

"Then you'll have to tell your body to quit giving you away."

"My body reacts, it's all physical," she contended. "If my mind's not there, how can I have any pleasure?"

"Be a little more honest with yourself, sweetheart," he said, "If you plan to stay with me, there will be more days like today, and I'll expect a better showing from you."

"What I went through was not enough?"

"Just a taste, just a taste."

He took the knotted scarf from around her waist and pulled it away. Then he pushed the leather skirt back over her hips, so that it was straight around her body. He shook out the scarf, and began to wrap it around her again with a flourish to match the way Maya had fashioned it.

"There, you almost look presentable—go fix your hair, but not too tidy. I like it mussed."

He was being so affectionate and incredibly sweet, a side of him that made her feel magical inside. She let his gentle eyes caress her for a minute, then retreated to the bath to fix her hair and make-up.

She wondered as she stared at herself in the mirror why this place, and Damien, and the women—those ghastly women—had so upset her.

One thing she knew for certain, she was horny. She felt as if there were a thousand hungry dragons crashing through her on a rampage. She wished that Miles had just flung her down and screwed her silly, but she hadn't words to ask the favor; and likely, he wouldn't have granted her the pleasure.

When she returned to him, she still had no answer to his question about her anger. As it was, Miles was too preoccupied with returning to his gathering to talk to her about it. He did offer one word of advice, as they were leaving the room. "It's a grand joke, Tessa, that's all it is. Treat it like one, and you'll have a much better time."

"That's how you see this afternoon, a joke?"

"Yes," he answered. "Frankly, I hadn't planned that you and Damien would be interrupted. It began as just a friendly sharing between friends, an initiation that you needed to endure, for reasons that will become clear in time. But the others, they were interesting accidents, comical ones at that." Seeing the twinkling expression in his eye, she could tell he was sincere.

A joke?

Comical?

Was that so ridiculous? Perhaps all the anger was for nothing. Had she passed a test or failed one? She supposed that only time would tell.

Resuming her place on Miles' arm, the two waltzed back to the dining room, where lunch was just being finished. Since she had had nothing to eat, Miles stopped at a tray of unserved plates of food; with some curious onlookers stealing glances at them, he fed her with his fingers. She giggled and laughed at the mess he made, like a bride being fed wedding cake on her wedding day, even as the poached salmon made a mess on her lips and chin.

Her earlier upset seemed incredibly silly now and she felt foolish for being so angered.

After wiping her face on a napkin, the two strolled to where Damien and his prissy wife Adelle were shaking hands with other art patrons.

"I hope you enjoyed yourself, Damien," Tessa said boldly.

Damien nodded at her coolly. Ah! That impeccable cool! Men like him would never be rattled, or taken off guard. But that wasn't the point. She had the satisfaction of satisfying the man in a way that his little woman never could.

Lust like hers made her an uncommon piece of art.

CHAPTER FOURTEEN

"WHERE DID HE take you?" Martine asked. She was leaning against a display case that Tessa was arranging with artifacts from the Mesopotamian era. Martine's slit skirt was rising high on her hips.

"A luncheon," Tessa replied.

"Ah." Martine nodded.

"Haven't you seen him lately?" Tessa asked.

"Not for a week," Martine said.

"Ooooo, you think he's lost interest?" Tessa was not above sparring with Martine, especially when it came to Miles.

"No," she answered indignantly.

"Well, he's left me for a week at a time, I suppose it's within his standard operating procedure," Tessa admitted, as she tried hiding her pleasure at Martine's abandonment, if that's what it was.

"So how was the luncheon?" Martine asked.

Tessa spent some moments considering a reply. Exactly how much did she want to reveal about her afternoon with Miles? Her relationship with Martine had always had its prickly side—they never seemed to want to get along, and yet, they did have some of the best sex ever. Perhaps it was time for a truce.

"Enlightening," Tessa finally admitted.

"How so?" her roommate asked. Tessa had been carefully fixing her artifacts, with a precision that annoyed Martine. It was like everything else with Tessa. Perfect, it had to be perfect.

"Oh, a roomful of his stuffy art patrons, and then there was me, dressed in a leather skirt and silk scarf like some art patron from the fiery dungeons. At least that's the way I must have looked to them." She said it with an amused smile on her face. "Unfortunately, I didn't appreciate the humor of it, right off. Miles had to point it out to me, after I'd faltered a bit giving his Mr. Big Bucks the show he wanted."

"Mr. Big Bucks?"

"The guy who buys the videos."

"Oh, that's interesting, what's he like?"

"Old. Distinguished. And definitely weird."

"Weird? How?"

"I don't know," she thought back. "I guess it was his eyes, they were really queer, in the old sense of the word."

"Sounds like something right up your alley."

"Not really, not like that. He made me uncomfortable." Martine shifted her stance, raising a foot to rest against a foot-high stool Tessa had used to reach the top of a display case. Her skirt was rising even higher on her leg. It wouldn't have taken much to bend down and see Martine's cunt peeking out from underneath. "Did Miles pierce you again?" Martine asked abruptly.

The question came like lightning, out of a clear cool sky, just as Tessa was almost enjoying a good old-fashioned woman-to-woman sharing with Martine. She hedged a little, trying not to look Martine in the eye.

"C'mon bitch, tell me. He did, didn't he?"

"So what if he did?"

"I want to see," Martine said. Martine was horny, practically rubbing her hips against the display case. All the usual signs were there, including the manner of nasty dominance that normally rose when she wanted Tessa to submit to her.

"So, when we get home," Tessa offered.

"No. Here. Now," Martine countered.

"I'm working now, and you should be too."

"Oh, don't give me lectures about your job responsibilities, you who fly off with Miles at the drop of a hat."

"I work independently, you know that. Right now, I have a five o'clock deadline on this exhibit."

"That's okay, it won't take but a moment to please me, oh precious one."

Tessa eyed her. Here it was again, the choice to fight or surrender to Martine. This time, however, there was a little voice inside her head that began to speak in tandem with all the thoughts that would object to Martine's command. It was a simple reminder of the night they'd spent together, Tessa under Martine's lash. The point of the night was all too apparent before it was over. Miles, in his inimitably crafty way, had led her to the undeniable truth—that she really desired Martine's dominance, nearly as much as she desired his. That thought, at this new moment, rose nastily before her like some obnoxious yet wondrously delicious beast.

"Lift up your skirt," Martine commanded, impatiently. She didn't share Tessa's interminable quandaries.

"Right here?" Tessa asked.

"Yes, there's no one around," Martine replied.

"But someone could come around the corner in seconds."

"Then you'll be embarrassed at worst, at best titillated. Raise that skirt. It's only four fuckin' inches."

Tessa would never have hesitated this way in front of Miles. God, he would have punished her ass if she'd resisted him this way. Still, Martine was not Miles. Tessa glanced around one more time, then pulled at her skirt so that it rose in the center, right before Martine's watchful eyes. The three rings sparkled in the light.

"My God, they're beautiful," Martine admired them. "Did Vincent do these?"

"How do you know Vincent?" Tessa asked in surprise.

"He did the dragon tattoo on my thigh a few years back. Miles and I thought it was an interesting coincidence."

"Did he screw you too?" Tessa asked.

"Did he screw you?" Martine asked, as if she was offended by the question.

Tessa pushed her skirt back down over her pussy and shrugged. "So we don't tell each other everything," Tessa replied.

Martine chuckled. "He did, didn't he?" she said, reading Tessa's mind anyway. She didn't need an answer. “He was always one of my favorite fucks,” Martine offered.

“More than once?” Tessa inquired curiously.

“Gawd yes. We had quite an affair, but he kept trying to poke my body with a bunch of holes like yours.”

“I’m surprised you haven’t pierced yourself,” Tessa remarked.

“It doesn’t suit my style—I think of it as something that submissives do.”

“And Vincent wanted you to be submissive?”

“Oh, he never really tried. What really broke us apart was his bitch. I couldn’t stand her.”

“Maya?”

“I quit seeing him when she rolled around, we didn’t get along.” Martine punctuated her comments with a snarl.

“I think they’re married,” Tessa said.

“That’s too bad, the streets could use a good one like Vincent. He’s so civil while he’s pummeling you, so decent.”

“That’s an interesting judgment. Surprising, coming from you. I didn’t think being decent was important to you,” Tessa said, “You’ve never been very particular about the men you fuck.”

“Oh, and you are?”

“You’re probably right about that,” Tessa conceded. “Except for now. I think Miles is changing me.”

There they were again, Tessa thought, at one of those almost tender moments when they were connecting as friends.

“That’s what I mean, Tessa. The thing with Vincent, it’s like Miles. He’s decent, really decent— and a scoundrel, a pervert, a real nasty scene-maker, but he respects you and me. Isn't that why we both like him?"

"Yeah. I suppose it is," Tessa mused. Strange the two of them agreeing on something. "You can even see where he's vulnerable," Tessa continued. "There are little chinks in his armor."

"All men are vulnerable," Martine offered as if she knew them all.

She would know, Tessa thought, since she was an expect at finding a man's weakness.

Lest the moment be too sweet and friendly, Martine changed on a dime. "Raise it again slut, I want it now," she ordered.

This time she didn't give Tessa much choice—her hand reached in and pulled the skirt up, finding its way to the rings. She yanked on the clit ring so hard it brought a muffled cry from Tessa.

Tessa tried not to move or make the slightest peep, though she knew that it would only be moments before Martine would have her panting for some release. She might as well give in.

Martine's fingers continued to play, with one finger poking its way inside Tessa's cunt. "This canyon of yours is like a raging river," she observed.

"How poetic of you," Tessa replied. She felt stabs of need rise inside her belly, waves beginning to commence. "You really shouldn't be doing this here."

"Oh, but it's so fun, wondering if you're going to get caught. Wouldn't you love to see the curator's face right now, his beady little eyes staring into your lust. He'd know for sure what a naughty little whore you really are. I'm sure he's wondered, the way you flaunt your private parts around here like they were just another display."

Tessa wanted to remind Martine that she was no different, but she couldn't find the words. She was losing touch with anything but the rising need of her pussy to come.

"That's it cunt," Martine purred at her. She leaned in closer to Tessa, so she could whisper in her ear. Inserting three fingers in the soppy puss, she rammed them in and out. Tessa widened her stance to accommodate the intrusion. She was ready to peak and unable to keep herself from thrusting her groin into Martine's fist. "I'll have it all in here next time, slut, I'll fuck you with my fist."

Tessa reacted to the threat with her hips. They moved in lusty unison to the pounding hand, wishing she would fuck her harder still.

"You want it now, don't you?" Martine murmured.

"Please not here," Tessa whispered.

"There's no one around, let's try," Martine said.

"No, please, not now."

"You want it slut, admit it. You want my whole hand up your little whoring cunt, jamming its way to the center of your belly."

"No, please, no." She denied the desire with little conviction.

"Admit it bitch," Martine seethed, her mouth against Tessa's ear, so the woman could not ignore her order.

"Admit it, or I'll raise a ruckus, and bring out the posse."

"Martine, no."

"Admit it!" she hissed in her ear.

"Yes, I want your fist inside me," Tessa gasped. Their bodies were so close, their hot breath mixed, the slightly stale smell of smoke on Martine's, a hint of mint from a lozenge still lingering on Tessa's. They were close, but not close enough. Martine backed off for a brief moment.

"Raise you leg, so I can get the right angle," she ordered.

With her foot now resting on the stool where Martine's had been, her skirt was hiked so high that even her butt showed from behind—from the direction that she would be discovered, if she was discovered. They had to be quick, but she had to have Martine's fist inside her. Her cunt opened like the petals of a flower opening wide, the dew of her female center dripping down her legs. The woman had Tessa too far gone for her stop, not even if someone happened around the corner.

Martine kneeled down on the floor between Tessa's legs, so that she could get the proper angle with her hand. Three fingers in her cunt became four, and then Martine's slim wet hand slipped inside all the way, filling her full. Fuller than Miles had filled her, fuller than Vincent had, fuller than any of the dozens of cocks that had widened her well-exercised cunt over time. She bucked on Martine's hand, feeling the fingers come together inside her to make a fist. The brutal reality of her submission hadn't escaped her, but it wasn't time to consider that thought. She was moving rapidly now, each thrust of that rude fist drawing her closer to a climax. Closer yet, she collapsed forward against Martine's smaller but firmly set body. The two worked in unison, bringing Tessa to a fine edge, then to a vibrant orgasm.

"Aaaaaaaahhhhhhh, yessssss," she murmured softly. She squeezed the offending fist with muscles that tightened around it, just as they might tighten around a cock.

"Yes baby, that's right, you love it, Tessa, yes you do," Martine encouraged her.

"Aaaaaaahh, that's perfect," Tessa exclaimed softly, and she went as limp as she could go without collapsing altogether.

As Martine withdrew her hand, she brought it to Tessa's lips. "Lick it darling, think of it as my nectar." Tessa's lips lapped the wet fist. Her only thought was how empty her cunt felt, how large and open and empty.

"See, there was no one to interrupt you," Martine reminded Tessa. They exchanged places with Tessa too weak to stand, sitting down on the stool.

"Why do you do these things to me?" Tessa wondered aloud.

"Because you love them, and so do I. You'd better plan on getting your ass fucked tonight. I bought a strap-on this morning." Martine picked up her purse, and was rummaging around inside its wide girth. She pulled out a bag, and withdrew a pink dildo attached to straps, and a harness to fit around her waist.

"Put that thing away," Tessa said.

"Oh, now you're going to get proper again?" Martine said.

"We may run out of luck."

"Well look at it for a minute, slut—just think of me ramming it down your tight dark hole, after you've sucked me off a few times. I figure you really owe me at least a dozen good comes. I've been treating you so well lately."

Tessa looked up at her. She had to smile at Martine's serious expression. The woman was totally sincere about her "gifts" to her. "You really have an interesting way of putting things," Tessa said. She was feeling the life return to her limbs.

"You just have to accept it, Tessa, you'll be a lot happier when you do."

"I don't know. Somehow with you, it's never been easy."

"I know, but think about the sex. You love it." Martine was trying to be kind in her own odd way.

Tessa didn't reply.

"So, where's he taking you next?" Martine asked.

"Miles?"

"Of course Miles."

"I don't know."

"To Damien's Ball?"

"He won't tell me," Tessa admitted.

"Really?" Martine looked surprised. "He's taking me."

"Ah." Tessa answered, trying to get ahold of the jealously that was suddenly racing through her again.

CHAPTER FIFTEEN

WHEN TESSA THOUGHT about it for any length of time, she realized that she was pissed, royally pissed that Miles was taking Martine to the ball, and that he still couldn't make up his mind about her.

The event of the season. This was the one whispered, gossiped, and rumored about for weeks before and after the main event. Tessa's sources however, never really knew when the party took place, or where, or who was *really* there and not just making up stories. But that didn't matter—fantasies about such parties were Tessa's specialty, even though she'd never donned leather, or worn chains, or had a studded collar around her neck. She regularly got off on the idea, imaging a perfect night of submissive bliss with Miles and his friends.

Yet as time passed, the graphic scenes in her head

were not enough. She had to experience it for herself. Was she imagining it right? Did she really understand what happened at these affairs? As Miles' submissive, did she look and feel and breathe the part of a submissive with the right sort of depth and attitude? Sometimes she felt terribly defiant for a submissive, though that was something Miles didn't often complain about.

Miles would tell her that soirees aren't important. What was between the two of them was all that mattered. And that really was the truth; all the pleasure she was getting from him should be enough to last forever, just the way it was. How could she ask for more?

But then, there was all that bottled-up curiosity. She could just imagine the sight of a hundred men and women in Latex and leather and everything else, doing all sorts of despicable things to each other!

She hoped there would be feathers, lots of feathers on masks—she loved masks, even though Miles would find them both confining and dishonest. Miles' strict values required ultimate honesty. He wouldn't want to cloak her, even for the perceived mystery...

Damien's Ball was an obsession. Thoughts of it flashed through her head, even as she and Miles drove through downtown traffic on their way to dinner.

They rode in silence, and while Tessa was considering her unmet desires, Miles was still considering Tessa. Not just whether he would take her to the ball, he was considering her from a more substantial point of view. He'd taken a dozen submissives to this annual ball over the years, some on the drop of the hat, little pawing submissive twits whose affections hardly amounted to a decent orgasm when it was all over.

Tessa had been different from the beginning, and nothing that had transpired over the past few months had changed his initial impression of her. She was not a typical submissive. She was prone to talk too much and question things that no decent submissive would consider questioning. But then, she hadn't been schooled in the proper decorum, and that was his job. If she wasn't progressing, it was as much his fault as hers.

The only problem was, he didn't really want to train her the way she *should be* trained.

And as for taking her the party, there was a selfish inclination to hold onto her for himself. He knew she wouldn't change her mind about him and suddenly fly off with some other dom. It was a pure and simple selfish desire to keep her bound to him and him alone. The other side of his dilemma was fear that he couldn't risk bridling her so tightly or when he did release her, she'd bolt away. These were stupid musings and he knew it, but they passed through his brain anyway.

He thought about her too much. It was that changeable nature, half priss, half flagrant slut, that craved attention and abandonment and everything else in-between, all at the same time. She was insatiable. He wondered if he could be enough for her?

She made him laugh.

She made him want to stare at her for hours, paint, draw, sculpt her face in its hundred expressions.

Her hold on him was getting stronger. That was probably why he was fucking Martine every time his loins got hot. It was a protection against Tessa, especially since his submissive was so rattled by her rather predictable roommate.

They waited at an intersection for some time, light changing three times before they inched forward to make it through the left turn, away from the jumbled mass of humanity at this ungodly hour.

Miles was lost in his thoughts of Tessa, when she spoke. Her voice lifted him from a glowering reverie, jerking him out of a silence that was becoming uncomfortable for her.

"You know, Miles, I've always wanted to be the belle of the ball," she said.

He glanced at her suspiciously. "You're asking about the soiree again, aren't you?"

"Yes," Tessa admitted.

"You know what that means, don't you?"

"Leather, whips, my rings. They should do. The marks, the bondage, aren't they enough to prove my readiness? I can't go on forever imagining this wild horrid orgy of self-indulgence and not have it."

"Of course you can," Miles said, "if that's what pleases me."

"Miles," she was exasperated, and showing it. "You've whipped me silly, shown me off, given me to Damien and Martine..."

"Quit whining, Tessa," he cut her off. "It's more than those things." He was exasperated too, mostly exasperated with not having made a decision. He was not an indecisive man.

"I just thought that this was what you were training me for?"

"I'm training you for *me*, no one else."

"But isn't the big scene the *pièce de résistance?*"

"It is, sometimes. But I'm not committed to anything."

"There are those pictures you have hidden in the closet," she ventured warily.

"You've been through my closets?"

"I'm very snoopy."

"I guess you are. I should paddle your butt until it's raw for that," he suggested, though she looked too charming to reprimand.

"Okay," she agreed smiling. "But what about them? The pictures. Those dark black and whites, the costumes, they make me soak my underwear."

"Underwear?" he asked.

"*If* I wore them," she corrected herself.

"Those pictures were from another time."

"A time that's past?" she queried.

"I don't do those anymore, art evolves; you are the evolvement of my art."

She smiled, liking what he said, but she couldn't drop the matter of the ball. "So, you're not taking me," she said.

"I didn't say that." He clammed up. His mouth shut tight, and she couldn't get another word from him about it for days.

CHAPTER SIXTEEN

A WEEK LATER, Miles and Tessa arrived in front of the old brick home just as the sun was setting. Tessa gazed in awe at the spooky sight that greeted her. The strange light made the sky above glow yellow-orange, like some ominous sign of the dark things to come. The night was made even more portentous by Miles' attitude. He was still cold and brooding. As many times as his coldness had made her shudder, she was still unaccustomed to the effect.

The limo pulled into the circular drive in front of the mansion. It was not as expansive a place as Tessa had imagined it might be, yet it was large and imposing, wedged between other antiquated houses in a neighborhood of the wealthy. Quite oddly, the lights inside the house glowed with the same hue as the setting sun.

Entering, the two stood side by side in the foyer, waiting.

"Damien will be with you shortly," the maid told them curtly, then she left them by themselves.

"Is this the soiree?" Tessa whispered to Miles.

"No," he answered. She was surprised.

"Then what?" she asked.

"Quit asking questions," he replied. He held her hand tightly on his arm.

Tessa wished they would sit down—the four-inch heels he insisted on hurt her feet. She was glad she had such tiny feet, they looked very good in spike heels. Miles thought so too. At the moment, though, with her feet aching, she thought it was a little too much to ask that she negotiate her way in heels so high.

When a side door opened, they were greeted by a cloud of cigar smoke billowing from the room beyond. The smell was pungent but sweet.

"Please come in," another maid said, holding the massive oak door open for them.

Miles dropped Tessa's hand and let her walk behind him into Damien's study. It was a pleasantly gracious room for the kind of man that liked to drink and smoke and read, and do whatever old men do long into the night. With a half-dozen overstuffed chairs and a worn leather couch appropriately arranged, it could easily accommodate quite a gathering of men. Gazing about the room, Tessa noticed five men, including Damien, but not one woman other than herself.

Tessa was bewildered by the group, their purpose not obvious to her. Her presence on Miles' arm caused little more than a ripple through the other guests. Damien himself was sitting behind his desk at one end of the room, smoking a cigar. Tessa thought he looked different than he had weeks before when she met him. That didn't surprise her, considering the rapid transformations he'd made during their inglorious session together. On this occasion, he was cruder than he appeared before. Perhaps his earlier refinement was for the women at the luncheon; now among men, he took on a typically masculine attitude, with little polish or gleam. He was more appealing to Tessa this way.

"You wanted to see her," Miles addressed Damien. He looked up from some papers, as Miles walked Tessa through the middle of a heated conversation.

"Good evening, Miles," one gentleman said, interrupting his harangue long enough to greet his friend.

"G'd evening Miles."

"G'd evening."

The one salutation triggered another, which triggered another, but the idle small talk was brief. Once Tessa and Miles were standing in front of Damien's desk, the other men returned to their chatter about stock prices.

There was something odd in Miles' manner, but Tessa had little time to consider it, since she was quickly the focus of both men's attention.

"I was unimpressed with your little trinket," Damien began, "and surprised you were still keeping her around. When you mentioned the ball, I thought we should talk."

"You weren't unimpressed with the movies," Miles reminded him. "But, frankly Damien, I don't really care about your considerations. Take it or leave it—she doesn't have to be at the party."

Tessa was surprised to hear Miles talk so sharply to his "major patron."

"I'm sure something can be worked out," Damien assured him a little more kindly.

Damien leaned back in his chair and stared her. Despite his more consistent attitude this time, he was still unsettling. His eyes bore into her with a ghastly intensity that made her want to turn and run from the room. Anticipating her trepidation, Miles grabbed her arm and held her fast, just for good measure.

"Actually, Miles, I wanted to see how I'd use her," he said. "Unfortunately, I didn't get a good look at her at the luncheon. Not good enough anyway. She is the kind that requires a good bit of thought. Is she trained on a leash?" he asked.

"No, and I don't plan to, at least not before the soiree."

"Really?" Damien replied in wonder. "You'll have to tell me your reasoning on that."

"Anytime," Miles said, "anytime but now."

Damien nodded at him, respecting his wishes. "So if I collar her, what will that mean?" Damien asked. "Will I have a petulant little bitch on my hands all night, or will I be able to use her as I wish?"

"I can't say, Damien, but Tessa learns quickly. I imagine she'll handle the collar well, after all she's wanted one around her neck for some time."

"And you've denied her, how interesting," Damien observed.

"I don't tell you how to train your servants or your sluts, please don't tell me how to train mine."

The tension between the two men frightened Tessa. This sparring had a darker side she didn't like. There was much they weren't saying. Though she knew her position was to surrender unconditionally, she still had a healthy dose of curiosity that wanted to jump right in with a dozen questions for them both.

She kept her mouth shut.

"Miss Cotille, or shall I call you Trinket? I rather like that name for you."

Tessa didn't reply, just nodded to him as he addressed her.

"Remove your clothes, all but your stockings and your shoes."

Tessa was taken off guard by his demand.

"Tessa," Miles said sharply when she didn't reply.

Jerked awake by the command, Tessa reached behind her to the zipper on her skirt. It came down quickly, the slip of material dropping easily to the floor. She briskly unbuttoned the sheer black fabric of her blouse and tossed it to her side on a chair.

It was just that simple. She was sure Miles was pleased with her quick disrobing. Standing in nothing but black gartered stockings and twinkling gold, she was stunning, stunning enough to quiet the men behind them, who now turned to gaze at her nakedness.

"Great ass," one man exclaimed. "Can I have her, Damien?" he called out in a drunken bellow.

"Not tonight friend," Damien calmed him with his definitive voice.

The men stared at the scene in silence, letting Damien hold court in his own way. Everyone could see by his kingly bearing, the pomposity in this voice, and the arrogance on his face, that he called all the shots. He expected the others, including Miles, to shut up. Why these men bowed to Damien wasn't clear, it was simply a given. Tessa couldn't see why he would have that kind of power. It must have been money that he held over their heads.

While the others behind her might have been lusting for her body, Damien was incredibly cold and matter-of-fact. He could easily win points from Vincent. For that matter, maybe he'd taught the doctor/piercer his detached style.

"I want another piercing," Damien finally announced, after what seemed an interminable time. Tessa, for all her nakedness, was sweating, little beads forming between her breasts. Her hands were cold and clammy, and if she was honest with herself, she would have recognized that she was growing wet between her legs.

"Another?" Miles questioned.

"Something high on her pubic mound. I want her labia pulled wide."

"A spreader would handle it," Miles said.

"I want this more permanent. She's too damned sassy for her own good. A bar, some kind of gold rod to hold apart her labia, fixed with studs on the end through that plump flesh of hers. It will remind her of her place. She's not nearly humble enough to suit me."

Miles met eye to eye with his mentor/patron. The stark contrast between the two men was impressive. Damien icy, Miles passionately cold. Damien a man of power and financial worth, Miles a man of infinite soul and artistic inspiration. But in this place, Damien had cards in his hand that were not Miles' to play. Their "eye to eye" was tortuous to watch. So much was going on beneath the surface of their confrontation. Tessa could feel it, like another burning fire in her belly, though she didn't wholly understand what was separating the two.

"I'm sure Vincent can fashion something suitable," Damien broke the silence.

"I'm sure," Miles replied.

"Just be sure she's trained with a collar when she comes, or she'll have a much rougher time than any of us will enjoy."

"I have great faith in this one. She'll not disappoint you," Miles said.

"Humph." It was all the reply Damien would utter. He waved them off and rose from his chair to join his watchful companions.

"A game of poker?" he suggested to them.

The group moved to an elegant felt-covered card table at the other end of the room.

"Will you join us, Miles?" Damien suggested.

"I think I will," Miles replied promptly.

Tessa was surprised that Miles agreed to stay—the natural rhythm of the night should have dictated a brusque retreat. Instead, he pulled up a chair with the others, leaving Tessa standing alone, with no clothes and no instructions. When he finally motioned for her, it was to point to a chair in the corner, opposite him.

Tessa sat in the high-backed velvet chair for nearly three hours, fighting off the urge to sneeze from the fumes of cigar smoke. She waited on the men, bringing them drinks as they instructed her. Otherwise, she was ignored by them all, including Miles, who assumed a visage as icy as Damien's. Only an occasional glance suggested that a couple of the men deliberately restrained their urge to play with her.

Tessa decided early on that this humbling interlude was a gesture by Miles to Damien: a message to him perhaps, that his submissive was indeed up to the task of compliant service. With that in mind, Tessa played the part carefully, making certain not to falter at any point, for any reason.

When they left, Miles continued his vacant icy manner. Tessa had hoped they would be together for a night, and was disappointed to find him dropping her at her apartment with no further sexual escapades. She would have begged to have him whip her raw, if only he would display some of the passion beneath the surface of his wintry cold. This ice was horrid to endure.

"I'll be arranging things with Vincent," he announced, as the apartment elevator came to a stop with a sudden jerk.

"For when?"

"Now how would I know that right now?" he snapped.

"I guess I'm anxious," Tessa offered.

"Much too anxious," he replied.

Tessa entered the elevator and was on her way, without any inkling of affection between them.

CHAPTER SEVENTEEN

TESSA'S DOORBELL BLARED its obnoxious noise until it finally woke her. Glancing at the clock, she saw it was 10 A.M., too early for a morning she had planned to sleep in.

She pulled herself from the bed and threw a robe around her, dashing to the door. The bell still buzzed offensively, doing so until she finally opened it.

With a broad smile and fitful laughter, Martine pushed her way past Tessa, with Miles and Vincent trailing.

"Why didn't you use your key?" was on the tip of Tessa's tongue, but she was too surprised by the men to speak at all.

"What's going on?" she asked.

"Why, I'd think you'd have that all figured out," Miles said, cheerfully. His mood was one hundred and eighty degrees opposite what it had been two nights before, when he'd left her at the elevator. His quick changes always took her off guard.

Tessa had suspected that Miles and Martine were spending the night together when her roommate slipped out of the apartment the night before with that typically vague smile of lust written all over her arrogant face.

"We just had breakfast," Martine announced, looking at Tessa haughtily. "Then we grabbed Vincent to come along. I've been dying to see you pierced, my love. I've always wondered what it would look like seeing a needle poke through your unwilling flesh."

"You are horrible," Tessa said.

The three plopped down in the living room with an unabashed insouciance. Tessa had never seen Miles so exuberant.

"I suppose if you've had breakfast, I don't need to make you coffee?" she asked.

"Do you have any beer?" Miles asked.

"In the morning?" Tessa countered.

"It's almost noon," he said.

"It is not!" she snapped back, to her surprise and theirs.

Miles didn't seem to care what she said, or how she said it, though he did look as if he was keeping count of all her faults for later.

"C'mere," he said, motioning her to him. "C'mere." She hesitated, but he was patient. Her robe had fallen open because she hadn't taken the time to tie it. But she didn't bother covering anything. Why should she be modest, when they all had a thorough knowledge of her body, sex and all?

Presenting herself to Miles with a pout on her face amused him. His expression was positively wicked, and though she knew what was likely to follow, she wondered what bizarre scheme he'd cooked up to accompany the ritual. The three of them looked much too inspired to have some mundane ceremony in mind. Martine was looking as amused as Miles was. Vincent was eying Tessa with a studied interest that sent a quick chill through her from head to toe.

Tessa stood to Miles' left side as he lounged in a chair looking up at her. She realized that this was one of the few times that he'd been in her apartment. And unlike the times before, he was planning to stay. Why here? Why now? she wondered. Why not pierce her in the dark confines of Maya's salon or the created theater of the garret? Her apartment was bright and cheerful, with sunlight streaming through the half-closed blinds, hardly the place for decadent piercing rituals.

Miles fingered her nether jewelry as he looked at her face. She was aroused by his play, but she remained placid, giving nothing away—although the juice spilling from her would soon reveal the pleasure he was bringing her.

"So you're ready to have yourself pierced again?" he asked.

"I guess so." It must be the rod Damien had ordered for her that he had in mind.

Miles' amusement didn't cease nor did Tessa's worry over his strangeness. His eyes danced lightning hot. The more he stared at her, the more intense they were becoming. She felt herself breathing hard, her heart pounding deep inside her chest. She looked down to see her breasts moving rhythmically up and down, with an overtly erotic sensuousness. What had begun as a startling invasion of her morning was quickly becoming a rush so profound she could hardly stay on her feet.

The longer Miles stared at her, the more his eyes darkened. As always, the environment around him followed his mood, and this day was no different. The sun, though it did not hide behind clouds, nor was it swallowed up by some descending spaceship, suddenly seemed less shrill; the rays of light that bathed the room softened to make their surroundings as warm and succulent as her pussy was feeling, as mysterious as Miles' aura.

The three: Miles, Martine, and Vincent, moved in unison, rising to surround their waiting submissive. Martine stood right in front of her and pushed the robe from her body with a gentle tug. She leaned in and kissed her mouth, as Vincent, from behind, drew Tessa's hands above her and fastened them securely in wrist cuffs.

The low marble coffee table between the living room couches was quickly cleared, and Miles led her to it. He gently eased her down to its glacial cool surface and laid her back as if it were an alter. Her hands were stretched over her head, tied by ropes to the legs of the table. Her legs were spread as wide as they would go, Vincent carefully adjusting them exactly where he wanted them. He bound her ankles with ropes and secured them in their awkward position, so that her pussy was open wide. Miles buckled a leather strap around her waist and tied it down tightly against the table. She was secured against any movement. Only her head was still free to roam from side to side, as she watched the silent ritual of her bondage.

Martine attached clamps and chains to Tessa's gold nipple rings. The chains were like reins for Martine to pull, each tug jolting her immobile body. Tessa immediately reacted in her pussy.

"So juicy," Martine murmured, as she kneeled between Tessa's bound legs and pushed her fingers inside her cunt. "Squeeze," she told her. Tessa squeezed the cock-like fullness inside her, moaning softly as she did.

Martine bent over her crotch and licked her clit, winding her tongue around the jewelry and parting her labia so that she could make a quick journey into the interior of Tessa's cunt. The surrendering Tessa tried to squirm as the pleasure mounted, but there was no way to move, no physical response possible equal to the exquisite feelings that were charging through her.

Vincent kneeled down beside Martine and pushed a fat pillow under Tessa's hips. Her cunt stood out prominently, the jewels gleaming, dragging her inner lips and hood of her clit like weights. Often, they felt heavy, tugging at her as if they were to remind her where all her thoughts should remain.

"He wants her open," Vincent stated in his typical cool reserve. He pulled a gold bar from his pocket and showed it to them. Like its predecessors, this piece of jewelry reflected back the shiny gold of its earthy color. It was three inches long, smooth and round on the ends, so that it would not cut her skin. Welded rigidly at either end of the rod were posts that would soon pierce her pubic lips and be held fast with tiny screws.

"I worked it especially for her. I trust it fits," Vincent said. The fact that it might be too big for her labia to handle filled the next moment with rightful suspense. Four pairs of eyes stared at the simple decoration in baited anticipation.

Though Martine had continued to play with Tessa and her toys, she finally backed away when Vincent was ready. She moved off, still hanging onto the chains that attached to Tessa's pierced nipples. She proceeded to tug at them enough so that her bound slave wouldn't forget the pain. Tessa tried to wriggle against it, but her movements were pointless. And she knew it.

For some moments, they all watched as Vincent pushed Tessa's outer labia back, opening her cunt wide.

"Here?" he asked Miles.

"I should think that would do. How does it fit?"

"I'm not often wrong in my estimations, and I wasn't wrong this time. It will be a little uncomfortable at first, but then, that is the point, isn't it?" he stated coldly. "She'll get used to it."

Miles nodded. He had wanted this for her. He had imagined it many times. He knew Tessa would wear the bar, not just because he wanted her to, but because it fit her unorthodox personality. He wasn't completely happy that Damien had insisted on this so soon. He had had other plans in mind for this addition to Tessa's anatomy. But, then, perhaps he was being too cautious with her.

Looking down on her now, he was glad he hadn't waited. His little lamb of a submissive was so deliciously spread out for them, he couldn't keep his cock from rising and he wouldn't want to.

"It fits perfectly," Vincent said, showing him how the bar would be wedged high between her labia and held with studs. Her cunt could not close unless the rod were removed.

As she was poked and prodded, tugged and pinched, she lay back in her forced surrender, wondering if she would wear this ornament forever. What her captors seemed to have in mind was something as enduring as the color of her eyes or the shape of her nose.

"My God, that's perfect, Miles," Martine gasped. "What a fine badge of submission! Knowing my roommate, she'll never stop being horny for us. She hardly has an off day anyway, but now, it's almost as good as if you'd branded her with fire."

"It is a breathtaking sight," Miles observed. "Do it," he ordered Vincent.

"You know all my cautions, don't you?" Vincent asked.

"Of course," Miles replied. "Do it."

He stood back, looking down while Vincent worked, admiring the skill of the man's fingers as they began their task.

Martine stroked Tessa's face, her eyes looking into Tessa's eyes.

"It's going to hurt," Tessa exclaimed, her body tensing anxiously.

"Just let it turn you on," Martine said. She tugged at the nipple rings, as if that pain would somehow ease the one down below. As Tessa tensed even more in reply, the heavy needle pierced her flesh.

"Noooooooooo," she cried as a searing sensation shot through her. She tried to twist away, without success. "Yeeeeeawwwwww." The woeful sound of

Tessa's voice crashed nastily against their ears, though it didn't worry the others as much as its cause pleased them.

Her cunt throbbed in ways it never had before. If only she could release some of the terrible tension that made her so afraid. But she couldn't move. "Nooooooo, please no more," she pleaded.

"It's done," Vincent announced, to her surprise.

"Done?" She looked up to verify his words.

"It's done. But perhaps you can't see it from your position," he offered. "There's a little blood, but we'll watch it carefully." He dabbed at her sore cunt for some moments.

The three, in choreographed unison, backed away, leaving Tessa on her altar without a hand to comfort her. They moved to the other side of the room where Tessa could not hear them speak. That was okay with her, she was getting used to the feelings in her pussy. The rod had been cold when she first felt it, though now, the metal was beginning to warm with the warmth of her own body. It was little consolation though. The foreign presence splaying her open was a defilement far more sobering than any of the other studs and rings had been. They were sassy decorations, statements of submission perhaps, but this was equal to being bound permanently.

With the rod in place, her splayed pubic lips exposed her clitoris and vagina to any sunshine or breath of air that crossed them; it made her whole cunt twitch, her hole spasm involuntarily.

"So, my love," Miles' voice brought her out of her reverie, as he returned to her side. He looked down on her, reaching low enough to pick up the chains. He tugged them as Martine had done. "How does it feel?"

"Strange."

He nodded, the answer acceptable.

"You're ready then for Damien's Ball. At least your body is ready. Match your mind to the state of your cunt, and you'll have a successful soiree. Otherwise, you'll hate it." The way he spoke to her, he sounded as if he doubted her fitness for the role. Even more disturbing was the hint of mockery in his voice. It challenged her to remember the moments when his warmth had embraced her, the times he'd said "I love you" clear out of the blue, the instants of pure bliss when it seemed that they were inextricably one in their crazed sexual desires. Now, the icy chill was so profound, she wondered if she'd misread him all these months.

"So she's mine," Martine said, slithering up to Miles side. Her hand met his crotch in front, her fingers fondling what looked to be a stiff dick.

Miles pushed the woman down to her knees, while his eyes remained on Tessa.

Martine opened the fly to his jeans, and pulled out the long shaft, its purple head inside her mouth in moments.

Tessa turned her eyes away.

"Tessa, look at me," he ordered.

She didn't want to see Martine satisfy him, and she was bold enough to defy him, at least for an instant.

Seeing her eyes retreat, Miles pushed Martine aside and bent over Tessa, pulling at the chains so hard she thought her nipples would be ripped off.

"Yeeeeawwwww, noooooo," she squealed. She watched her breasts and nipples stretch out tight. He didn't stop. She cried out, but he didn't release them.

"Are you going to defy me, bitch?" he asked. He kneeled beside her, his face in her face.

"Pleeeeese," she was beginning to cry.

"What is it bitch?" he demanded, not moved by tears.

"No, no pleeeese." She was desperate, could hardly think through the pain. "Please, I'm sorry."

"You damn well better be," he said, releasing the chains for an instant, then tugging them again.

"Oh God," she cried. He grabbed her chin and forced her eyes on him.

"You watch us, slut. You watch her take my cock. Don't you dare take your eyes off of us for a second. You hear me?"

"Yes." Her frightened eyes were fixed on him.

He eased his grasp on the chains, though he didn't drop them. Standing again, Martine resumed the blowjob, taking the thick prick inside her mouth, with a pleasure she would not often show any man. Throwing the facts in her roommate's face was motivation enough. She bobbed up and down on Miles' shaft, and then feeling him about to explode, she backed away and let his come spew out on her face for Tessa to see.

Miles groaned lustily as he looked down at his bound slave.

"Maybe you're not ready for Damien's Ball," Miles remarked when he put his cock back inside his pants, and Martine had risen from her knees. "Untie her," he ordered Martine, "and let her sulk for awhile. Let her think about being submissive for a while—she's a far cry from the good little whore she needs to be."

He left with a look of disgust across his face.

Vincent had left earlier, so Tessa was left alone with Martine.

"I would have liked to have sucked this pussy of yours so prettily laid out, but you don't deserve it," Martine said. She was sounding as arrogantly disdainful as Miles.

Martine undid her bonds: her wrists, ankles, knees, and the strap around her waist. But she didn't bother to help Tessa from the table. Over an hour under the strain of the ropes had left her weak. She felt her wrists; they were sore and marked where the cuffs had cut into her. She must have strained more than she realized. She rubbed them to get the feeling back. Her legs ached; they'd stiffened into their strained awkward positions.

Worst of all was the bar at her cunt. It stretched her flesh as she sat against the hard surface of the coffee table/altar. The bar's presence would be an obsessive nagging complaint until she got used to it, until her flesh conformed to the way it was unnaturally pulled; that is, if she ever got used to it.

Tessa had expected this piece of submissive garb to excite her, but at the moment it was only a flaming annoyance. She was glad that Miles and Vincent had left, glad that Martine was ignoring her, off in the kitchen somewhere. She pulled herself to her feet and quietly retreated to her bedroom.

CHAPTER EIGHTEEN

TESSA DANCED. She threw herself into a savage abandon, jostled and jolted by a throng of dancers around her.

The polished young man who had whisked her onto the dance floor was hypnotized by her groin, the way it pulsed against his when they were close, the way it gyrated lasciviously for him as he watched.

She was gorgeous. He didn't know her name, but the moment she walked in the door of the club, he knew she was the woman he'd hit on that night. She was hot. A real nasty slut.

The more she danced, the more she turned him on. Her long blonde hair moved sensuously as she moved. He couldn't wait to run his hands through it. Her miniskirt was riding so high on her thighs that he could see the lacy tops of her black stockings. She had smooth hips, firm legs, and the hint of a very fine crotch at the bottom of it all. And if he wasn't mistaken, her nipples were pierced. He could see the hint of it through the lacy bra beneath her sheer blouse. He could see the dark shades of her aureoles, the hard buds, and a glint of gold twinkling through the creamy fabric.

He'd sleep with her. He had it all figured. After all, he was the hottest stud in the club on any night. The best dancer, he wooed women with a easy self-assurance and he made love like Casanova.

There was a provocative smirk on her face. Her eyes danced like fireflies on a summer night. What a tease this chick was, what an outrageous wanton slut. He couldn't wait to get her in bed. He bet she fucked for hours, that she sucked cock, that she even took it in that tight little ass. Ooooo yes, that's what I want, he thought to himself, that tight little ass, oh man, what a score....

Her hips seemed to confound physics the way they moved so nastily. She had her hand on the edge of her mini-skirt, and teased him, pretending she was going to pull it up. Yes, gawd, yes, he thought, do it babe, show me that cunt. His eyes were ready to explode from his sockets, as little by little the skirt rose higher on her hips, until he could see a little flesh at the bottom, smooth-shaved pussy. God, she'd shaved! He reached in with his hand and felt the moist wet skin. He planted his lips on hers, pushing his tongue between them, mimicking what he wanted to do with his cock.

She backed away from him, her lips glistening from the kiss. She was showing him more. My god! The little slut's gonna show me her puss, right here on the dance floor! She raised the center of her skirt. Goddamn! She's pierced! he exclaimed silently. A little more and her pussy was practically bared for his eyes, What the hell, there's a bar pierced into her pubic mound, holding her pussylips wide open! Damn what a slut! His cock was hard as a rock, precome seeping all over his Jockeys.

She flashed him a wicked smile, her nostrils flared.

She lowered her skirt just enough so she was decent again, though he could still catch peeks of her naked flesh when she rocked back and forth in front of him. She reached out and pulled his hand to her crotch, nestling in against him. Groin to groin they danced.

He thought he'd died and was jetting to heaven... though heaven would soon vanish, even more quickly than it had appeared.

As the music played and the slut writhed in front of him, Young Casanova caught a glimpse of a man from the corner of his eye. Behind the blonde, his figure loomed darkly. With his slicked-back black hair tied into a ponytail, his black shirt, black jeans, and black cowboy boots, he looked like some creature from hell, a fashionable hell perhaps, but with the nasty accompanying expression on his face. He was not one to tangle with.

Her boyfriend perhaps. Damn just my luck, he groaned to himself.

The dark man whispered in the woman's ear. She answered. Then he grabbed her by the arm. Young Casanova watched his gorgeous blonde temptress disappear into the crowd, only a brief wave of her hand and the wink of an eye to remain in his memory as a memento of what he might have had that night.

His limousine was waiting for them.

It happened so fast, her head was spinning wildly.

She'd heard his voice in her ear just as she was showing off her lusty jewelry to a peach of guy, with tight buns and a terrific sense of rhythm. She was having some fun. And why not? she thought to herself. Hibernating in her apartment for three days, nursing the agony of the bar in her cunt, made her feel pent-up and restless. Getting out was the best thing she could do for herself. She couldn't wait around forever. When the fourth night came, Martine was out the door in a flash, off to see Miles, Tessa presumed.

She'd be damned if was going to stay home another night alone, so she dressed like a lusty whore and planned to act like one.

But when he spoke to her on the crowded dance floor, his unexpected voice rattled her like an earthquake.

"You have plans to exhibit your finery to the entire place?" He spoke as if he thought her some immoral harlot, his judgmental tone wreaking havoc on her brain. He was furious with her, she could tell by the passion emanating from his calm reserve. It made her body soar sky high.

"How did you find me?" she whispered, still dancing to the perplexed glances of her impromptu lover.

"I know your habits, I know your weaknesses."

He made her feel promiscuous, as if dancing was a sin. But her body liked that feeling too. Naughty, like a little girl breaking rules. Maybe he'd spank her for the offense.

"You're leaving now," he'd said. She wouldn't protest. His voice grabbed her as surely as if she was tethered on a leash.

She'd smiled to her gentleman fellow. Poor man would have to spend his evening in fantasy, she remembered thinking.

Miles pushed her into the waiting limousine.

"On the floor," he ordered.

She was too shocked to react right off and sat down on the seat. Her faux pas was greeted with an instantaneous response from Miles: The palm of his hand hit hard against her face, practically knocking her to the floor where she belonged.

Tessa was immediately in tears, though she moved to a submissive pose at his feet.

"You have forty-eight hours of unquestioned obedience to survive. Let's just hope you can live up to your own expectations."

It must be Damien's Ball, she thought.

"You weren't at your apartment when I arrived tonight," Miles said.

"You expected I'd be there?" Tessa questioned, trying not to be testy. "You gave me no orders after our last encounter."

"You still have problems anticipating your dominant's will. I thought you were more intuitive than that."

"I thought my deportment was so unacceptable that you'd left forever."

"Don't be melodramatic, Tessa. Your behavior is as

transparent as glass. You're damned impatient and defiant. Those are not virtues in a submissive. In fact, they could be your undoing, especially when you defy all previous assumptions with the stunt you pulled tonight."

"But you're spending your nights with Martine," she protested. "Isn't that some kind of clue to your intentions?"

"Yes—I wouldn't be screwing Martine if I'd left you."

"Oh, so that's supposed to be some sign of your affection for me? She's just a way to get to me? She means that little to you?" Her voice was high-pitched, quite unlike her normal tone.

He jerked her head with his hand, her chin held fast, so she was looking directly into his face.

"Shut up!" he said icily. "My relationship with Martine is no business of yours. For a woman in your position, you're making blunders you will regret." He let go of her chin. "Put your face on the floor," he ordered.

Tessa bent down with her head resting on the floor, her face pressed against the plush blue carpeting. Her fingers played with the tufts of fuzz. His hand pushed her down even more, so her breasts were pressed against the carpet. He smacked her ass until she was sure it was bright red.

"I'm sorry, Miles," she said meekly when he stopped.

"You don't know what sorry is, not yet," he said.

He sat back in silence, content to watch her grovel before him.

"This is Damien's Ball, isn't it?" she asked, her voice quiet and inoffensive.

"Could be Damien's hell for you!" He leaned forward and smacked her again, until she groaned from the pain.

He sat back again and stared at her tear-stained face and smudged make-up. She was beautiful, even like this. He softened looking at her.

"Perhaps you *are* ready, after what I saw earlier."

"You mean at the club?"

"Blatantly tawdry. I don't excuse your willfulness, but you did capture the essence of a good exhibitionist," he commented.

"It was my mood," she said.

"Well, don't forget the mood, you're going to have to marshal all your forces tonight."

This was not the beginning that Tessa had hoped for. She'd always imagined a heady wine, a lush dinner, and a seductive eroticism between the two. He'd help her dress. She'd pant with delicious expectations. By the time they'd arrived at Damien's vulgar ball, they'd both be ready for one hell of a night!

On the floor at his feet, with an angered Miles looming over her, the trip to the ball took on a considerably different aspect, one that Miles seemed unready to change.

In Damien's house, Miles escorted Tessa to a room on the other side of the house from the one she'd been in days before. It was a simple living room, furnished with leather couches and a softer palette of colors than those that decorated Damien's masculine study. This room, with a vase of fresh-cut flowers on the coffee table, had a woman's touch.

Miles didn't speak, and Tessa offered no conversation. Their earlier discussions in the limo had failed to restore the tender bond they'd shared in the past. Tessa assumed this was the way he wanted things to remain, for he did nothing to thaw his icy demeanor. As they waited, Miles strolled about the room gazing at paintings Tessa realized were likely his work. Tessa remained three steps inside the door in frozen silence.

Their wait wasn't long. Minutes later, Damien and two valets came through a door at the other end of the room.

"She's yours Damien. I have places to go," Miles said.

Damien nodded first at Miles, then at Tessa, his own impeccable cool intact.

"I wouldn't suggest you hold back on her, she's been insolent and shamelessly indiscreet. I'd have already flogged her backside until it was raw if I hadn't known I'd be bringing her here tonight."

"It isn't my job to discipline your recalcitrant concubine, Miles. This is a night of pleasure," Damien said.

"Then pleasure yourselves with her. You have free reign. I'll return, tomorrow at this time?" he asked.

"If she's finished. You know we don't interrupt anything."

"Of course not." Miles turned to leave. "And Damien," he said looking back, "I trust you'll find her gold rod to your liking." He didn't give Tessa the satisfaction of even a single glance, leaving her with the feeling that she was simply so much dust on his feet to be wiped away.

In turn, Damien was as brusque with her as Miles. He turned to his two valets, one male, one female.

"Get her ready," he ordered, then he too left the room.

Tessa was quickly led back through the main French doors, through the foyer into the back of the house. Up two flights of stairs, she was brought into an attic room on the third floor. The room was unfinished, like attics in her imagination, except for a wild variety of leather hanging on the walls, an old-fashioned wardrobe, like the one in Miles' garret, and a professional make-up table with bright lights surrounding a mirror.

The valets guiding her were silent, shoving her to one side of the room, while they took their places with other valets on the other side. There were two other submissive women standing with her, and they were soon joined by three men, looking like dutiful slaves with the collars fixed around their necks.

A woman of obvious dominant inclinations stood between the two groups.

"You," she directed her comments to the six submissives, "are trinkets for this night, nothing more than baubles, for the pleasure of the guests at this ball. You are here because you have expressed the will and the desire to be of service in this most humbling way."

Tessa stared at the woman as she spoke. Her remarkable garb was the first suggestion, that at least some of what she expected at Damien's Ball was about to happen. The woman was clothed in black leather, exactly as Tessa imagined the most severe dominatrix. She was statuesque, especially so in thigh-high leather boots that sported five-inch heels. She wore a black lace waist-cinching corset that pushed her generous tits into two jiggling mountains above the leather; to finish her attire, she wore black leather gloves up to her elbows. Her voluminous hair was teased to an extraordinary height, befitting the kind of character she was striving to portray.

She continued her speech in smooth even tones, thankfully, without the hint of disgust that Tessa noted in both Miles and Damien.

"From this moment on, you have no will of your own, your needs and desires are of no concern to anyone here, to any of the valets," she nodded to the several men and women on the opposite side of the room, "to me, or to Damien's guests. Your sole purpose is to serve in whatever way you're required. You will be lavishly whipped, fucked, and made to perform all manner of acts that you might find hideous in other situations. In this place, however, whatever base and immoral acts are required of you, you will do without question, knowing they will provide great pleasure to your masters.

"If you are not gagged, you will not speak. There will be no protests of any kind. The valets will give you each a safe word. That is required for certain safety reasons, however," she deliberately raised her voice so that her message was not missed, "you were chosen to be trinkets because Damien knows you'll have few, if any, limits."

The dom paused to let her words sink in, then continued.

"We are not completely without compassion, and you are expected to trust the dominants at this party. Safe words should be unnecessary. Your valet will be with you the entire night—you are in their charge between your excursions with Damien's guests. They are there to assist any way they can, to make this a most satisfying evening. Your valet will now prepare you." The dominatrix nodded to them haughtily, then clicked her boots together at the heels, and walked briskly out of the room.

Tessa was taken to one corner of the attic by a man only a little taller than she. He was young, perhaps her age, but what he might have lacked in years, he certainly made up for in his carriage. He was like a youthful Miles, with eyes as piercing as her own dominant's and a jaw that was set as firmly as Miles' often was. His lean, muscled body was clothed in a pair of baggy pajama-type pants. He had a leather band around his left arm and a gold earring through his nipple. His feet were bare.

He was quick with his work. He undressed her, the skirt and top hastily thrown to the floor. Once he gazed at her naked body, he let out a brief gasp, seeing her piercings. He was taken aback by the rod that spread her cunt. After the initial impact, he proceeded about his business, placing a three-inch leather collar about her neck, a wide leather belt with a half dozen heavy rings about her waist, and wide leather cuffs, also fixed with rings, to her wrists and ankles. She would remain barefoot.

The valet then moved her to a make-up table, where he ordered her to sit. With efficient skillful motions, as if he were a make-up artist in his other life, the valet applied heavy rouge, eyeliner, shadows in a whole palette, and a thick coating of red lipstick. There was some pride in his work, for he pushed her chair around so that she could look in the mirror. The results were stunning, in a bizarre sort of way. Her face was Tessa, but so much more. Toying with her long blonde locks, he styled her hair in a inspired work of art, twisting it into a beautifully braided bun that suited her submissive status. The total effect, the leather, the hair, and the make-up, transformed her into a seductive creature of the night, half-sensuous woman, half animal.

Tessa and the other trinkets were led on leashes downstairs to Damien's grand ballroom. At the door, the number four was clamped to Tessa's collar. For the remainder of Damien's ball she would be known as Trinket Four.

With their valets leading them, the six trinkets were taken into a lavish room, with gleaming chandeliers, violin music, and the sounds of bright chattering guests.

There were several hundred people inside, dressed not expressly for sex or for sadomasochistic games, but for a fine dress ball: some in long sequined gowns, others with daring cleavage in front and back and skirts slit nearly to the hip. There were some that were garbed in the finery of sexual domination, leather, chains, and lace.

As Tessa was marched through the throng of people, she and the other trinkets were stared at with wide-eyed looks of haughty arrogance. For a moment, Tessa relived the bizarre day at Miles' luncheon, thinking these men and women were clones of those other horrid people, if not the very same ones. But the further she went, the more apparent it became that the night *was* for sex! A glimpse of tit, a pussy flashed, a hand fondling asscheeks, lust permeated the room with a cloud of sexual expectation.

Each trinket in turn was positioned at a particular point in the ballroom where there was a pedestal waiting for them. When Tessa reached the two-foot-high granite column, her valet pulled her up short on her leash. Helping her up the awkward step, she stood heads above Damien's guests, exhibited in all her seductive splendor. Trinket Four.

Her valet joined her on the pedestal, long enough to secure her wrists to a sturdy hook hanging over her head. Clothed and bound, Trinket Four remained standing alone as the first rustle of excitement rippled through the crowd and died away. She and her fellow trinkets would be left ignored until their services were required, their valets standing patiently beside them.

CHAPTER NINETEEN

"THIS ONE," the woman said.

"She's a fine one," the man at her side replied.

"I love blondes, you know that," the woman said. "They do show their marks much more quickly than brunettes with darker skin."

The man nodded to the valet, and Trinket Four was slowly released from the hands-over-head agony that had gone on for nearly two hours.

"We'll whip her here to begin with," the woman said. She herself was a brunette, with hair pulled back from her face and fixed in a bun at the base of her neck. She wore a gown that draped deeply in front and back, the inside of her breasts bobbing into view with each move she made. Her rear cleft was visible as she walked with a swish to her hips.

"Grab your legs," the woman ordered, looking up at the slave on the pedestal.

Trinket Four strained to comply. Her arms and legs ached, but she was nonetheless determined not to falter, especially when this was the first demand that had been made on her.

She bent down, grabbed her ankles and locked her knees, afraid the lash might cause her to loose her balance. She clenched, waiting for the first blow to strike.

The brunette bitch was in front of her, admiring the line of her body, the fine pose she'd managed to strike. It was commendable. She pulled the trinket's hair and looked into the silent face of submission.

"Whip her buttocks raw, then bring her to me," she said to one of the men accompanying her. She dropped the slave's head and walked away.

The lash was brutal, coming down on the trinket's body with one blow after another. There were moans and faint cries.

"Do we gag her?" one attendant questioned.

"No, let her whimper, it will be all the worse for her when we get her down," the other one countered.

The lash resumed its journey over Trinket Four's slave ass, cut piled upon cut, burning into the creamy tender skin. She was a valiant one, the perpetrators thought. The two men, on orders from their mistress to whip the slave's butt, played games of their own to see what might knock the chosen trinket off her pedestal. The slave held her position with some determination, though it was not a war that she could ever win.

Her valet caught her when a flurry of lashes whisked through the air from the two vile whips, and she could take no more. She fell off her pedestal to the sounds of laughter coming from the masters with the whips.

This first lashing of the night, an apt icebreaker, was watched by scores of guests that used this trinket's woe as a source of inspiration. In particular, Trinket Four was observed in her moment of agony by eyes that had seen her in such positions on other occasions, by eyes belonging to the master that had initiated her into the world of punishment. He was a brooding man, who was not making sport of the night, as he had done so many times before when he lent his hand in a whipping or commanded one of Damien's trinkets. He was content this time to explore the ballroom and its fascinating pleasures, though his mind was forever welded to just one poor trinket/slave, who now wiggled her red ass in the air.

He thought she wouldn't see him, that it would be safe enough to observe, but one fleeting glance during one fleeting moment, when Trinket Four opened her eyes, gave him away. His face, though expressionless, renewed the slave's courage. To this trinket's surprise, her master had lied about being there, though she had no time or will to contemplate a relationship that was best forgotten for the rest of the night.

The first punishment complete, the trinket/slave was led to a side room on her leash. She crawled on hands and knees across a crowded floor of people that were not inclined to notice her. She was stepped on. She wanted to cry out when her fingers were smashed, but as if her valet anticipated her cry, he jerked on her leash to remind her of the required silence.

The small anteroom was like a scene from the

Arabian Nights, pillows covering the floor, incense giving off heavy smoke, and a pungent smell permeating the air.

The brunette Mistress was waiting for her prize, reclining on the pillows with a long thin buggy whip poised in her hand.

"Bow, slave, at my feet," she ordered Trinket Four.

The slave crawled forward with her head to the floor, reaching the brunette's feet just as the buggy whip flashed through the air and landed across her back.

She jerked and moaned, stunned.

"So easily pained?" the Mistress questioned. "I'd better not have claimed a cowardly trinket." The lash made several brisk trips through the air, landing each time with an emphatic crack against the slave's back.

This time she was quiet, not a peep from her mouth.

"That's better," the Mistress purred, "Come here between my legs." The trinket/slave crawled between the woman's legs and began to lap at the juicing cunt presented her. The Mistress leaned back, the immediate joy of her trinket's careful work apparent in the blissful expression on her face.

"Oooooooo my lord, what a tongue," the woman seethed, her heavy breathing becoming heavier still, as she was quickly pushed toward a smashing come. As much as she might have wanted to wait, there was too much sexual heat floating around the room to fend off any orgasm for long. She bucked and churned against her trinket's tongue, her juices spilling out all over the attentive face.

The slave backed off in silence once the Mistress

had been served. She kept her head pressed to the pillow, honoring the swift bond that had been forged between them.

"Come here, slave," the woman ordered.

Trinket Four crawled higher on the pillows, till the woman raised her chin with a nurturing hand and looked into her slave's surrendering eyes.

"Rise up so I can see your jewelry," she said. "I'm so fascinated by piercing, and yours is quite appealing."

The slave pulled herself to her knees at the Mistress's side, letting the woman's hand stray over her nipples, toying with the studs and the rings, twisting and pulling them until the trinket winced in pain.

"Oh, does that hurt?" the Mistress wondered aloud, her voice veiled in mockery. "Ah, but I like these best," she said, petting her the opened cunt. "This bar is so lovely. Does it hurt?"

Her slave remained silent.

"You may speak," the Mistress informed her.

"Only when I move too quickly or in the wrong direction," Trinket Four replied.

"So does your Master plan to leave this here forever?" the Mistress asked.

"I don't know," her slave replied.

"How open it makes you, how exposed." The Mistress looked as if she'd like to use her tongue against the moistening flesh. But she had other ideas first. "Hand me that small crop," she said to one of her male attendants. She had urges to satisfy, pain to inflict.

The small crop was perfect. It was soon cracking against the exposed cunt with ruthless cuts going every which way over thighs, cunt, and labia. Small whimpers escaped her lips. And where it hit against the slave's jewelry, she cried out with a bloodcurdling scream. She could hardly stay upright.

"Now for your ass again, it's looking too pale," the Mistress said. She pushed her slave around, her attendants shoving her head against the pillows. The crop whisked through the air again, raising fiery red stripes across the slave bottom. She couldn't help her distressed moans and occasional cries.

"A dildo please," the Mistress ordered. One was quickly placed in her hand. By the way her male attendants readily served her, it was clear they feared the same fate as the slave now bowing humbly at her side.

"Grease her," she ordered. An attendant moved forward with a jar of cream in hand and began to rub it into the slave's rear hole.

"Yes, grease it deeply." The Mistress watched attentively. "You'll both be in there soon, I love to watch a good ass rape." Finishing, the man backed away so that his Mistress could insert the dildo in its proper place. Clutching it in one hand, she shoved the huge plastic prick against the trinket's sphincter, forcing it to give way.

"Yeaaaaahhhhhhh!" the slave cried aloud.

"Does it hurt?" the Mistress asked in a singsong voice, happily amused. She loved listening to that gasp of pain and the tiny cries that ensued thereafter as she rammed the huge cock in and out of her little slave. "You take this well," she observed. "You must have had this treatment before." Her slave began to wriggle her rear against the offending prick with a moan of pleasure escaping her lips.

"Answer me you whore!" the Mistress demanded. The palm of her free hand began to slap her slave's raw asscheeks. "Does it hurt?"

"It's unbearable," the trinket gasped. She practically collapsed on the pillows, with force and desire butting heads together in her violated rear end.

"How wonderful for all of us," the Mistress said, hearing the anguished moans muffled into the pillows below. The poor little thing was hardly able to contain herself.

"In her ass!" the dom roared at last, as she pulled the dildo from Trinket Four's wide-open ass. Two eager cocks waited impatiently to force their way inside the submissive rear hole. The more anxious of the two moved forward on his Mistress's command and impaled the slave with a forceful shove.

"Oh gawd!" she cried.

The attendant smirked delightedly, pulling vigorously in and out, just as the dildo had done.

"Gawd no!" the slave cried again. The cock was not as easy to manage as the dildo. She hoped for some compassion from the man that rammed her ass, but he was eager. He was too often denied his pleasure by his Mistress to not take every advantage he could of succulent slave flesh and a tight rear channel.

He cried his own exuberant cries with a gleeful smile, looking out at the audience that gathered around to watch.

"She's so humbled," one woman said.

"I find it uplifting," another spoke.

"How can they find it in them to give themselves this way, I'll never know," a third remarked.

The Mistress of the hour, reclining happily on her

pillows, sneered lewdly at the crowd. She was a happy Mistress with her two submissives and a borrowed trinket. Every whim, every urge, was satisfied.

Trinket Four did not finish with the trio until she had satisfied the two men with her ass and the Mistress once more with her mouth.

By the time she was returned to her pedestal, the evening's festivities were well underway. The elegant clothes that adorned Damien's guests were strewn in corners and closets. Soft naked flesh-on-flesh encounters were going on throughout the ballroom, in several side rooms, and in parlors beyond.

Trinket Four had hardly resumed her place on the pedestal before she was summoned again. Her valet led her away to another Master desiring the use of her available orifices.

She was whipped with a cat-o'-nine-tails, buggy whip, and assorted leather instruments, spanked with paddles, and impaled with dildos and cocks. Her backside was raw to touch, her openings stretched and sore from use. She was made to pad about the ballroom on hands and knees until her knees ached and she didn't think she could move another inch.

The time passed as if in a dream; sometimes it seemed that it dragged forever, though she was vaguely aware that day had dawned, the morning light had come and gone, and afternoon sunlight had disappeared to give way to another night.

Crawling up on her pedestal for the last time, the valet no longer insisted that she stand tied arms over her head. Trinket Four remained with her eyes closed until she felt her valet tug at her collar again.

Her eyes popping open, she stared into his passive face.

"Again?" she whispered wearily. Her limbs could hardly move, and she no longer cared whether "submissive protocol" was breached by her faint protest.

The valet did not reply, though he didn't scowl in response to her plea. Instead, he pulled her to her feet, not her knees, and led her from the ballroom past sleeping bodies. As they made their silent journey, only a rare sensuous movement caught their eye. The feeling of exhausted satisfaction rippled through the ballroom on a listless breeze. Someone had thrown open a window, and a whiff of fresh air caught their nostrils as they returned to the attic stairway.

In the attic, the valet undressed her, removing the collar, the leather belt, and the cuffs.

"You were a fine trinket/slave" he said. He looked weary too, though a twinkle in his eye flashed through the fatigue. He was very kind now, whereas all night and day he'd been just another master for her to obey.

"I was once Trinket Four," he told her.

She smiled at his admission. Strange bonds, strange times create.

Dressed, she was led back to the foyer, to a chair where she was left by herself. She nodded off, wanting only to sleep.

"Tessa!" She heard her name spoken sharply, hardly recognizing it. Opening her eyes, she saw Miles towering above her.

CHAPTER TWENTY

WHEN SHE FINALLY woke again, it was afternoon, a sumptuous lazy sunshine flooding the room. The cushion of downy comforters cocooned her naked body. She ached too much to be really comfortable, but she didn't want to move. She dozed again, not waking until daylight had vanished and a hurricane lamp on the far side of the room was the only light to see by.

This time, Tessa had to rise, her bodily functions demanding attention. Finding a sumptuous looking bathtub next to the toilet, she filled it with hot soapy bubbles, and slipped into the silky warm water to soak. She hoped forever.

When she finally pulled herself out of the tub and dried her body with a thick bath towel, she felt as tired as when she first sank into the water. The bath had soothed her aches and pains away, so that she wanted to sleep again.

It was not until she was nearly dry that she looked down to see that the bar had been removed from her cunt, her labia once again allowed to close over her womanly bud. She felt strange without it. She wondered when it was removed and by whom, though memory cheated her of the specific instant of recollection. She was satisfied to put the puzzle from her head in favor of sleep.

It was morning when she woke again—she could tell by the songs of birds outside the open window. Only then did she realize that someone had been attending to her as she slept, opening windows, closing them, leaving food and tea by her bedside, and removing it untouched when she was too tired to eat.

Now she was ravenous and anxious to see Miles. She was in his house, she recognized the room, though it wasn't the one she'd stayed in that other time, months ago. She recognized the paintings on the wall. There was a picture of a woman with her cunt spread open. It was one of her. Like a message painted in rough pigment on this canvas, he reminded her that he was watching over her; like Pygmalion, her creator loomed, his subtle designs around her even when she slept.

Seeing clothes laid out for her, she quickly dressed and left the room, thinking that all her impending needs would be cared for somewhere downstairs.

She was flashing back to months before, walking into the sunroom where Miles sat eating breakfast. The greatest difference between this time and before, was that the table was set for two.

"Awake at last?" he said, smiling broadly. Traces of anger, expressions of scorn, and the cold that could flash so brilliantly on his face were now replaced with his impeccable calm.

She sat down where he pulled out a chair.

She stared at him forever, wondering what to say. Forty-eight hours between them—she didn't know where to start. "You removed the bar," popped into her head and out of her mouth. It was a bizarre first statement to utter after everything that had happened.

Even Miles was surprised by her comment.

"I never thought it permanent Tessa—sometimes I like the look of your womanhood in its natural state," he explained. "So is that all you can think to ask about?" He smiled at her, charmed by her befuddlement.

Tessa blushed, a zillion thoughts cramming her brain until it pounded crazily. She said nothing.

"A muffin?" Miles asked, uncovering a half-dozen steamy dark muffins in a breadbasket. They were filled with nuts and raisins, their scent making her mouth water.

"Oh my God yes!" She took one, trying not to appear too anxious, though she would look back later and remember how quickly she ate it, the hunger surging in her. There was a vast emptiness needing to be filled. She was afraid she couldn't stop eating as Miles looked at her with dispassionate interest.

"Another?" he offered.

She took the second muffin, and allowed Miles to serve her a plate with fresh fruit and scrambled eggs.

"These are wonderful!" she exclaimed taking a first bite of the eggs. "What's in them?"

"Thank you for noticing," Miles said, still awed by her hunger and enthusiasm, "I made them myself, there's buttermilk, a little dill, and some red sauce."

"They're perfect!" She continued eating, content to let Miles' eyes caress her.

Finally slowing down, he took her hand in his. "I have meetings all day, Tessa, so I won't be here. Please make yourself at home, but don't you dare leave. I'll blister your butt if you do—I want to see you tonight."

"You're leaving now? But I have so much to say," she lamented.

"Do you really?" he asked.

She'd polished off two muffins, the plate of eggs and fruit, and two cups of coffee. She was no longer hungry. Either the natural need to eat was finally satiated, or it was simply suppressed by Miles' unexpected announcement. Disappointment had hit her like a brick. "Just tell me before you go, were you there all evening?"

"I was."

"You saw everything?" She only remembered seeing his face once, during the first punishment.

"Every lash on that pretty bottom, every cut of the crop across your pussy, every forced or gentle entry."

Tessa shuddered thinking back. "I didn't see you," she said.

"And you shouldn't have, your mind should have been elsewhere."

Tessa knew it hadn't been. Despite pain and constant torture, there was always a prominent corner of her mind focused on Miles. "I did see you that first time, when I was on the pedestal."

"That was a mistake," Miles admitted. "You peeked."

"There was no rule to close my eyes," Tessa reminded him with a dash of irritation.

He observed her for some moments. "You know, you're not likely to change, Miss Feisty" he said.

"What does that mean?" Tessa asked.

"You performed well for twenty-four hours, in fact you were nearly flawless, but you don't really want to surrender, you fight it."

She looked crestfallen.

He chuckled darkly. "But then…staying away from your submissive desires is like staying away from chocolate candy, isn't it?" he said. "You can't do it."

"You're unhappy with me," Tessa said, feeling herself jolted from the halcyon bliss to cruel reality.

"No, I'm not at all unhappy with you. My only consideration, Tessa, is not can you be the perfect trinket for Damien's Ball, but can you satisfy me?"

"What more would I have to do?" she asked.

Miles viewed the voluptuous curves of Tessa's torso, her breasts and nipples bulging against the thin fabric of the lacy purple T-shirt he'd given her to wear. Her golden hair was shining, falling softly past her shoulders. He saw her as he had seen her in the club that first night, bright, fresh, and willing to be molded. She hadn't changed much. Except that she was less flighty, less drawn to men with half her depth, more willing to acknowledge her more flagrant, abusive desires. She was more confident, he thought, more earthbound goddess than airy sprite.

"Let's find out tonight what you have to do," he finally said, pushing away from the table and rising to his feet. A hand dropped down to caress her shoulder. He leaned down and kissed her on the mouth, his tongue reaching in to penetrate her deeper than the surface of her lips.

"Tonight...." he said as he turned away, the word dropped like some magical mantra into the magical air of morning.

She waited for him, curling up in an overstuffed chair, her feet tucked under her, the three-inch patent leather pumps remaining on the floor. She was in one of a half dozen places she could have chosen in the ridiculously monstrous house. She wondered as she roamed through it why he bothered with the massive stone fortress, living alone the way he did. Maybe it was a family home, maybe it was the eccentric artist that demanded this space to create. Then again, he created most of his work in the garret, or so she thought.

Tessa had dressed two hours before, and waiting was a miserable business. If only he'd told her when he'd be home, but he'd omitted a lot of details when he spoke with her at breakfast. She had to improvise. The T-shirt and tiny skirt he'd left for her in her room weren't right for evening, so she took liberties, thumbing through the closet in her room for something that reflected the way she felt about the approaching night with Miles.

She was looking for elegance, finally finding a black cotton sheath, cut low in the back and front. It clung like second skin to every body curve.

She paraded around the house in the dress and heels she'd found, and the make-up that she discovered in the bathroom. Between 9:00 A.M. and 5:00 P.M., she must have changed her look a hundred times, experimenting like a teenager with the dazzling colors on her cheeks and eyes. A dozen faces from Damien's Ball returned to her memory. Leather bitches, soft submissives...androgynous, sexual, animal-like faces of some Master's sexual vision.

Still, she didn't know what Miles' vision for her was, and what he wanted that night. Finally deciding on the usual "Tessa Cotille" make-up, she threw her hair into a flouncy pile atop her head and descended the staircase to wait for her master.

"You seem to be sleeping now, most anytime I find you."

"What?" She pulled up inside the enormous chair, unaware of how utterly seductive she looked to him.

"Come here," he said, holding out his hand and drawing her into his arms.

"Lick my lips," he said.

Her tongue obeyed, making excursions about his lips and mouth.

"Let me see you." He pushed her further from him and waited. "Raise your skirt."

With inchworm tugs, she raised the sheath, higher, and higher still on her thighs, until it was pleated at her hips, the skin of her cunt peeking from below.

He licked his middle finger and held it for her to see, then stepped forward and poked it between her cuntlips, straight as an arrow into her vagina. She jerked against him and moaned.

He pumped her for several seconds, then withdrew.

With a firm hand on either side of her, he pushed the black sheath up and over her head, throwing it to the floor.

She was naked, he was clothed; it was the way he wanted her.

He took her hands behind her back, pinning them at waist level, and held them there with one hand. With the other hand he slapped her. First her breasts, then her cunt.

"Ow, ouch, please," she breathed in. She was still sore everywhere.

"Shush. Lick my lips," he ordered.

He offered her his lips to satisfy. The tracing of her tongue across his mouth had always sent him into paroxysms, heated spasms of energy that stiffened his dick.

They were eye to eye: his pleasure in her mouth-to-mouth attentiveness, hers in the slaps, each rude sting making her cunt twitch, the inside of her vagina throb. He rapped her pussy several times in a row at unmeasured intervals. Like Chinese water torture, she didn't know when he would strike it again. He snickered diabolically, his eyes darkening as he retreated into an animalistic state of base satisfaction.

He slapped her cunt.

"Please don't, I hate it," she moaned.

"You lie."

He slapped her face, hard enough for her head to jerk to the side. "You like this too, don't you?" When she didn't reply, he slapped her again. "Tell me."

"I love it. I hate it, but I love it."

"Don't qualify the truth bitch, you love it, it makes you frantic." He teased her. Several times his hand came down to her shivering mound and stopped. Without thinking once, she squealed.

He chuckled.

Then his hand slapped her with a sound smack.

"Oh gawd," she retorted quietly, her body doing a simple shimmy, while her cunt juiced.

He felt her between her legs where it was sticky and wet and her clitoris was hard. His fingers rubbed the bud, and she felt a savage stirring emanating everywhere about her cunt.

"I want to come," she told him. Her body was bursting with pent-up, locked away, repressed sexual fever. Her belly burned hot, swelling, as if she had reservoir ready to spill.

"Ah! Not yet," he said sharply.

He pushed her from him. "Grab that dress and run upstairs, third room on the left." His room.

Tessa stared at him and turned to pick up the black sheath. When she was bent over, he smacked her with the palm of his hand. She tried jerking away, and he grabbed her by the waist, and paddled her rear end with a least two dozens smacks.

"Ouch, damn it hurts, please Miles no." He ignored her mournful pleas, spanking her even more fiercely. He loved the rising red on her ass. He released her when it was red top to bottom.

"Now you can go," he said.

She hesitated, looking into his icy-hot eyes.

"Go, go, run," he ordered, looking as if he was shooing a cat away.

She bolted, hastening naked across the foyer and up the stairs. He followed for a few feet, whacking her rear, until he was certain that she was on her way.

"And don't turn on the lights," he called to her, as she reached the top of the stairs.

She heard him as she hurried to the third room on

the left. Opening the door, she breathed again. He hadn't followed her, she could catch her breath. But he'd be there soon.

She could have orgasmed in an instant, but she didn't dare touch her pussy.

Miles entered with a candle in his hand, a long taper with a flame dancing.

He stared at her from the same dark devilish place he'd been downstairs. This wasn't romance, this was sex. She remembered that gladly. He was taking her deeper than she'd been before, even though the trappings of sadomasochism were absent. It didn't matter.

She was sparked, frightened.

He walked toward her and stared at her some seconds.

"Play with your pussy," he ordered.

"But I'll come."

"Don't come, not till I tell you."

She leaned back with her hand between her legs, her fingers to the side of her hard bud, in just the right place.

"Put a finger in your ass," he said.

Another finger found her asshole and pushed at the entrance.

"Deeper," he ordered. The candle lit his face; he looked like a demon. "Deeper in your ass, two fingers."

She let the fingers penetrate deeper still, her ass-end wanting more. He was there with lube when it was too dry and she slipped further inside with as much of her hand as she could fit in her awkward self-rape.

He stood over her watching. Having thrown off his pants, he was stroking his fat prick. He moved closer still, the candle leaning out over her. She looked up to see a bubble of hot melted wax at the cradle beneath the flame, ready to spill over.

Another Chinese torture. The anticipation ripped through her as if the wax had already struck the mark. She was panting from the surging in her pussy and the awaited burn.

When the hot wax spilled, it splashed onto her belly and her shaved mound.

"Yeeeawww." Her body sizzled. "Please no..." Her eyes flickered in the candle's light, as if she were a demon whore rising from a darkened cavern.

Hot wax spilled again. Her well-attended cleft churned in reply. She drew breath through her teeth, hissing.

Miles placed the candle on a table behind him and drew a small whip from a drawer.

"Open your legs and remove your hand." He meant the hand that played with her cunt. She was getting too close. This orgasm would take forever, if he could manage it.

He cut her between her legs, where the bruises and healing cuts were still visible. She didn't like it, but it was in her loins too deep for her to resist too avidly. She mostly moaned protests, which she expected him to ignore and he did.

Her inner thighs were red again; there were red marks rising on her belly and against the tender shaved skin. The lashes made her howl.

He descended to the bed, throwing her legs over his shoulders, penetrating her cunt, leaned against her, making her legs ache. Yet her pussy, so deeply penetrated, wanted him inside her deeper still, as far as he could go. She eagerly thrust against him, but he immediately changed positions when she got too close to a climax.

Rolling her over on top of him, she screwed his cock with a squeezing pussy.

"Fuck me bitch." He remained still, while she did dances on the shaft. Pulling in and out, gently, wildly, while her muscles pulsed and pulled. She wanted to intoxicate him with her seductive massage, so that he'd be overcome and ram the blessed rod straight through the ceiling of her cunt.

But he was determined to make her play, to stall the finish as long as he could. It was another torture for loins that wanted only fast, hard-driving, reckless fucking.

With his cock still inside her, he pulled himself up, Tessa sitting on his cock, moving gently for a sweet moment of softer screwing. They hugged naked torsos, her breasts, her nipples, her jewelry pressed against his hairy chest, the cushion of her pierced and yielding flesh an affirmation that she was his.

Falling down on their sides, they almost spilled into laughter, but there was another round of going yet to traverse.

He turned her on her side, with her bottom pressed into his groin behind her. She lay in the cradle of his arms, held tight by unyielding strength. She sucked his finger in her mouth, like she would his cock if it were offered. But now, instead, his cock was poised at her anus, planning to push inside.

She felt his hand first, fingering her anus, where her

own fingers had played. Then his cock pressed against the sphincter and shoved.

She raised one leg to make his journey easier.

He was in.

He moved in slowly, as she gasped with ripples of pain, sharp shooting violating pain. It seemed no matter how many times she'd been taken in the ass, it was a testy process getting used to the assault. The ripples eased. And then, as always, the crudest sensations became electrifying to her, in ways that made no sense, except that she knew she craved his cock in her ass. It was her pleasure to satisfy him, to have him as deep inside her as he could go, coming with her taut muscles milking him dry.

Thoughts swam through her brain. She couldn't see him. She couldn't look in his eyes. She could hardly play with herself, or him with her. In this position of captive surrender there was nothing but the feel of cock in ass to focus on. There was no hardened penis pressing at her face, or pussy there for a suck, diverting her attention, or whips or paddles or lusty master/slave talk; just his arms, Miles' dark hairy muscled arms, holding her tightly to him, as he moved at will inside her rear.

She was yielding, opening wider, letting more than just his cock inside her. There was a steady stream of power nestling in. She felt as if she were melting into his body heat, into his flesh, so that there were no spaces between them, just Tessa, an open vessel: submissive, acquiescent, reduced.

He picked up speed and rammed her with barbarous jolts. She gasped, feeling as if there were supernovas bursting inside her, flares igniting fires from cunt to head and toes and back again. All in the space of seconds, minutes, maybe hours.

He pressed against her with cock spewing, as if it could really pump her full.

Then he withdrew, dripping sperm. She groveled between his legs, lapping the remainders with her tongue, until he pulled her up and slapped her face.

"Come now," he demanded. His fingers toyed with her.

She strained to comply, not quite at a peak, too many discordant harmonies singing every which way, all clamoring to find the common melody of her body's natural peaking rhythms.

She fought with herself to find the edge.

It was right between her legs, where his fingers prodded and his hand tugged nastily at her labia. He spanked her, slapped her, drove her toward her end. But the end was not coming in his time frame. He pushed her own hands away and punished her with more slaps and pokes and pinches.

They were groin to groin now, face to face, her body tense, his relaxed. The control that held her captive, as if she was just another piece of himself, wouldn't settle for her fretful, headstrong attempts to regain control. "Come bitch—*now,*" he ordered. He pinched her clitoris, while her hand rubbed, and knowing she was about to orgasm, he pushed her hands away and rubbed himself.

"Ah, ah, ah, ah yes..." Her face contorted, a silent scream issuing from her open mouth. Whimpers followed, as waves of pleasure rushed over her, enveloping them both in a cocoon of electric unseen energy. Tangible to the touch, invisible to the eye.

"It's never happened like that before," she said in a quiet moment the next morning. She was sitting on his lap. They were surrounded by the green of the lush conservatory. She felt the warmed skin of her bottom with her hand, where he'd just spanked her. It was punishment, just the beginning of punishment. He informed her of that, said she "deserved it," for exposing her cunt in the club three nights before without permission. She thought he was half kidding, just an excuse to redden her oh-so-tender flesh again. But he was serious.

"What's never happened like that?" he asked.

"Last night, it defies description," she said. It was something that she thought about for hours after he had fallen asleep next to her. "Everything that's happened before, with everyone else, and the cameras, and Martine, and Damien, and all the bitch ladies, it was never like it was last night. But I can't describe it."

"You belong to me, maybe that's the difference."

"But I've belonged to you before."

He shook his head no. "You belonged to your imagination, *and* every dime-store sex novel you could lay your hands on, and every rumor of abusive lusts fulfilled in alleys and anonymous beds. I gave you that," he said, "and a good deal more. But last night, we gave each other something else."

His eyes were noncommittal, neither flashing darkly nor brimming with affection. Just wholly sincere.

She understood and said no more. Some things are impossible to define. She had decided that, and so had he. She might have sought that perfect definition, the way to say it in words, but words didn't work here.

Only feelings mattered. How could she put into words what passed between them, the ebb and flow of eroticism, submission, succumbing that abused her, filled her, and brought her such peace. No, it wasn't necessary to define, even if it were possible. "I belong to you," she affirmed, as his hand reached inside her blouse, fondled her breast, and played with the stud that pierced her.

ANAÏS NIN AND FRIENDS

WHITE STAINS

$6.95/609-X

Written by Anaïs Nin, Virginia Admiral, Caresse Crosby, and others for a dollar per page, this breathtaking volume was printed privately and soon became an underground legend. After more than fifty years, this collection of explicit but sophisticated musings is back in print.

DENISE HALL

THE COMPANION

$6.95/676-6

Carla spends her days answering phones at the Sureware Customer Service Center, a sterile workplace she'd be happy to leave. One day, an anonymous admirer calls with an intriguing proposition. How would she like working for him—as his personal phone sex operator? He offers to pay royally for Carla's long-distance attentions, and the lovely young woman finally agrees to the arrangement. In no time, Carla becomes the ultimate exhibitionist!

JUDGMENT

$6.95/590-5

Judgment—a forbidding edifice where unfortunate young women find themselves subject to the wiles of their masters. Abandoned to the whims of Judgment's thrilling masters, Callie descends into the depths of this prison, discovering a new capacity for sensuality....

S. CRABB

CHATS ON OLD PEWTER

$6.95/611-1

A compendium of tales dedicated to dominant women. From domineering check-out girls to merciless flirts on the prowl, these women know what men like—and are highly skilled at reducing men to putty in their hands.

ALISON TYLER & DANTE DAVIDSON

BONDAGE ON A BUDGET

$6.95/570-0

The ultimate guide to low cost lust! Filled with delicious scenarios requiring no more than simple household items and a little imagination, this guide to DIY S&M will explode the myth that adventurous sex requires a dungeonful of expensive paraphernalia.

JEAN SADDLER

THE FASCINATING TYRANT

$6.95/569-7

A reprint of a classic tale from the 1930s. Jean Saddler's most famous novel, *The Fascinating Tyrant* is a riveting glimpse of sexual extravagance in which a curious young man discovers his penchant for flagellation and sadomasochism.

ROBERT SEWALL

THE DEVIL'S ADVOCATE

$6.95/553-0

Clara Reeves appeals to Conrad Garnett, a New York district attorney, for help in tracking down her missing sister, Rita. Clara soon finds herself being "persuaded" to accompany Conrad on his descent into a shocking demimonde where unspeakable pleasures await....

LUCY TAYLOR

UNNATURAL ACTS

$7.95/552-2

"A topnotch collection" —*Science Fiction Chronicle*

A tunning collection of speculative erotic fiction from this acclaimed writer. *Unnatural Acts* plunges deep into the dark side of the psyche and brings to life a disturbing vision of erotic horror. Unrelenting angels and hungry gods play with souls and bodies in Taylor's murky cosmos: where heaven and hell are merely differences of perspective.

NIGEL MCPARR

THE TRANSFORMATION OF EMILY

$6.50/519-0

The shocking story of Emily Johnson, live-in domestic. Without warning, Emily finds herself dismissed by her mistress, and sent to srve at Lilac Row—the home of Charles and Harriet Godwin. In no time, Harriet has Emily doing things she'd never dreamed would be required of her—all involving the erotic discipline Harriet imposes with relish. Little does Emily realize that, as strict and punishing as Harriet Godwin is, nothing could compare to the rigors of her next "position..."

ERICA BRONTE

LUST, INC.
$6.50/467-4
Explore the extremes of passion that lurk beneath even the most businesslike exteriors. Join in the sexy escapades of a group of professionals whose idea of office decorum is like nothing you've ever encountered!

OLIVIA M. RAVENSWORTH

DOMESTIC SERVICE
$6.95/615-4
Though married for twenty-five years, Alan and Janet still manage to find sensual excitement in each other's arms. Sexy magazines fan the flames of their desire—so much so that Janet yearns to bring her own most private fantasy to life. Janet persuades Alan to hire live-in domestic help—and their home soon becomes a most infamous household!

GERALD GREY

NEW YORK SECRETS
$6.95/675-8
A young woman arrives in Old New York, intent on realizing her dream of being a writer. She meets with Mr. Keating, an established and influential magazine editor and publisher. To her shock, Keating suggests that she turn her talents to sex fiction. She agrees—not knowing that Keating actually has the most severe erotic training in mind for his new authoress.

THE QUALITY OF MERCY
$6.95/650-2
James Adams arrives in Vienna intent upon receiving a thorough university education. All seems in order until he encounters Gizelle, a randy servant. With James, Gizelle is anything but subservient—little by little, she gains control of the young man's raging libido, until he is powerless in her hands!

LONDON GIRLS
$6.50/531-X
In 1875, Samuel Brown arrives in London, determined to take the glorious city by storm. Randy Samuel quickly distinguishes himself as one of the city's most notorious rakehells. Young Mr. Brown knows well the many ways of making a lady weak at the knees—and uses them not only to his delight, but to his enormous profit!

ATAULLAH MARDAAN

KAMA HOURI/DEVA DASI
$7.95/512-3
"Mardaan excels in crowding her pages with the sights and smells of India, and her erotic descriptions are convincingly realistic."
—Michael Perkins, *The Secret Record: Modern Erotic Literature*

Kama Houri details the life of a sheltered Western woman who finds herself living within the confines of a harem. *Deva Dasi* is a tale dedicated to the sacred women of India who devoted their lives to the fulfillment of the senses.

J. A. GUERRA, ED.

COME QUICKLY: For Couples on the Go
$6.50/461-5
The increasing pace of daily life is no reason to forego a little carnal pleasure whenever the mood strikes. Here are over sixty of the hottest fantasies around, in one extraordinary all designed especially for modern couples on a hectic schedule.

VISCOUNT LADYWOOD

GYNECOCRACY
$9.95/511-5
Julian is sent to a private school, and discovers that his program of study has been devised by stern Mademoiselle de Chambonnard. In no time, Julian is learning the many ways of pleasure and pain—under the firm hand of this beautifully demanding headmistress.

N. T. MORLEY

THE APPOINTMENT
$6.95/667-7
Vanya Garrison is married to a wealthy man, but she's beautiful enough to have plenty of fun on her own. Vanya knows just how to please a lover, and she practices her skills with almost any man who crosses her path! It takes a firm hand to control this pampered nymphomaniac; luckily, Dr. Rachel Quarry—Vanya's favorite shrink—provides a type of restraint and guidance unmatched in contemporary psychology. Dr. Quarry makes certain that all of Vanya's deep-seated issues are thoroughly explored!

THE CIRCLE
$6.95/627-8
Gina, a high-class "working girl," encounters a mysterious woman who pays her to indulge her kinky whims. Gina finds herself increasingly aroused by her encounters with Miranda, expanding her limits further than she could ever have imagined. Gradually, additional partners join in the fun, creating a circle of friends who just couldn't be closer!

THE OFFICE
$6.95/616-2
Lovely Suzette interviews for a desirable new position on the staff of a bondage magazine. Once hired, she discovers that her new employer's interest in dominance and submission extends beyond the printed page. Soon, Suzette is putting in plenty of overtime—as the bound sextoy of her demanding superior.

THE CONTRACT
$6.95/575-1
Beautiful Sarah is experiencing some difficulty in training her current submissive. Carlton proposes an unusual wager: if Carlton is unsuccessful in bringing Tina to a full appreciation of Sarah's domination, Carlton himself will become Sarah's devoted slave....

THE LIMOUSINE
$6.95/555-7
Brenda was enthralled with her roommate Kristi's desire to be dominated. Brenda decides to embark on a trip into submission, beginning in the long, white limousine where Kristi first met the Master.

VANESSA DURIÈS

THE TIES THAT BIND
$6.95/688-X
This best-selling account of real-life dominance and submission will keep you gasping with its vivid depictions of sensual abandon. At the hand of Masters Georges, Patrick, Pierre and others, this submissive seductress experiences pleasures she never knew existed....

CHARISSE VAN DER LYN

SEX ON THE NET
$5.95/399-6
Electrifying sex tales from one of the Internet's hottest authors. Encounters of all kinds—straight, lesbian, dominant/submissive and all sorts of extreme passions—are explored in thrilling detail.

M. S. VALENTINE

THE CAPTIVITY OF CELIA
$6.95/654-4
A scorching tale of erotic blackmail. Beautiful Celia wants nothing more than to be with her lover, Colin. But Colin is mistakenly considered the prime suspect in a murder, forcing him to seek refuge with his cousin, Sir Jason Hardwicke. In exchange for Colin's safety, Jason demands Celia's unquestioning submission—knowing she will do anything to protect the man she loves. Soon, Celia is indeed doing everything demanded of her, surrendering her inhibitions as a perverse ransom for Colin's safety. Little by little, she becomes the instrument each man uses for the satisfaction of his depraved appetites!

SACHI MIZUNO

SHINJUKU NIGHTS
$6.50/493-3
Using Tokyo's infamous red light district as his backdrop, Sachi Mizuno weaves an intricate web of sensual desire, wherein many characters are ensnared by the demands of their carnal natures.

PASSION IN TOKYO
$6.50/454-2
Tokyo—one of Asia's most historic and seductive cities. Come behind the closed doors of its citizens, and witness the many pleasures that await intrepid explorers. Men and women from every stratum of society free themselves of all inhibitions in this thrilling tour through the libidinous East.

MARTINE GLOWINSKI

POINT OF VIEW
$6.50/433-X
The story of one woman's erotic awakening. After her divorce, a lonely woman decides to expand her sexual horizons. With the assistance of a new, unexpectedly kinky lover, she discovers and explores her exhibitionist tendencies—until there is virtually nothing she won't do before the horny audiences her man arranges. Soon she is infamous for her unabashed sexual performances. An exhibitionist run wild!

AMANDA WARE

BOUND TO THE PAST

$6.50/452-6

Doing research in an old Tudor mansion, beautiful Anne finds herself aroused by James, a descendant of the property's owners. Together they uncover the perverse desires of the mansion's long-dead master—desires that bind Anne inexorably to the past—not to mention the bedpost!

RICHARD McGOWAN

A HARLOT OF VENUS

$6.50/425-9

A highly fanciful, epic tale of lust on Mars! Cavortia—the most famous and sought-after courtesan in the cosmopolitan city of Venus—finds love and much more during her adventures with some cosmic characters. A sexy, sci-fi fairytale, McGowan's interstellar epic is an unforgettable exploration of the outer limits of the sexual imagination.

M. ORLANDO

THE SLEEPING PALACE

$6.95/582-4

Maison Bizarre is the scene of unspeakable erotic cruelty; the *Lust Akademie* holds captive only the most luscious students of the sensual arts; *Baden-Eros* is the luxurious retreat of one's nastiest dreams.

CAROLE REMY

FANTASY IMPROMPTU

$6.50/513-1

Kidnapped to a remote island retreat, Chantal finds herself catering to every sexual whim of the mysterious Bran. Bran is determined to bring Chantal to a full embracing of her sensual nature, even while revealing himself to be something far more than human....

CHARLES G. WOOD

HELLFIRE

$5.95/358-9

A vicious murderer is running amok in New York's sexual underground—and Nick O'Shay, a virile detective with the NYPD, plunges into the case. He soon becomes embroiled in the Big Apple's notorious nightworld of dungeons and sex clubs, hunting a madman seeking to purge America with fire and blood sacrifices.

MARCO VASSI

THE STONED APOCALYPSE

$5.95/401-1/Mass market

"Marco Vassi is our champion sexual energist." —*VLS*

During his lifetime, Marco Vassi's reputation as a champion of sexual experimentation was worldwide. Funded by his groundbreaking erotic writing, *The Stoned Apocalypse* is Vassi's autobiography; chronicling a cross-country trip on America's erotic byways.

THE SALINE SOLUTION

$6.95/568-9/Mass market

"I've always read Marco's work with interest and I have the highest opinion not only of his talent but his intellectual boldness." —Norman Mailer

During the Sexual Revolution, Vassi established himself as an explorer of an uncharted sexual landscape. Through this story of one couple's brief affair and the events that lead them to desperately reassess their lives, Vassi examines the dangers of intimacy in an age of extraordinary freedom.

TINY ALICE

THE GEEK

$5.95/341-4

An offbeat classic of modern erotica, *The Geek* is told from the point of view of, well, a chicken who reports on the various perversities he witnesses as part of a traveling carnival. When a gang of renegade lesbians kidnaps Chicken and his geek, all hell breaks loose. A strange but highly arousing tale, filled with outrageous erotic oddities.

ROBIN WILDE

TABITHA'S TEASE

$6.95/597-2

When poor Robin arrives at The Valentine Academy, he finds himself subject to the torturous teasing of Tabitha—the Academy's most notoriously domineering co-ed. Adding to Robin's delicious suffering is the fact that Tabitha is pledge-mistress of a secret sorority dedicated to enslaving young men. Men suffer deliciously at the hands of Tabitha and her wicked beauties.

ANONYMOUS

LADY F
$6.95/642-1

It is the age of Queen Victoria and the moral price of pleasure is high. Master Kidrodstock—full as he is of wicked and uncontrollable impulses and urges—soon discovers just how high the price is when he encounters Lady F. Stunningly cruel and sensuous, this haughty lady leaves all men gasping—for more!

THE YELLOW ROOM
$6.95/631-6

The "yellow room" holds the secrets of lust, lechery, and the lash. There, demure Alice Darvell soon experiences a variety of extraordinary experiences. Another story follows the perversions of a sadistic heiress and her two lusty ladies.

DANIELLE: Diary of a Slave Girl
$6.95/591-3

At the age of 19, Danielle Appleton vanishes. The frantic efforts of her family notwithstanding, she is never seen by them again. After her disappearance, Danielle finds herself doomed to a life of sexual slavery, obliged to become the ultimate instrument of pleasure to the man—or men—who own her and dictate her every move and desire.

ROMANCE OF LUST
$9.95/604-9

"Truly remarkable...all the pleasure of fine historical fiction combined with the most intimate descriptions of explicit love-making." —*The Times*

One of the most famous erotic novels of the century! This collaborative work of sexual awakening in Victorian England was repeatedly been banned for its "immorality"—and much sought after for its vivid portrayals of sodomy, sexual initiation, and flagellation.

PROTESTS, PLEASURES AND RAPTURES
Invited for an allegedly quiet weekend at a country Vicarage, a young woman is stunned to find herself surrounded by shocking acts of sexual sadism. Soon her curiosity is piqued, and she begins to explore her own capacities for cruelty—leading to an all-out search for an appropriately punishable partner. Latent depravity explodes!204-3/$4.95

SUBURBAN SOULS
$9.95/563-8

Focusing on the May–December sexual relationship of nubile Lillian and the more experienced Jack, all three volumes of *Suburban Souls* now appear in one special edition—guaranteed to enrapture readers with its detail.

THE MISFORTUNES OF COLETTE
$7.95/564-6

The tale of one woman's erotic suffering at the hands of a sadistic man and woman. Beautiful Colette is the victim of an obscene plot guaranteed to keep her in erotic servitude. Passed from one lustful tormentor to another, Colette wonders whether she is destined to find her greatest pleasures in punishment!

TITIAN BERESFORD

CINDERELLA
$6.95/606-5

An exploration of the erotic potential of this famous fairy tale. Castle dungeons and tightly corseted ladies-in-waiting, naughty viscounts and cruel masturbatrixes—nearly every conceivable method of kinky arousal is explored and described in lush, vivid detail. A fetishist's dream and a masochist's delight!

CHIDEWELL HOUSE and Other Stories
$6.95/554-9

What keeps Cecil a virtual, if willing, prisoner of Chidewell House? One man has been sent to investigate the sexy situation—and reports back with tales of such depravity that no expense is spared in attempting Cecil's rescue. But what man would possibly desire release from the breathtakingly corrupt Elizabeth?

JUDITH BOSTON
$6.50/525-5

Edward would have been lucky to get the stodgy companion he thought his parents had hired for him. But an exquisite woman arrives at his door, and Edward finds that his lewd behavior never goes unpunished by the unflinchingly severe Judith Boston!

MARY LOVE

ANGELA
$6.95/545-X

Angela's game is "look but don't touch," and she drives everyone mad with desire, dancing for their pleasure but never allowing a single caress. Soon her sensual spell is cast, and she's the only one who can break it!

MASTERING MARY SUE
$6.95/660-X
Mary Sue is a rich nymphomaniac whose husband is determined to declare her mentally incompetent and gain control of her fortune. He brings her to a castle where, to Mary Sue's delight, she is unleashed for a veritable sex-fest!

LIZBETH DUSSEAU

THE APPLICANT
$6.95/670-7
Hilary answers a personal ad, hoping to find someone who can meet her very special erotic needs. She makes an appointment to meet the couple behind the advertisement, and is thrilled to find them abundantly skilled in sensual domination. Liza is a flawless mistress and, together with her husband, Oliver, she trains Hilary to be the perfect personal servant, tireless in her efforts to meet the demands of her superiors.

TRINKETS
$6.95/668-5
A woman toys with the idea of erotic submission, never thinking her dream might come true. But it does, and Tessa finds herself gleefully subordinate to an eccentric artist's every whim. In no time, the domineering Miles fashions her into the ultimate erotic bauble—to be shown off in public, but fully enjoyed in private....

THE BEST OF LIZBETH DUSSEAU
$6.95/630-8
Dusseau's explorations of male-dominant lust have made her a favorite with fans of contemporary erotica. This volume is full of heroines who are unafraid to put everything on the line in order to experience pleasure at the hands of a virile man...

MEMBER OF THE CLUB
$6.95/608-1
A restless woman yearns to realize her most secret, licentious desires. There is a club that exists for the fulfillment of such fantasies—a club devoted to the pleasures of the flesh, and the gratification of every hunger. When its members call she is compelled to answer—and serve each in an endless quest for satisfaction.... A thrilling tale of the ultimate sex club.

LYN DAVENPORT

THE GUARDIAN II
$6.50/505-0
The tale of submissive Felicia Brookes continues. No sooner has Felicia come to love Rodney than she discovers that she has been sold—and must now accustom herself to the guardianship of the debauched Duke of Smithton. Surely Rodney will rescue her from the domination of this depraved stranger. *Won't he?*

AMARANTHA KNIGHT

The Darker Passions: THE PIT AND THE PENDULUM
$6.95/639-1
Edgar Allen Poe's deadly pit is trans- formed into the site of a thousand unbearable pleasures, a carnal playground frequented by the perverse members of a secret society devoted to sensual experimentation. One young woman, herself blessed with extraordinary talents, is about to discover what has made the Pit of Delights a legend....

The Darker Passions: FRANKENSTEIN
$6.95/617-0
The mistress of erotic horror sets her sights on Mary Shelley's darkest creation. What if you could create a living, breathing human? What shocking acts could it be taught to perform, to desire, to love? Find out what pleasures await those who play God....

The Darker Passions: CARMILLA
$6.95/578-6
Captivated by the portrait of a beautiful woman, a young man finds himself becoming obsessed with her remarkable story. Little by little, he uncovers the many blasphemies and debaucheries with which the beauteous Laura filled her hours—even as an otherworldly presence began feasting upon her....

THE PAUL LITTLE LIBRARY

LUST OF THE COSSACKS
$6.95/664-2
A countess enjoys watching lovely peasant girls submit to her perverse lesbian manias. She tutors her only male lover in the joys of erotic torture and in return he lures an innocent ballerina to the estate, intent on presenting her to the countess as a plaything. A breathtaking tale of innocence lost.

ALIZARIN LAKE

THE INSTRUMENTS OF THE PASSION
$6.95/659-6
All that remains is the diary of a young initiate, detailing the rituals of a mysterious cult institution known only as "Rossiter." Behind sinister walls, a beautiful woman performs an unending drama of desire and submission.

MISS HIGH HEELS
$6.95/632-4
It was a delightful punishment few men dared to dream of. Who could have predicted how far it would go? Forced by his wicked sisters to dress and behave like a proper lady, Dennis Beryl finds he enjoys life as Denise much more! Petticoats and punishments make for a delicious romp!

CLARA
$6.95/548-4
The mysterious death of a beautiful woman leads her old boyfriend on a harrowing journey of discovery. His search uncovers an unimaginably sensuous woman embarked on a quest for deeper and more unusual sensations!

LUSCIDIA WALLACE

THE ICE MAIDEN
$6.95/613-8
Edward Canton has everything he wants in life, with one exception: Rebecca Esterbrook. He whisks her away to his remote island compound, where she learns to shed her inhibitions. Fully aroused for the first time in her life, she becomes a slave to desire!

SARA H. FRENCH

MASTER OF TIMBERLAND
$6.95/595-6
A tale of sexual slavery at the ultimate paradise resort—where sizzling submissives serve their masters without question. Each lucky visitor lives out her fantasy of complete submission to a dominant man. No one leaves Timberland without exploring the furthest reaches of desire. One of our best-selling titles, this trek to Timberland has ignited passions the world over.

JOHN NORMAN

TRIBESMEN OF GOR
$6.95/677-4
"Surrender Gor"—so read the message received by the Priest-Kings. The gauntlet had been thrown: either Gor submits to the Others, or resigns itself to destruction. Tarl Cabot rouses himself to action on behalf of the Priest-Kings and the world they rule. Cabot heads to the great wasteland of the Tahari, fighting his way amongst feuding clans, treacherous slavers, a voluptuous woman warlord, and the ferocious powers from the worlds of steel.

MARAUDERS OF GOR
$6.95/662-6
Tarl Cabot has struggled to free himself from the control of Gor's powerful Priest-Kings, but to no avail. Now he finds that mission challenged by a threat emanating from the planet's forbidding northern lands. There, a menacing alien force waits for Tarl, who faces an awesome choice: protect his own position as a rich merchant-slaver, or risk everything to defend the freedom of his world....

HUNTERS OF GOR
$6.95/592-1
Tarl Cabot ventures into the wilderness of Gor, pitting his skill against brutal outlaws and sly warriors. His life on Gor been complicated by three beautiful, very different women: Talena, Tarl's one-time queen; Elizabeth, his fearless comrade; and Verna, chief of the feral panther women. In this installment of Norman's million-selling sci-fi phenomenon, the fates of these uncommon women are finally revealed....

CAPTIVE OF GOR
$6.95/581-6
On Earth, Elinor Brinton was accustomed to having it all—wealth, beauty, and a host of men wrapped around her little finger. But Elinor is now a pleasure slave of Gor, a world whose society insists on her subservience, and Elinor finds herself succumbing—with pleasure—to her powerful Master....

RAIDERS OF GOR
$6.95/558-1
Tarl Cabot descends into the depths of Port Kar—the most degenerate port city of the Counter-Earth. There Cabot learns the ways of Kar, whose residents are renowned for the grip in which they hold their voluptuous slaves....

THE ENGLISH GOVERNESS
$6.95/622-7
When Lord Lovell's son was expelled from his prep school for masturbation, he hired a very proper governess to tutor the boy—giving her strict instructions not to spare the rod to break him of his bad habits. Upon her arrival in Lord Lovell's home, governess Harriet Marwood reveals herself a force to be reckoned with—particularly by her randy charge. In no time, Master Lovell's onanism is under control—as are all other aspects of his life.

MASQUERADE READERS

THE 50 BEST PLAYGIRL FANTASIES
$7.95/648-0
A steamy selection of women's fantasies straight from the pages of *PLAYGIRL*—the leading magazine of sexy entertainment for women. Contemporary heroines pursue liaisons with horny men from every walk of life in these tales of modern lust.

Rhinoceros

CHRISTA FAUST

CONTROL FREAK
$7.95/633-2
"Christa Faust is a Veronica in a world of Betties."
—Quentin Tarantino

"Takes the reader on an odyssey of the spirit leading to places that most of us have neither the imagination nor the courage to envision." —John Pelan

Caitlin McCullough, an author of cheap detective novels who has a nose for the sensational, is fascinated by the grisly particulars of a brutal murder. As Caitlin's investigation into Eva's wild life and brutal death draws her deeper into the labyrinth of New York's infamous sexual playground, she finds herself perversely attracted to the killing's prime suspect—a notorious SM club owner.

JOHN NORMAN

IMAGINATIVE SEX
$7.95/561-1
The author of the Gor novels outlines his philosophy on relations between the sexes, and presents fifty-three scenarios designed to reintroduce fantasy to the bedroom.

LEOPOLD VON SACHER-MASOCH

VENUS IN FURS
$7.95/589-1
The alliance of Severin and Wanda epitomizes Sacher-Masoch's obsession with a cruel goddess and the urges that drive the man held in her thrall. Exclusive to this edition are letters exchanged between Sacher-Masoch and Emilie Mataja—an aspiring writer he sought as the avatar of his desires.

M. CHRISTIAN, ED.

A MIDSUMMER NIGHT'S DREAM: Many Tales From One Story
$7.95/679-0
"This is a book about—and yet not about—William Shakespeare's play, *A Midsummer Night's Dream*. It is...a book of expositions on the intertwining love lives of a dozen or so beings, some of this earth, others not—all creations of the Bard, all living in one of his most imaginative works. An anthology of erotic interpretations on the play, on Theseus and Hippolyta, Hermia and Lysander, Demetrius and Helena, Oberon and Titania, Bottom and, not least of which, Puck—this is a place where remarkable writers have taken these wonderful characters and pushed them out, beyond their familiarity in *A Midsummer Night's Dream*." —from the Introduction

EROS EX MACHINA: Eroticizing the Mechanical
$7.95/593-X
As the millennium approaches, technology is not only an inevitable, but a desirable addition to daily life. *Eros Ex Machina* explores the thrill and danger of machines—our literal and literary love of technology. Join over 25 of today's hottest writers as they explore erotic relationships with all kinds of gadgets, and devices.

THOMAS S. ROCHE

NOIROTICA: An Anthology of Erotic Crime Stories (Ed.)
$6.95/390-2
A collection of darkly sexy tales, taking place at the crossroads of the crime and erotic genres. Here are some of today's finest writers, all of whom explore the extraordinary and arousing terrain where desire runs irrevocably afoul of the law. A groundbreaking collection of contemporary erotica.

MASQUERADE BOOKS

NOIROTICA 2: Pulp Friction (Ed.)
$7.95/584-0
Another volume of criminally seductive stories set in the murky terrain of the erotic and noir genres. Thomas Roche has gathered the darkest jewels from today's edgiest writers to create this provocative collection.

DARK MATTER
$6.95/484-4
"*Dark Matter* is sure to please gender outlaws, bodymod junkies, goth vampires, boys who wish they were dykes, and anybody who's not to sure where the fine line should be drawn between pleasure and pain. It's a handful." —Pat Califia

"Here is the erotica of the cumming millennium.... You will be deliciously disturbed, but never disappointed."
—Poppy Z. Brite

DAVID MELTZER

UNDER
$6.95/290-6
The story of a 21st century sex professional living at the bottom of the social heap. After surgeries designed to increase his physical allure, corrupt government forces drive the cyber-gigolo underground, where even more bizarre cultures await....

ORF
$6.95/110-1
He is the ultimate musician-hero—the idol of thousands, the fevered dream of many more. And like many musicians before him, he is misunderstood, misused—and totally out of control. From agony to lust, every last drop of feeling is squeezed from a modern-day troubadour and his lady love in their relentless descent into hell. Long out of print, Meltzer's frank, poetic look at the dark side of the sixties returns.

KATHLEEN K.

SWEET TALKERS
$6.95/516-6
"If you enjoy eavesdropping on explicit conversations about sex... this book is for you." —*Spectator*

A explicit look at the burgeoning phenomenon of phone sex. Kathleen K. ran a phone-sex company in the late 80s, and she opens up her diary for a peek at the life of a phone-sex operator. Transcripts of actual conversations are included.
Trade /$12.95/192-6

LAURA ANTONIOU, ED.

SOME WOMEN
$7.95/573-5
Introduction by Pat Califia
"Makes the reader think about the wide range of SM experiences, beyond the glamour of fiction and fantasy, or the clever-clever prose of the perverati." —*SKIN TWO*

Over forty essays written by women actively involved in consensual dominance and submission. Professional mistresses, lifestyle leatherdykes, whipmakers, titleholders—women from every conceivable walk of life lay bare their true feelings about issues as explosive as feminism, abuse, pleasure and public image.

NO OTHER TRIBUTE: Erotic Tales of Women in Submission
$7.95/603-0
A volume sure to challenge Political Correctness in a way that few others have. Tales of women kept in bondage to their lovers by their deepest passions. Love pushes these women beyond acceptable limits, rendering them helpless to deny anything to the men and women they adore.

BY HER SUBDUED: Erotic Tales of Women's Power
$6.95/281-7
These tales all involve women in control—of their lives and their lovers. So much in control that they can remorselessly break rules to become powerful goddesses of those who sacrifice all to worship at their feet.

ROMY ROSEN

SPUNK
$6.95/492-5
Casey, a lovely model poised upon the verge of super-celebrity, falls for an insatiable young rock singer—not suspecting that his sexual appetite has led him to experiment with a dangerous new aphrodisiac. Soon, Casey becomes addicted to the drug, and her craving plunges her into a strange underworld.... A knowing tour through the world of the hip and beautiful.

BUY ANY 4 BOOKS & CHOOSE 1 ADDITIONAL BOOK, OF EQUAL OR LESSER VALUE, AS YOUR FREE GIFT

MOLLY WEATHERFIELD

SAFE WORD: CARRIE'S STORY II
$7.95/665-0

The sequel to Molly Weatherfield's best-selling look at contemporary dominance and submission, *Carrie's Story*. Carrie leaves behind her life with Jonathan, intent on proving herself with the demanding gentleman who has chosen her as his own. Whisked away to Greece, Carrie learns new, more rigorous methods of sexual satisfaction. When her year of training is complete, Carrie faces a decision—life on her own, or in the embrace of her beloved but estranged Jonathan....

CARRIE'S STORY
$7.95/652-9

"I was stunned by how well it was written and how intensely foreign I found its sexual world.... And, since this is a world I don't frequent... I thoroughly enjoyed the National Geo tour." —*bOING bOING*

"Hilarious and harrowing... just when you think things can't get any wilder, they do." —*Black Sheets*

Weatherfield's bestselling examination of dominance and submission. "I had been Jonathan's slave for about a year when he told me he wanted to sell me at an auction...." A rare piece of erotica, both thoughtful and hot!

GARY BOWEN

DIARY OF A VAMPIRE
$6.95/331-7

"Gifted with a darkly sensual vision and a fresh voice, [Bowen] is a writer to watch out for." —Cecilia Tan

Rafael, a red-blooded male with an insatiable hunger for the same, is the perfect antidote to the effete malcontents haunting bookstores today. The emergence of a bold and brilliant vision, rooted in past and present.

AMELIA G, ED.

BACKSTAGE PASSES: Rock 'n' Roll Erotica from the Pages of *Blue Blood* Magazine
$6.95/438-0

Amelia G, editor of the goth-sex journal *Blue Blood*, has brought together some of today's most irreverent writers, each of whom has outdone themselves with an edgy, antic tale of modern lust.

CYBERSEX CONSORTIUM

CYBERSEX: The Perv's Guide to Finding Sex on the Internet
$6.95/471-2

You've heard the objections: cyberspace is soaked with sex, mired in immorality. Okay—so where is it!? Tracking down the good stuff—the real good stuff—can waste an awful lot of expensive time, and frequently leave you high and dry. An easy-to-use guide for those intrepid adults who know what they want.

GERI NETTICK WITH BETH ELLIOT

MIRRORS: Portrait of a Lesbian Transsexual
$6.95/435-6

Born a male, Geri Nettick knew something just didn't fit. Even after coming to terms with her own gender dysphoria, and taking steps to correct it, she still fought to be accepted by the lesbian feminist community to which she felt she belonged. An inspiring true story of self-discover and acceptance.

LAURA ANTONIOU ("Sara Adamson")

"Ms. Adamson creates a wonderfully diverse world of lesbian, gay, straight, bi and transgendered characters, all mixing delightfully in the melting pot of sadomasochism and planting the genre more firmly in the culture at large. I for one am cheering her on!" —Kate Bornstein

THE MARKETPLACE
$7.95/602-2

The first title in Antoniou's thrilling Marketplace Trilogy, following the lives an lusts of those who have been deemed worthy to participate in the Marketplace—the ultimate BD/SM arena.

THE SLAVE
$7.95/601-4

The Slave covers the experience of one submissive who longs to join the ranks of those who have proven themselves worthy of entry into the Marketplace. But the price of admission, while delicious, is staggeringly high....

THE TRAINER
$6.95/249-3

The Marketplace Trilogy concludes with the story of the trainers, and the desires and paths that led them to become the ultimate figures of authority.

THE CATALYST

$6.95/621-9

Different from a lot of SM smut in that it depicts actual consensual SM scenes between just plain folks rather than wild impossible fantasies, *The Catalyst* is both sweet-natured and nastily perverse. —*Blowfish*

After viewing an explicitly kinky film full of images of bondage and submission, several audience members find themselves deeply moved by the erotic suggestions they've seen on the screen. A modern BD/SM classic, and this popular author's debut.

JOHN WARREN

THE TORQUEMADA KILLER

$6.95/367-8

Detective Eva Hernandez gets her first "big case": a string of murders taking place within New York's SM community. Eva assembles the evidence, revealing a picture of a world misunderstood and under attack—and gradually comes to face her own hidden longings. An edge-of-the-seat thriller from this popular fetish author.

THE LOVING DOMINANT

$7.95/600-6

Everything you need to know about an infamous sexual variation, and an unspoken type of love. Warren, a scene veteran, guides readers through this rarely seen world, and offers clear-eyed advice guaranteed to enlighten the novice and seasoned erotic explorer alike. A best-selling erotic manual.

TAMMY JO ECKHART

AMAZONS: Erotic Explorations of Ancient Myths

$7.95/534-4

The Amazon—the fierce woman warrior—appears in the traditions of many cultures, but never before has the erotic potential of this archetype been explored with such energy and imagination. Powerful pleasures await anyone lucky enough to encounter Eckhart's legendary spitfires.

PUNISHMENT FOR THE CRIME

$6.95/427-5

Stories that explore dominance and submission. From an encounter between two of society's most despised individuals, to the explorations of longtime friends, these tales take you where few others have ever dared....

T. TAORMINO & D. A. CLARK, EDS.

RITUAL SEX

$6.95/391-0

These writers understand that body and soul share more common ground than society feels comfortable acknowledging. From memoirs of ecstatic revelation, to quests to reconcile sex and spirit, *Ritual Sex* provides an unprecedented look at private ritual.

AMARANTHA KNIGHT, ED.

DEMON SEX

$7.95/594-8

Examining the dark forces of humankind's oldest stories, the contributors to *Demon Sex* reveal the strange symbiosis of dread and desire. Stories include a streetwalker's deal with the devil; a visit with the stripper from Hell; the secrets behind an aging rocker's timeless appeal; and many more.

SEDUCTIVE SPECTRES

$6.95/464-X

Tours through the erotic supernatural via the imaginations of today's best writers. Never have ghostly encounters been so alluring, thanks to otherworldly characters well-acquainted with the pleasures of the flesh.

SEX MACABRE

$6.95/392-9

Horror tales designed for dark and sexy nights—sure to make your skin crawl, and heart beat faster. A cast of stellar talents makes this a compelling volume, and an important title in the emerging genre of erotic horror.

FLESH FANTASTIC

$6.95/352-X

Humans have long toyed with the idea of "playing God": creating life from nothingness, bringing life to the inanimate. Now Amarantha Knight collects stories exploring not only the act of Creation, but the lust that follows.

JEAN STINE

THRILL CITY

$6.95/411-9

Thrill City is the seat of the world's increasing depravity, and this classic novel transports you there with a vivid style you'd be hard pressed to ignore. Raging passions bring together lonely, depserate souls in this vision of contemporary Babylon.

GRANT ANTREWS

LEGACIES
$7.95/605-7
Kathi Lawton discovers that she has inherited the troubling secret of her late mother's scandalous sexuality. In an effort to understand what motivated her mother's desires, Kathi embarks on an exploration of SM that leads her into the arms of Horace Moore, a mysterious man who seems to see into her very soul. As she begins falling for her new master, Kathi finds herself wondering just how far she'll go to prove her love—until finally proving herself in ways she had never imagined.

SUBMISSIONS
$7.95/618-9
Suddenly finding himself a millionaire, Kevin Donovan thinks his worries are over—until his restless soul tires of the high life. He turns to the icy Maitresse Genevieve, hoping that her ministrations will guide him to some deeper peace....

ROGUES GALLERY
$6.95/522-0
A stirring evocation of dominant/submissive love. Two doctors meet and slowly fall in love. Once lovely Beth reveals her hidden, kinky desires to Jim, the two explore the forbidden acts that will come to define their affair.

MY DARLING DOMINATRIX
$7.95/566-2
When a man and a woman fall in love, it's supposed to be simple, uncomplicated, easy —unless that woman happens to be a dominatrix. One couple exlores the outer limits and inner depths of desire in this unpretentious love story that captures the richness of this special kind of love without leering or smirking.

TUPPY OWENS

SENSATIONS
$6.95/3081-4
Tuppy Owens takes a rare peek behind the scenes of *Sensations*—the first big-budget sex flick. Originally commissioned to appear in book form after the release of the film in 1975, *Sensations* is finally available to fans of modern erotica.

PHILIP JOSÉ FARMER

A FEAST UNKNOWN
$6.95/276-0
"Sprawling, brawling, shocking, suspenseful, hilarious..."
—Theodore Sturgeon

Lord Grandrith—armed with the belief that he is the son of Jack the Ripper—tells the story of his remarkable life. His story progresses to encompass the furthest extremes of human behavior.

FLESH
$6.95/303-1
Commander Stagg explored the galaxies for 800 years. Upon his return, the hero Stagg is made the centerpiece of an incredible public ritual—one that will take him to the heights of ecstasy, and drag him toward the depths of hell.

ALICE JOANOU

THE BEST OF ALICE JOANOU
$7.95/623-5
"Outstanding erotic fiction." —*Susie Bright*

The best from this major name in the renaissance of American erotica. This volume includes excerpts from *Cannibal Flower*, *Tourniquet* and *Black Tongue*—the titles that announced her talent to the world.

BLACK TONGUE
$6.95/258-2
"Joanou has created a series of sumptuous, brooding, dark visions of sexual obsession, and is undoubtedly a name to look out for in the future." —*Redeemer*

Exploring lust at its most florid and unsparing, *Black Tongue* is redolent of forbidden passions.

SOPHIE GALLEYMORE BIRD

MANEATER
$6.95/103-9
Through a bizarre act of creation, a man attains the "perfect" lover—by all appearances a beautiful, sensuous woman, but in reality something far darker. Once brought to life she will accept no mate, seeking instead the prey that will sate her hunger.

MICHAEL PERKINS

THE SECRET RECORD: Modern Erotic Literature
$6.95/3039-3
Michael Perkins surveys the field with authority and unique insight. Updated and revised to include the latest trends, tastes, and developments in this misunderstood genre.

AN ANTHOLOGY OF CLASSIC ANONYMOUS EROTIC WRITING
$6.95/140-3
The best passages from the world's erotic writing. "Anonymous" is one of the most infamous bylines in publishing history—and these excerpts show why!

SAMUEL R. DELANY

THE MAD MAN
$8.99/408-9/Mass market
"Delany develops an insightful dichotomy between [his protagonist]'s two worlds: the one of cerebral philosophy and dry academia, the other of heedless, 'impersonal' obsessive sexual extremism. When these worlds finally collide...the novel achieves a surprisingly satisfying resolution...."
—*Publishers Weekly*

Graduate student John Marr researches the life of Timothy Hasler: a philosopher whose career was cut tragically short over a decade earlier. Marr begins to find himself increasingly drawn toward shocking sexual encounters with the homeless men, until it begins to seem that Hasler's death might hold some key to his own life as a gay man in the age of AIDS. Surely this legendary writer's most mind-blowing and explicit novel.

LIESEL KULIG

LOVE IN WARTIME
$6.95/3044-X
Madeleine knew that the handsome SS officer was dangerous, but she was just a cabaret singer in Nazi-occupied Paris, trying to survive in a perilous time. When Josef fell in love with her, he discovered that a beautiful woman can be as dangerous as any warrior.

Badboy

MICHAEL BRONSKI, ED.

FLASHPOINT: Gay Male Sexual Writing
$7.95/687-1
Michael Bronski has astutely selected twenty-four stories which explore the diversity of gay male sexuality. The stories are well-written, and in most cases, even excellently so.... Savor this worthy assortment of gay male sexual writing. And believe you me, you will desire repeated visits to Michael Bronski's excellent collection.
—*Lambda Book Report*

Today's hottest volume collection of contemporary gay erotica. Cultural critic Michael Bronski presents work from more than twenty of the genre's best writers, exploring areas such as enlightenment, violence, true life adventures, trans- formations and more.

DAVID MAY

MADRUGADA
$6.95/574-3
Set in San Francisco's gay leather community, *Madrugada* follows the lives of a group of friends—and their many acquaintances—as they tangle with the thorny issues of love and lust. Uncompromising, mysterious, and arousing, David May weaves a complex web of relationships in this unique story cycle.

PETER HEISTER

ISLANDS OF DESIRE
$6.95/480-1
Red-blooded lust on the wine-dark seas of classical Greece. Anacraeon yearns to leave his small, isolated island and find adventure in one of the overseas kingdoms. Accompanied by some randy friends, Anacraeon makes his dream come true—and discovers pleasures he never dreamed of!

KITTY TSUI ("Eric Norton")

SPARKS FLY
$6.95/551-4
A chronicle of modern gay life, set in America's most famous gay neighborhood. Tsui chronicles the highest highs—and most wretched depths—of life as Eric Norton, a beautiful wanton living San Francisco's high life. *Sparks Fly* traces Norton's rise, fall, and resurrection, vividly marking the way with the personal affairs that give life meaning.

MICHAEL FORD, ED.

BUTCHBOYS:
Stories For Men Who Need It Bad
$6.50/523-9
A big volume of tales dedicated to the rough-and-tumble type who can make a man weak at the knees. Some of today's best erotic writers explore the many possible variations on the age-old fantasy of the dominant male.

JOHN PRESTON

MR. BENSON
With a new introduction by Michael Bronski
$6.95/637-5
"Something in the character of Jamie and Aristotle Benson struck a nerve in adventuresome gay America that has simply never been duplicated.... This seminal work of American SM literature is now back in print in its unexpurgated entirety to be savored as both a piece of history and a damn good read."
—*Inches*

A classic erotic novel from a time when there was no limit to what a man could dream of doing.

HUSTLING: A Gentleman's Guide to the Fine Art of Homosexual Prostitution
$6.50/517-4
"Fun and highly literary. What more could you expect form such an accomplished activist, author and editor?" —*Drummer*

John Preston solicited the advice and opinions of "working boys" from across the country in his effort to produce the ultimate guide to the hustler's world.
Trade $12.95/137-3

THE ARENA
$4.95/3083-0
Preston's take on the ultimate sex club–where men go to abolish all personal limits. One young man is introduced to the pleasures that await members of the Arena—and soon establishes himself as one of the club's most dedicated members. Only the author of *Mr. Benson* could have imagined so perfect an institution for the satisfaction of male desire.

TALES FROM THE DARK LORD
$5.95/323-6
Twelve stunning works from the man *Lambda Book Report* called "the Dark Lord of gay erotica." The ritual of lust and surrender is explored in all its manifestations in this heart-stopping triumph of authority and vision.

TALES FROM THE DARK LORD II
$4.95/176-4

THE HEIR•THE KING
$4.95/3048-2
Two legendary novellas in one volume. *The Heir*, written in the lyric voice of the ancient myths, tells the story of a world where slaves and masters create a new sexual society. *The King* tells the story of a soldier who discovers his monarch's most secret desires.

The Mission of Alex Kane

DEADLY LIES
$4.95/3076-8
Politics is a dirty business and the dirt becomes deadly when a smear campaign targets gay men. Who better to clean things up than Alex Kane!

STOLEN MOMENTS
$4.95/3098-9
Houston's evolving gay community is victimized by a malicious newspaper editor who is more than willing to boost circulation by printing homophobic slander. He never counted on Alex Kane, fearless defender of gay dreams and desires.

SECRET DANGER
$4.95/111-X
Alex Kane and the faithful Danny are called to a small European country, where a group of gay tourists is being held hostage by brutal terrorists.

LETHAL SILENCE
$4.95/125-X
Chicago becomes the scene of the right-wing's most homophobic plan— facilitated by unholy political alliances. Alex and Danny head to the Windy City to battle the mercenaries who would squash gay men underfoot.

WILLIAM J. MANN, ED.

GRAVE PASSIONS:
Gay Tales of the Supernatural
$6.50/405-4
A collection of the most chilling tales of passion currently being penned by today's most provocative gay writers. Unnatural transformations, otherworldly encounters, and deathless desires make for a collection sure to keep readers up late at night.

WWW.MASQUERADEBOOKS.COM

MATT TOWNSEND

SOLIDLY BUILT
$6.50/416-X
The tale of the relationship between Jeff, a young photographer, and Mark, the butch electrician hired to wire Jeff's new home. For Jeff, it's love at first sight; Mark, however, has more than a few hang-ups. But lust saves the day, as both studs obey their deep desires....

JAY SHAFFER

ANIMAL HANDLERS
$4.95/264-7
In Shaffer's world, every man finally succumbs to the animal urges deep inside. And if there's any creature that promises a wild time, it's a beast who's been caged for far too long.

FULL SERVICE
$4.95/150-0
Shaffer is one of today's best chroniclers of masculine passion. No-nonsense guys bear down hard on each other as they work their way toward release in this fine assortment of fantasies.

BARRY ALEXANDER

ALL THE RIGHT PLACES
$6.95/482-8
Stunningly sexy stories filled with hot studs in lust and love. From modern masters and slaves to medieval royals and their subjects, Alexander explores the mating rituals men have engaged in for centuries—all in the name of desire...

J. A. GUERRA, ED.

COME QUICKLY: For Boys on the Go
$6.50/413-5
Here are over sixty of the hottest fantasies around—all designed to get you going in less time than it takes to dial 976. J. A. Guerra has put together this volume especially for you—a busy man on a modern schedule, who still appreciates a little old-fashioned action.

SCOTT O'HARA

DO-IT-YOURSELF PISTON POLISHING
$6.50/489-5
Sex-pro Scott O'Hara drew upon his powers of seduction to lure you into a world of hard, horny men long overdue for a tune-up.

D. V. SADERO

IN THE ALLEY
$4.95/144-6
A breathtaking collection of stories from this popular writer. Hardworking men bring their special skills and impressive tools to the most satisfying job of all: capturing and breaking the male animal.

SUTTER POWELL

EXECUTIVE PRIVILEGES
$6.50/383-X
No matter how serious or sexy a predicament his characters find themselves in, Powell conveys the sheer exuberance of their encounters with a warm humor rarely seen in contemporary gay erotica.

GARY BOWEN

WESTERN TRAILS
$6.50/477-1
Gay lit's brightest stars tell the sexy truth about the many ways a stud found to satisfy himself—and his buddy—in the Wild West.

MAN HUNGRY
$5.95/374-0
A riveting collection of stories from one of gay erotica's new stars. Dipping into a variety of genres, Bowen crafts tales of lust unlike anything being published today.

ROBERT BAHR

SEX SHOW
$4.95/225-6
Luscious dancing boys. Brazen, explicit acts. Take a seat, and get very comfortable, because the curtain's going up on a very special show no discriminating appetite can afford to miss.

KYLE STONE

THE HIDDEN SLAVE
$6.95/580-8
"This perceptive and finely-crafted work is a joy to discover. Kyle Stone's fiction belongs on the shelf of every serious fan of gay literature."
—Pat Califia

A young man searches for the perfect master. An electrifying tale of erotic discovery.

BUY ANY 4 BOOKS & CHOOSE 1 ADDITIONAL BOOK, OF EQUAL OR LESSER VALUE, AS YOUR FREE GIFT

HOT BAUDS 2
$6.50/479-8
Stone conducted another heated search through the world's randiest gay bulletin boards, resulting in one of the most scalding follow-ups ever published.

HOT BAUDS
$5.95/285-X
Stone combed cyberspace for the hottest fantasies of the world's horniest hackers. A collection of sexy, shameless, and eminently user-friendly tales.

FIRE & ICE
$5.95/297-3
A collection of stories from the author of the adventures of PB 500. Stone's characters always promise one thing: enough hot action to burn away your desire for anyone else....

FANTASY BOARD
$4.95/212-4
Explore the future—through the intertwined lives of a collection of randy computer hackers. On the Lambda Gate BBS, every horny male is in search of virtual satisfaction!

THE CITADEL
$4.95/198-5
The sequel to *PB 500*. Micah faces new challenges after entering the Citadel. Only his master knows what awaits....

THE INITIATION OF PB 500
$4.95/141-1
An interstellar traveller crash lands on a strange planet—where he is held and trained as the sexual slave of a powerful warrior.

RITUALS
$4.95/168-3
Via a computer bulletin board, a young man finds himself drawn into sexual rites that transform him into the willing slave of a mysterious stranger. His former life is thrown off, and he learns to live for his Master's touch....

JASON FURY

THE ROPE ABOVE, THE BED BELOW
$4.95/269-8
A vicious murderer is preying upon New York's go-go boys. In order to solve this mystery and save lives, each studly suspect must lay bare his soul—and more!

ERIC'S BODY
$4.95/151-9
Follow the irresistible Jason through sexual adventures unlike any you have ever read—touching on the raunchy, the romantic, and a number of highly sensitive areas in between....

LARS EIGHNER

WANK: THE TAPES
$6.95/588-3
Eighner gets back to basics with this look at every guy's favorite pastime. Studs bare it all and work up a healthy sweat during these provocative discussions about masturbation.

WHISPERED IN THE DARK
$5.95/286-8
A volume demonstrating Eighner's unique combination of strengths: poetic descriptive power, an unfailing ear for dialogue, and a finely tuned feeling for the nuances of male passion.

AMERICAN PRELUDE
$4.95/170-5
Eighner is one of gay erotica's true masters, producing wonderfully written tales of all-American lust, peopled with red-blooded, oversexed studs. This volume is one of his best, exploring the many manifestations of gay lust.

TOM BACCHUS

RAHM
$5.95/315-5
Tom Bacchus brings to life an extraordinary assortment of characters, from the Father of Us All to the cowpoke next door, the early gay literati to rude, queercore mosh rats.

BONE
$4.95/177-2
Queer musings from the pen of one of today's hottest young talents. Tom Bacchus maps out the tricking ground of a new generation.

DAVID LAURENTS, ED.

SOUTHERN COMFORT

$6.50/466-6

A collection of tales focusing on the American South—stories reflecting not only the Southern literary tradition, but the many sexy contributions the region has made to the iconography of the American Male. New voices and old favorites examine the myths of the region in this scintillating volume.

WANDERLUST: Homoerotic Tales of Travel

$5.95/395-3

A volume dedicated to the special pleasures of faraway places. Celebrate the freedom of the open road, and the allure of men who stray from the beaten path....

THE BADBOY BOOK OF EROTIC POETRY

$5.95/382-1

Erotic poetry has long been the problem child of the literary world—highly creative and provocative, but somehow too frank to be considered "art." *The Badboy Book of Erotic Poetry* restores eros to its place of honor in gay writing.

AARON TRAVIS

SLAVES OF THE EMPIRE

$6.95/646-4

"Aaron Travis' epic of gladiator sex, slavery and sadism is not good porn—it's great. Not only is the story told well, but it is populated by real people who are at once pornographic archetypes and complex models of psychology. Caught between the real and the fantastic, Travis has given us the best of both worlds." —Michael Bronski

"*Slaves of the Empire* has more sexual excitement than any novel of Roman times I have ever read. It is Aaron Travis' masterpiece." —*Drummer*

BIG SHOTS

$5.95/448-8

Two fierce tales in one electrifying volume. In *Beirut,* Travis tells the story of ultimate military power and erotic subjugation; *Kip,* Travis' hypersexed and sinister take on *film noir,* appears in unexpurgated form for the first time. Together, these stories make this Travis's most overwhelming volume.

EXPOSED

$4.95/126-8

Cops, college jocks, ancient Romans—even Sherlock Holmes and his loyal Watson—cruise these pages, fresh from the pen of one of our hottest authors.

IN THE BLOOD

$5.95/283-3

Early tales from this master of the genre. Includes "In the Blood"—a heart-pounding descent into sexual vampirism.

THE FLESH FABLES

$4.95/243-4

One of Travis' best collections. Includes "Blue Light," as well as other stories that established him as one of gay erotica's masters.

KEY LINCOLN

SUBMISSION HOLDS

$4.95/266-3

From tough to tender, the men between these covers stop at nothing to get what they want. A collection of originality and scalding sensuality.

JR

FRENCH QUARTER NIGHTS

$5.95/337-6

Sensual snapshots of the many places where men get down and dirty—from the steamy French Quarter to the steam room at the old Everard baths.

CLAY CALDWELL

SOME LIKE IT ROUGH

$6.95/544-1

Here are the best of Caldwell's darkest tales—filled with enough virile masters and slaves to satisfy the the most demanding reader.

JOCK STUDS

$6.95/472-0

Swimmers, football players—whatever your sport might be, there's a man here waiting to peel off his uniform, and claim his reward for a game well-played....

ASK OL' BUDDY

$5.95/346-5

Set in the underground SM world—where men initiate one another into the secrets of the rawest sexual realm of all. And when each stud's initiation is complete, he takes part in the training of another hungry soul....

STUD SHORTS
$5.95/320-1
"If anything, Caldwell's charm is more powerful, his nostalgia more poignant, the horniness he captures more sweetly, achingly acute than ever." —Aaron Travis

A new collection of this legend's latest sex-fiction. Caldwell tells all about cops, cadets, truckers, farmboys (and many more) in these dirty jewels.

TAILPIPE TRUCKER
$5.95/296-5
Trucker porn! Caldwell tells the truth about Trag and Curly—two men hot for the feeling of sweaty manflesh. Together, they pick up—and turn out—a couple of thrill-seeking punks.

SERVICE, STUD
$5.95/336-8
Another look at the gay future. The setting is the Los Angeles of a distant future. Here the all-male populace is divided between the served and the servants—guaranteeing the erotic satisfaction of all involved.

QUEERS LIKE US
$4.95/262-0
For years the name Clay Caldwell has been synonymous with the hottest, most finely crafted gay tales available. *Queers Like Us* is one of his best: the story of a randy mailman's trek through a landscape of available studs.

CALDWELL/EIGHNER

QSFX2
$5.95/278-7
Other-worldly yarns from two master storytellers—Clay Caldwell and Lars Eighner. Both eroticists take a trip to the furthest reaches of the sexual imagination, sending back ten scalding sci-fi stories of male desire.

CALDWELL & AARON TRAVIS

TAG TEAM STUDS
$6.50/465-8
Two legendary talents team up for a volume of high impact erotica. Wrestling will never seem the same, once you've made your way through this assortment of sweaty studs. But you'd better be wary—should one catch you off guard, you might spend the night pinned to the mat....

BOB VICKERY

SKIN DEEP
$4.95/265-5
So many varied beauties no one will go away unsatisfied. No tantalizing morsel of manflesh is overlooked—or left unexplored!

LARRY TOWNSEND

LEATHER AD: M
$5.95/380-5
John's curious about what goes on between the leatherclad men he's fantasized about. He takes out a personal ad, and starts a journey of discovery that will change his life.

LEATHER AD: S
$5.95/407-0
The tale continues—this time told from a Top's perspective. A simple ad generates many responses, and one man puts these studs through their paces....

BEWARE THE GOD WHO SMILES
$5.95/321-X
A mindblowing trip through the gay past, via this author's notoriously twisted imagination. Two lusty young Americans are transported to ancient Egypt—where they are embroiled in warfare and taken as slaves by barbarians. The two finally discover that the key to escape lies within their own rampant libidos.

THE CONSTRUCTION WORKER
$5.95/298-1
A young, hung construction worker is sent to a building project in Central America, where he is shocked to find some ancient and unusual traditions in practice. Of special interest are the sexual ways of the men he encounters—all of whom believe man-to-man sex to be the only acceptable norm! The young stud quickly fits right in (and quite snugly)—until he begins to suspect that an almost supernatural force moves beneath the constant sexual shenanigans.

MIND MASTER
$4.95/209-4
Who better to explore the territory of erotic dominance than an author who helped define the genre. One gifted man exploits his ability to control others.

THE LONG LEATHER CORD
$4.95/201-9
Chuck's stepfather never lacks money or male visitors with whom he enacts intense sexual rituals. As Chuck comes to terms with his own desires, he begins to unravel the mystery behind his stepfather's secret life.

THE SCORPIUS EQUATION
$4.95/119-5
The story of a man caught between the demands of two galactic empires. Our randy hero must match wits—and more—with the incredible forces that rule his world.

MAN SWORD
$4.95/188-8
The *trés gai* tale of France's King Henri III, who encounters enough sexual schemers and politicos to alter one's picture of history forever! Witness the unbridled licentiousness of one of Europe's most notorious courts.

THE FAUSTUS CONTRACT
$4.95/167-5
Another thrilling tale of leather lust. Two cocky young hustlers get more than they bargained for in this story of lust and its discontents.

CHAINS
$4.95/158-6
Picking up street punks has always been risky, but here it sets off a string of events that must be read to be believed. The legendary Townsend at his grittiest.

RUN NO MORE
$4.95/152-7
The sequel to *Run, Little Leather Boy.* This volume follows the further adventures of Townsend's leatherclad narrator as he travels every sexual byway available to the S/M male. Soon, Wayne's experiencing more than even he had dreamed possible....

THE GAY ADV. OF CAPTAIN GOOSE
$4.95/169-1
A rollicking tale of gay lust on the high seas. Handsome Jerome Gander is sentenced to serve aboard a ship manned by the most hardened criminals. In no time, Gander becomes one of the most notorious rakehells Olde England had ever seen. On land or sea, Gander hunts down the Empire's hottest studs.

DONALD VINING

CABIN FEVER AND OTHER STORIES
$5.95/338-4
"Demonstrates the wisdom experience combined with insight and optimism can create." —*Bay Area Reporter*

Eighteen blistering stories in celebration of the most intimate of male bonding, reaffirming the importance of both love and lust in modern gay life.

DEREK ADAMS

THE MARK OF THE WOLF
$5.95/361-9
The past comes back to haunt one well-off stud, whose desires lead him into the arms of many men—and the midst of a mystery.

MY DOUBLE LIFE
$5.95/314-7
Every man leads a double life, dividing his hours between the mundanities of the day and the pursuits of the night. Derek Adams shines a little light on the wicked things men do when no one's looking.

HEAT WAVE
$4.95/159-4
Derek Adams sexy short stories are guaranteed to jump start any libido—and *Heatwave* contains his very best.

MILES DIAMOND & THE CASE OF THE CRETAN APOLLO
$6.95/381-3
The further adventures of this popular private dick. Hired to track a cheating lover, Miles finds himself involved in a highly unprofessional capacity! When the jealous Callahan threatens not only Diamond but his studly assistant, Miles counters with a little undercover work—involving as many horny informants as he can get his hands on!

MILES DIAMOND & THE DEMON OF DEATH
$4.95/251-5
The return of the intrepid Miles Diamond. Miles always find himself in the stickiest situations—with any stud he meets! This adventure promises another carnal carnival, as Diamond investigates a host of horny guys—each of whom hides a secret Miles is only too willing to expose!

THE ADV. OF MILES DIAMOND
$4.95/118-7
The debut of this popular gay gumshoe. To Diamond's delight, "The Case of the Missing Twin" is packed with randy studs. Miles sets about uncovering all as he tracks down the delectable Daniel Travis.

KELVIN BELIELE

IF THE SHOE FITS
$4.95/223-X
An essential volume of tales exploring a world where randy boys can't help but do what comes naturally—as often as possible! Sweaty male bodies grapple in pleasure.

JAMES MEDLEY

THE REVOLUTIONARY and Other Stories
$6.50/417-8
Billy, the son of the station chief of the American Embassy in Guatemala, is kidnapped and held for ransom. Billy gradually develops a close relationship with Juan, the revolutionary assigned to guard him—and soon, lust complicates an already explosive situation.

HUCK AND BILLY
$4.95/245-0
Young lust knows no bounds—and is often the hottest of one's life! Huck and Billy explore the desires that course through their bodies, determined to plumb the depths of passion. A thrilling look at desire between men.

FLEDERMAUS

FLEDERFICTION: Stories of Men and Torture
$5.95/355-4
Fifteen blistering paeans to men and their suffering. Unafraid of exploring the furthest reaches of pain and pleasure, Fledermaus unleashes his most thrilling tales in this volume.

VICTOR TERRY

TYING KNOTS
$6.95/636-7
From an encounter with a lusty German who begs a position of service on the farm of a horny American couple, to a gay leather couple who test the limits of their love and lust in an effort to secure a hefty inheritance, these stories are among the very best and hottest of this veteran eroticist's career.

MASTERS
$6.50/418-6
Terry's butchest tales. A powerhouse volume of boot-wearing, whip-wielding, bone-crunching bruisers who've got what it takes to make a grown man grovel.

SM/SD
$6.50/406-2
Set around a South Dakota town called Prairie, these tales offer evidence that the real rough stuff can still be found where men take what they want despite all rules.

WHIPS
$4.95/254-X
Cruising for a hot man? You'd better be, because these WHiPs—officers of the Wyoming Highway Patrol—are gonna pull you over for a little impromptu interrogation....

MAX EXANDER

DEEDS OF THE NIGHT: Tales of Eros and Passion
$5.95/348-1
MAXimum porn! Exander's a writer who's seen it all—and is more than happy to describe every inch of it in pulsating detail. A whirlwind tour of the hypermasculine libido.

LEATHERSEX
$4.95/210-8
Lleather clad lust draws together only the most willing and talented of tops and bottoms—for an all-out orgy of limitless surrender and control....

MANSEX
$4.95/160-8
Unrelenting tales of men who like to take control—and those who so willingly abandon themselves to desire.

"BIG" BILL JACKSON

EIGHTH WONDER
$4.95/200-0
"Big" Bill Jackson's always the randiest guy in town. From the bright lights and back rooms of New York to the open fields and sweaty bods of a small Southern town, "Big" Bill always manages to cause a scene!

1-800-375-2356

SEAN MARTIN

SCRAPBOOK

$4.95/224-8

From the creator of *Doc and Raider* comes this hot collection of life's horniest moments—all involving studs sure to set your pulse racing!

MICHAEL LOWENTHAL, ED.

THE BADBOY EROTIC LIBRARY Vol. 2

$4.95/211-6

A second volume of scalding outtakes, taken from *Mike and Me, Muscle Bound, Men at Work, Badboy Fantasies*, and *Slowburn*.

ERIC BOYD

MIKE AND ME

$5.95/419-4

Mike joined the gym squad to bulk up on muscle. Little did he know he'd be turning on every sexy muscle jock in Minnesota! Hard bodies collide in a series of horny workouts.

MIKE AND THE MARINES

$6.50/497-6

Mike takes on America's most elite corps of studs! Join in on the never-ending sexual escapades of this singularly lustful platoon!

ANONYMOUS

A SECRET LIFE

$4.95/3017-2

A gay erotic classic. Meet Master Charles: eighteen and quite innocent, until his arrival at the Sir Percival's Academy, where the lessons are supplemented with a crash course in pure sexual heat!

SINS OF THE CITIES OF THE PLAIN

$5.95/322-8

indulge yourself in the scorching memoirs of young man-about-town Jack Saul. Jack's sinful escapades grow wilder with every chapter!

THE SCARLET PANSY

$4.95/189-6

Randall Etrange travels the world in search of true love. Along the way, his journey becomes a sexual odyssey of truly epic proportions.

HARD CANDY

SIMON LEVAY

ALBRICK'S GOLD

$7.95/644-8

"Well-plotted and imaginative... Original and engaging."

—*Publishers Weekly*

"LeVay has done a fine job...Well-paced and imaginative."

—*The Advocate*

An acclaimed thriller from the man behind recent genetic theories of sexuality. Dr. Roger Cavendish finds himself faced with a mystery straight out of his worst nightmares. Violence is on the rise at ultraconservative Levitican University—and Cavendish becomes a reluctant gumshoe, busily involved in discovering what lies beneath this sudden rise in brutal crime. The truth seems to lie somewhere in the laboratory of Dr. Guy Albrick—a mysterious scientist who claims to "cure" homosexuals. Soon, Cavendish is in a race with time, struggling to unlock the secrets of Albrick's work as the wave of violence threatens to overtake him and all others in its path.

ROBERT PATRICK

TEMPLE SLAVE

$7.95/635-9

"Genuinely original—a story of triumph."

—*Harvard Gay & Lesbian Review*

Temple Slave tells the story of the Espresso Buono and the wildly talented misfits who called it home in the 60s. The Buono became the birthplace of underground theater—and the personal and social consciousness that would lead to Stonewall and the modern gay and lesbian movement. A riotous tour de force from one of gay Off-off Broadway's legendary writers.

KEVIN KILLIAN

ARCTIC SUMMER

$6.95/514-X

A critically acclaimed examination of the emptiness lying beneath the rich exterior of America in the 50s. With the story of Liam Reilly—a young gay man of considerable means and numerous secrets—Killian exposes the complexities and contradictions of the American Dream.

CHEA VILLANUEVA

BULLETPROOF BUTCHES
$7.95/560-3

"...Gutsy, hungry, and outrageous, but with a tender core... Villanueva is a writer to watch out for: she will teach us something." —Joan Nestle

One of lesbian literature's most uncompromising voices. Never afraid to address the harsh realities of working-class lesbian life, Chea Villanueva charts territory frequently overlooked in the age of "lesbian chic."

PAUL T. ROGERS

SAUL'S BOOK
$7.95/462-3

Winner of the Editors' Book Award

"A first novel of considerable power... Speaks to us all." —*New York Times Book Review*

The story of a Times Square hustler, Sinbad the Sailor, and Saul, a brilliant, self-destructive, dominating character who may be the only love Sinbad will ever know. A classic tale of desire, obsession and the wages of love.

ELISE D'HAENE

LICKING OUR WOUNDS
$7.95/605-7

Winner of a 1998 Firecracker Alternative Book Award

"A fresh, engagingly sarcastic and determinedly bawdy voice. D'Haene is blessed with a savvy, iconoclastic view of the world that is mordant but never mean." —*Publisher's Weekly*

This acclaimed debut novel is the story of Maria, a young woman coming to terms with the complexities of life in the age of AIDS. Abandoned by her lover and faced with the deaths of her friends, Maria struggles along with the help of Peter, HIV-positive and deeply conflicted about the changes in his own life, and Christie, a lover who is full of her own ideas about truth and the meaning of life.

STAN LEVENTHAL

BARBIE IN BONDAGE
$6.95/415-1

Widely regarded as one of the most clear-eyed interpreters of big city gay male life, Leventhal here provides a series of explorations of love and desire between men.

SKYDIVING ON CHRISTOPHER STREET
$6.95/287-6

"Positively addictive." —Dennis Cooper

Aside from a hateful job, a hateful apartment, a hateful world and an increasingly hateful lover, life seems, well, all right for the protagonist of Stan Leventhal's latest novel. An insightful tale of contemporary urban gay life.

MICHAEL ROWE

WRITING BELOW THE BELT: Conversations with Erotic Authors
$7.95/540-9

"An in-depth and enlightening tour of society's love/hate relationship with sex, morality, and censorship." —*James White Review*

Michael Rowe interviewed the best and brightest erotic writers and presents the collected wisdom in *Writing Below the Belt*. Includes interviews with such cult sensations as John Preston, Larry Townsend, Pat Califia, as well as new voices such as Will Leber, Michael Lowenthal and others. An acclaimed look at the lives and work of today's most important erotic artists.

The tale of one gay man's journey into adulthood, and the roads that bring him home. A best-selling title.

LARS EIGHNER

GAY COSMOS
$6.95/236-1

A collection of this author's provocative essays looking at the state of contemporary gay culture. Praised by the press, *Gay Cosmos* is an important contribution to the area of Gay and Lesbian Studies.

WALTER R. HOLLAND

THE MARCH
$6.95/429-1

Beginning on a hot summer night in 1980, *The March* revolves around a circle of young gay men, and the many others their lives touch. Over time, each character changes in unexpected ways; lives and loves come together and fall apart, as society itself is horribly altered by the onslaught of AIDS.

BRAD GOOCH

THE GOLDEN AGE OF PROMISCUITY

$7.95/550-6

"The next best thing to taking a time-machine trip to grovel in the glorious '70s gutter." —*San Francisco Chronicle*

"A solid, unblinking, unsentimental look at a vanished era. Gooch tells us everything we ever wanted to know about the dark and decadent gay subculture in Manhattan before AIDS altered the landscape." —*Kirkus Reviews*

A controversial look at life during the decadent 70s, *The Golden Age of Promiscuity* follows a young gay artist from rags to riches.

RED JORDAN AROBATEAU

WHERE THE WORD IS NO

$7.95/674-4

"Like the characters in her stories, Red Jordan Arobateau's writing is raucous and raw and rough-hewn.... Beautiful, crackling with a kind of sparse energy." —Nisa Donnelly

The story of Jesse, a young African-American man struggling with his dream of becoming a "player." Jesse wrestles with his sexual identity, choosing to hide his nascent bisexuality behind a bluff macho exterior. All that changes when Miss La-Di-Da, a fierce, unafraid drag goddess of the streets pierces the young man's armor—leaving Jesse no choice but to confront his own truths....

DIRTY PICTURES

$5.95/345-7

"This writer is a poet locked inside a reality so harsh she gasps for beauty—and finds it—using the same language and individualistic spelling and grammar as her characters. This is no paint-by-number genre dabbler, no weekend novelist out to supplement her income and self-image. She is the graffiti artist of lesbian literature, not respectable by a long shot, but chronicling for us the raw material of her world."

—Lee Lynch,*Lambda Book Report*

LUCY AND MICKEY

$6.95/311-2

"A necessary reminder to all who blissfully—some may say ignorantly—ride the wave of lesbian chic into the mainstream." —Heather Findlay

The volume that made Red Jordan a sensation. Here are the exploits of Mickey—an uncompromising butch—and her long affair with Lucy, the femme she loves.

JAMES COLTON

TODD

$6.95/312-0

A remarkably frank novel from an earlier age. With Todd, Colton took on the complexities of American race relations, becoming one of the first gay writers to explore interracial love between men.

THE OUTWARD SIDE

$6.95/304-X

Marc Lingard, a handsome, respected young minister, finds himself at a crossroads. Unnerved by the homophobic persecution of a local resident, Marc finds himself caving in to the desires he has so long denied.

FELICE PICANO

AMBIDEXTROUS

$6.95/275-2

"Makes us remember what it feels like to be a child..."

—*The Advocate*

Picano tells all about his formative years: home life, school face-offs, the ingenuous sophistications of his first sexual steps.

MEN WHO LOVED ME

$6.95/274-4

"Zesty...spiked with adventure and romance...a distinguished and humorous portrait of a vanished age." —*Publishers Weekly*

In 1966, Picano abandoned New York, determined to find true love in Europe. He becomes embroiled in a romance with Djanko, and lives *la dolce vita* to the fullest. Upon returning to the US, he plunges into the city's thriving gay community of the 1970s.

THE LURE

$6.95/398-8

A Book-of-the-Month-Club Selection

"Picano does for New York gay life what Arthur Hailey did for airports and hotels. He plays out the novel's secrets brilliantly, one deliberate card at a time... The subject matter plus the authenticity of Picano's research are, combined, explosive. Felice Picano is one hell of a writer." —Stephen King

After witnessing a brutal murder, Noel is recruited by the police,to assist as a lure for the homophobic killer. Provided with a false identity, he moves deep into the freneticism of gay highlife in 1970s Manhattan—where he discovers his own hidden desires.

DONALD VINING

A GAY DIARY
$8.95/451-8

"*A Gay Diary* is, unquestionably, the richest historical document of gay male life in the United States that I have ever encountered...." —*Body Politic*

Vining's *Diary* portrays a vanished age and the lifestyle of a generation frequently forgotten. An unprecedented look at the lifestyle of a pre-Stonewall gay man.

WILLIAM TALSMAN

THE GAUDY IMAGE
$6.95/263-9

"To read *The Gaudy Image* now...it is to see first-hand the very issues of identity and positionality with which gay men were struggling in the decades before Stonewall. For what Talsman is dealing with...is the very question of how we conceive ourselves gay." —from the introduction by Michael Bronski

Rosebud

ARTEMIS OAKGROVE

WARCLOUDS
$6.95/643-X

Silky, an outsider who's found grudging acceptance in her small community, suddenly finds her staid life changed by the arrival of Cloud—a thrilling but troubled butch still stinging from a recent defeat. In the meantime, Nighthawk, the woman who singlehandedly removed Cloud from her turf, rules her hard-won kingdom—and the women in it—with an iron fist, not knowing her greatest battles are yet to come....

NIGHTHAWK
$6.95/634-0

Artemis OakGrove, forebear of much of today's butch/femme fiction, follows the Nighthawk through various adventures. Butcher than butch, 'Hawk leaves her lovers indelibly marked and begging for more—even while she herself moves on in search of tomorrow's conquest. Tough, street-smart and unsentimental, Nighthawk is a figure of unforgettable power and sensuality.

DANIELLE ENGLE

UNCENSORED FANTASIES
$6.95/572-7

In a world where so many stifle their emotions, who doesn't find themselves yearning for honesty—even if it means bearing one's own secret desires? Danielle Engle's heroines do just that—and a great deal more—in their quest for total sexual pleasure.

RACHEL PEREZ

ODD WOMEN
$6.50/526-3

These women are sexy, smart, tough—some say odd. But who cares! An assortment of Sapphic sirens proves once and for all that comely ladies come best in pairs.

RED JORDAN AROBATEAU

THE BLACK BIKER
$6.95/624-3

Once again, the Oils Club witnesses the outrageous antics of the Outlaws—a gang of brave and uncompromising rebels, banded together against a hostile world. One day, a mysterious biker walks into Oils, looking for love, driven by lust, and hoping to leave a sorry past behind.

STREET FIGHTER
$6.95/583-2

Another blast of truth from one of today's most notorious plain-speakers. An unsentimental look at the life of a street butch—Woody, the consummate outsider, living on the fringes of San Francisco.

ROUGH TRADE
$6.50/470-4

Famous for her unflinching portrayal of lower-class dyke life and love, Arobateau outdoes herself with these tales of butch/femme affairs and unrelenting passions.

BOYS NIGHT OUT
$6.50/463-1

Incendiary short fiction from this lesbian sensation. As always, Arobateau takes a hard look at the lives of everyday women, noting well the struggles and triumphs each experiences.

RANDY TUROFF

LUST NEVER SLEEPS
$6.50/475-5
Highly erotic, powerfully real fiction. Turoff depicts a circle of modern women connected through the enduring bonds of love, friendship, ambition, and lust with accuracy and compassion. An acclaimed look at modern lesbian life and lust.

VALENTINA CILESCU

DARK VENUS: Mistress with a Maid, Volume 2
$6.50/481-X
Claudia Dungarrow's quest for ultimate erotic dominance continues in this scalding second volume! How many maidens will fall prey to her insatiable appetite?

BODY AND SOUL: Mistress with a Maid, Volume 3
$6.50/515-8
Dr. Claudia Dungarrow returns for yet another tour of depravity, subjugating every maiden in sight to her sexual whims. Though many young women have fallen victim to her unquenchable lusts, she has yet to hold Elizabeth in submission. Will she ever?

MISTRESS MINE
$6.50/502-6
Sophia sits in prison, accused of authoring the "obscene" *Mistress Mine*—the chronicle of her life under the hand of Mistress Malin.

ALISON TYLER

THE SILVER KEY: Madame Victoria's Finishing School
$6.95/614-6
In a Victorian finishing school, a circle of randy young ladies share a diary. Molly records an explicit description of her initiation into the ways of physical love; Colette reports on a ghostly encounter. Eden tells of how it feels to wield a switch; and Katherine transcribes the journey of her love affair with the wickedly wanton Eden.

COME QUICKLY: For Girls on the Go
$6.95/428-3
Here are over sixty of the hottest lesbian fantasies around. A volume of "quickies" designed for a modern girl on a modern schedule—who still appreciates a little old-fashioned action.

VENUS ONLINE
$6.50/521-2
Lovely Alexa spends her days in a boring bank job, saving her energies for the night—when she goes online, searching chat rooms for a partner willing to satisfy her kinky sexual desires. Soon Alexa—a.k.a. Venus—finds her real and online lives colliding sexily. BUt is she ready to confront the most ardent of her online lovers?

DARK ROOM:An Online Adventure
$6.50/455-0
Dani can't bring herself to face the death of her lover, Kate. Determined to keep the memory of her lover alive, Dani goes online under Kate's screen alias—where she discovers Kate's secret life, and the ways in which it led to her untimely death....

BLUE SKY SIDEWAYS & OTHER STORIES
$6.50/394-5
A variety of women, and their many breathtaking experiences with lovers, friends—and even the occasional sexy stranger. Short, sexy fiction from this acclaimed writer.

DIAL "L" FOR LOVELESS
$5.95/386-4
Katrina Loveless—a sexy private eye talented enough to give Sam Spade a run for his money. In her first case, Katrina investigates a murder implicating a host of lovely, lusty ladies.

AARONA GRIFFIN

LEDA/THE HOUSE OF SPIRITS
$6.95/585-9
Two novellas in one volume. Though in a relationship with Chrys, *Leda* decides to take a one-night vacation—at a local lesbian sex club.In the second story, lovely Lydia thinks she has her grand new home all to herself—but this *House of Spirits* harbors other souls, determined to do some serious partying.

PASSAGE & OTHER STORIES
$6.95/599-9
A story of one woman's awakening to true desire. Nina finds herself infatuated with a woman she spots at a local café. One night, Nina follows her, only to find herself enmeshed in an maze leading to a mysterious world where women test the edges of sexuality and power.

ANNABELLE BARKER

MOROCCO

$6.50/541-7

A young woman stands to inherit a fortune—if she can only withstand the ministrations of her guardian until her twentieth birthday. But liberty has its own delicious price....

SUSAN ANDERS

CITY OF WOMEN

375-9/$5.95

A collection of stories dedicated to women and the passions that draw them together. Designed strictly for the sensual pleasure of women, Anders' tales are set to ignite flames of passion from coast to coast. The residents of City of Women hold the key to even the most forbidden fantasies.

LINDSAY WELSH

BAD HABITS

$6.95/625-1

"If you like hot lesbian erotica, run—don't walk—and pick up a copy of *Bad Habits.*" —*Lambda Book Report*

When some dominant and discerning women begin to detect tell-tale signs of poor training in their servants, they know there's only one remedy. In no time, a certain group of young ladies is back in school, joyfully learning the real, burning truth of submission to Woman.

PROVINCETOWN SUMMER

508-8/$6.96

"These tales are extremely enjoyable...reading may be interrupted by increased passion." —Perception

This completely original collection is devoted exclusively to white-hot desire between women. From the casual encounters of women on the prowl to the enduring erotic bonds between old lovers, the women of *Provincetown Summer* will set your senses on fire! A nationally best-selling title.

SECOND SIGHT

$6.50/507-7

The debut of lesbian superhero Dana Steel! During an attack by a gang of homophobic youths, Dana is thrown onto subway tracks. Miraculously, she survives—and finds herself possessing powers that make her the world's first lesbian superhero.

NASTY PERSUASIONS

$6.50/436-4

A hot peek into the behind-the-scenes operations of Rough Trade—one of the world's most famous lesbian clubs. Join Slash, Ramone, Cherry and many others as they bring one another to the height of ecstasy.

MILITARY SECRETS

$5.95/397-X

Colonel Candice Sproule heads a specialized boot camp. Assisted by three dominatrix sergeants, Colonel Sproule takes on the submissives sent to her by military contacts. Then along comes Jesse—a butch recruit whose pleasure in being served matches the Colonel's own.

THE BEST OF LINDSAY WELSH

$5.95/368-6

Welsh was one of Rosebud's early bestsellers, and remains one of our most popular writers. This sampler is set to introduce some of today's hottest lesbian erotica to a wider audience.

NECESSARY EVIL

$5.95/277-9

One lovely submissive decides to create a Mistress who'll fulfill her heart's desire. Little did she know how difficult it would be—and, in the end, rewarding....

A VICTORIAN ROMANCE

$5.95/365-1

A young woman realizes her dream—a trip abroad! Soon, Elaine comes to discover her own sexual talents, as a hot-blooded Parisian named Madelaine takes her Sapphic education in hand.

A CIRCLE OF FRIENDS

$6.50/524-7

A close-knit group of women pair off to explore all the possibilities of lesbian passion, until finally it seems that there is nothing—and no one—they have not dabbled in.

SEXUAL FANTASIES (ED.)

$6.95/586-7

Bestselling author Lindsay Welsh selects a dozen sexy stories, ranging from sweet to spicy, from her favorite up-and-coming writers. *Sexual Fantasies* offers a look at the many desires of modern women.

LAURA ANTONIOU, ED.

LEATHERWOMEN III: The Clash of the Cultures
$6.95/619-7
Antoniou gathers the very best of today's cutting-edge women's erotica—concentrating on multicultural stories involving characters not frequently seen in this genre.

LEATHERWOMEN
$6.95/598-0
"...a great new collection of fiction by and about SM dykes." —*SKIN TWO*

A groundbreaking anthology. These fantasies, from the pens of new or emerging authors, break every rule imposed on women's fantasies. An unforgettable exploration of the female libido.

LOVECHILD

GAG
$5.95/369-4
Fearless verse addressing sex and freddom at the Millenium. These poems take on hypocrisy with uncommon energy, and announce Lovechild as a writer of unforgettable rage.

A Richard Kasak Book

PAT CALIFIA

DIESEL FUEL: Passionate Poetry
$12.95/535-2
"Dead-on direct, these poems burn, pierce, penetrate, soak, and sting.... Califia leaves no sexual stone unturned, clearing new ground for us all." —Gerry Gomez Pearlberg

Califia's first collection of verse. A must-read exploration of underground culture.

SENSUOUS MAGIC
$12.95/458-5
"*Sensuous Magic* is clear, succinct and engaging even for the reader for whom S/M isn't the sexual behavior of choice.... When she is writing about the dynamics of sex and the technical aspects of it, Califia is the Dr. Ruth of the alternative sexuality set...." —Lambda Book Report

The best-selling guide to alternative lovemaking available today.

SIMON LEVAY

ALBRICK'S GOLD
$20.95/518-2/Hardcover
"Well-plotted and imaginative... [Levay's] premise and execution are original and engaging." —*Publishers Weekly*

From the man behind the controversial "gay brain" studies comes a tale of medical experimentation run amok. Is Dr. Guy Albrick performing unethical experiments in an attempt at "correcting" homosexuality? Dr. Roger Cavendish is determined to find out, before Albrick's guinea pigs are let loose among an unsuspecting gay community...

MICHAEL BRONSKI, ED.

TAKING LIBERTIES: Gay Men's Essays on Politics, Culture and Sex
$12.95/456-9
Lambda Literary Award Winner
"Offers undeniable proof of a heady, sophisticated, diverse new culture of gay intellectual debate. I cannot recommend it too highly." —Christopher Bram

America's gay community is, in many ways, stronger than ever before—due largely to the diversity of opinions on the history and future of the tribe. Some of the gay community's foremost essayists—from radical left to neo-conservative—weigh in on such slippery topics as outing, pornography, pedophilia, and much more. One of the most acclaimed anthologies in the field.

FLASHPOINT: Gay Male Sexual Writing
$12.95/424-0
A thrilling and enlightening look at contemporary gay porn. Accompanied by Bronski's insightful analysis, each story illustrates the many approaches to sexuality used by today's gay writers.

HEATHER FINDLAY, ED.

A MOVEMENT OF EROS: 25 Years of Lesbian Erotica
$12.95/421-6
Tracing the course of the genre from its pre-Stonewall roots to its current renaissance, Findlay examines each piece, placing it within the context of lesbian community and politics.

BARRY HOFFMAN, ED.

THE BEST OF GAUNTLET
$12.95/202-7
Gauntlet has always published the widest possible range of opinions. The most provocative articles have been gathered by editor- in-chief Barry Hoffman, to make *The Best of Gauntlet* a riveting exploration of society's limits.

MICHAEL LASSELL

THE HARD WAY
$12.95/231-0
"Lassell is a master of the necessary word. In an age of tepid and whining verse, his bawdy and bittersweet songs are like a plunge in cold champagne." —Paul Monette

The first collection of renowned gay writer Michael Lassell's poetry, fiction and essays.

WILLIAM CARNEY

THE REAL THING
$10.95/280-9
"Carney gives us a good look at the mores and lifestyle of the first generation of gay leathermen. —Pat Califia

With a new introduction by Michael Bronski. A chilling epistolary novel set in the gay leather clubs of California, circa 1968. *The Real Thing,* out of print for over twnety-five years, returns from exile, to thrill and enlighten a new audience with its tale of the attitudes and practices of an earlier generation of gay leather- men.

EURYDICE

F/32
$10.95/350-3
"It's wonderful to see a woman...celebrating her body and her sexuality by creating a fabulous and funny tale." —Kathy Acker

A funny, disturbing quest for unity, *f/32* tells the story of Ela and her vagina—the latter of whom embarks on one of the most hilarious road trips in recent fiction. An award-winning novel.

GUILLERMO BOSCH

RAIN
$12.95/232-9
In a quest to sate his hunger for some knowledge of the world, one man is taken through a series of extraordinary encounters that change the course of civilization around him.

RANDY TUROFF, ED.

LESBIAN WORDS: State of the Art
$10.95/340-6
"This is a terrific book that should be on every thinking lesbian's bookshelf." —Nisa Donnelly

The best of lesbian nonfiction looking at not only the current fashionability the media has brought to the lesbian "image," but considerations of the lesbian past via historical inquiry and personal recollections.

ASSOTTO SAINT

SPELLS OF A VOODOO DOLL
$12.95/393-7
Lambda Literary Award Nominee.
"Angelic and brazen." —Jewelle Gomez

A spellbinding collection of the poetry, lyrics, essays and performance texts by one of the most important voices in the renaissance of black gay writing.

FELICE PICANO

DRYLAND'S END
$12.95/279-5
Dryland's End takes place in a fabulous techno-empire ruled by intelligent, powerful women. While the Matriarchy has ruled for over two thousand years and altered human society, it is now unraveling. Military rivalries, religious fanaticism and economic competition threaten to destroy the mighty empire.

LUCY TAYLOR

UNNATURAL ACTS
$12.95/181-0
"A topnotch collection..." —*Science Fiction Chronicle*

A disturbing vision of erotic horror. Unrelenting angels and hungry gods play with souls and bodies in Taylor's murky cosmos: where heaven and hell are merely differences of perspective; where redemption and damnation lie behind the same shocking acts.

CECILIA TAN, ED.

SM VISIONS: The Best of Circlet Press
$10.95/339-2
Circlet Press, publisher of erotic science fiction and fantasy genre, is now represented by the best of its very best—a most thrilling and eye-opening rides through the erotic imagination.